"S_____ M_____ __ _____ b_____ _____ _____ d a
_____ "Holiday Book Club" _____
by the *Los Angeles Times*

"Compulsively readable. . . . A perfect book for someone who loves thrillers and wants a . . . female main character who really can take care of herself."

—Nancy Pearl, National Public Radio

"Cain . . . skillfully maintains an edgy level of tension throughout the narrative."   —*The Boston Globe*

"There are echoes of Lisbeth Salander, Stieg Larsson's steely heroine, in Kick Lannigan . . . but she's a far more human and likable character than Lisbeth Salander could ever be. . . . *One Kick* gets off to a rapid start . . . well-engineered and fast-paced."

—*New York Times Book Review*

"*One Kick* is superb! From its breathtaking opening sequence, through scenes of wrenching evil and heart-clutching emotion to its roller-coaster finale, this novel will stay with you for a long time. And what a heroine. . . . Here's hoping for more Kick Lannigan soon!"

—#1 *New York Times* bestselling author Jeffery Deaver

"A wholly original heroine: gritty and determined to ensure her own survival, perfectly willing to put her elbow through someone's trachea, but loving with her adopted brother and elderly dog."

—*Oprah's Book Club 2.0* newsletter

ALSO BY CHELSEA CAIN

CHELSEA CAIN

ONE KICK

POCKET BOOKS

New York   London   Toronto   Sydney   New Delhi

Pocket Books
An Imprint of Simon & Schuster, Inc.
1230 Avenue of the Americas
New York, NY 10020

This book is a work of fiction. Any references to historical events, real people, or real places are used fictitiously. Other names, characters, places, and events are products of the author's imagination, and any resemblance to actual events or places or persons, living or dead, is entirely coincidental.

First Pocket Books paperback edition June 2015

POCKET and colophon are registered trademarks of Simon & Schuster, Inc.

For information about special discounts for bulk purchases, please contact Simon & Schuster Special Sales at 1-866-506-1949 or business@simonandschuster.com.

The Simon & Schuster Speakers Bureau can bring authors to your live event. For more information or to book an event, contact the Simon & Schuster Speakers Bureau at 1-866-248-3049 or visit our website at www.simonspeakers.com.

Manufactured in the United States of America

10 9 8 7 6 5 4 3 2 1

ISBN 978-1-4767-4987-7
ISBN 978-1-4767-4988-4 (ebook)

For Marc Mohan, and Eliza Fantastic
Mohan, and Lucy.

I fear not the man who has practiced
10,000 kicks once, but I fear the man
who has practiced one kick 10,000 times.

—*Bruce Lee*

PROLOGUE

THEY HAD TOLD HER what to do if the police ever
came. They had run drills—first thing in the morning; in the middle of the night; halfway through a
meal—until she could get to the trapdoor in the
closet from anywhere in the house in under a minute. She was an agile kid, and fast, and she practiced. When her father clicked the stopwatch and
gave her a proud nod, she felt a heat of happiness
burn in her chest.

She knew that he did it all for her. She saw the
toll the stress took, the creases at the corners of his
eyes, the gray strands in his gold hair; the pink of
his scalp showed through where his hair was thinning on top. He was still strong. She could still
count on him to protect her. Their property was in
a rural county, miles from the nearest house, and
he said he could hear a car coming as soon as it
turned onto the gravel lane. This is where he had
taught her to shoot. How to plant her feet so the
.22 would feel steadier in her hands. He told her
that if the police ever came, and he wasn't home,
that she should shoot anyone who tried to keep
her from getting to the trapdoor. He had walked

her around the house, showing her where every gun was stashed, making her say the location of each out loud so she would remember. "Under the kitchen sink." "Dining room buffet drawer." "Behind the books on the bookshelf." She wasn't scared. Her father was always home. If anyone needed shooting, he'd do it for her.

Rain battered the fragile farmhouse windows, but she felt safe, already dressed for bed in her cotton nightgown with the giraffes on it, a quilt wrapped around her shoulders. The smell of jar spaghetti sauce and meatballs—her favorite meal—still hung in the air, along with the burning wood crackling in the fireplace. The dining room table had been cleared. Her mother had disappeared into the kitchen. The Scrabble board was set up and she and her father studied their tiles. They played every night after dinner. It was part of her homeschooling. The fireplace in the living room flickered with a warm orange glow, but they played at the dining room table. Her father said it was better for her posture. He picked up a wooden Scrabble tile and moved it onto the board. *C*. He grinned at her, and she knew that look, knew he had a good one. He put another tile down. *A*. He was putting the next tile down when the sound of someone pounding at the front door echoed through the house. She could see the fear on his face, the way his eyelids twitched. He dropped the tile. *K*.

Her mother materialized in the kitchen doorway, a yellow dishrag still in her wet hands. Everything went still. Like the moment when a photograph is taken—that pause when the whole world waits, trying not to blink.

"It's Johnson," a familiar voice shouted from outside. "Storm put a tree down on my power lines. Phone's down. Everything. Can I use yours to call the sheriff?"

Her parents exchanged a tense glance and then her father tightened his fists on the table and leaned over them, not even noticing as he knocked over his Scrabble rack and all his tiles skidded across the tablecloth. Her mother had embroidered that tablecloth with bluebells and lupins. The *K* tile from her father's rack sat right there, on a bluebell, right in front of her. That tile alone was worth five points.

"I want you to go to the side window by the piano," her father told her. He said it in the serious whisper voice he used when she was to follow his instructions and not ask questions. His eyes darted toward her mother and then he put his hands through his fine fuzz of hair, so different from her own thick dark mop of tangles. "You should be able to see the Johnson place down the hill just past the lake," he told her. "Tell me if you see any lights on."

This was different from the drills. She could see it in the way her parents looked at each other. She wondered if she should be frightened, but when she inventoried her body for signs of fear, she found none. Her father had taught her the importance of preparation.

She calmly pushed her chair away from the table, stood, let the quilt fall to the floor, and made her way barefoot from the dining room into the living room. The fireplace cut an orange circle out of the darkness. She tiptoed alongside her mother's piano and tucked herself between it and the wall. Then she turned her gaze outside the water-streaked window into the blackness beyond. The cold air seeping in from outside made her forget about the fire. She peered in the direction her father had indicated. But there were no lights—only her own faint reflection flickering like a dying ember. She craned her head back toward the dining room. "I don't see any lights," Kick reported. "It's dark down there."

Her mother said her father's name, a little sound followed by a gulp, like she was swallowing it. Her father cleared his throat. "I'll be right with you!" he hollered toward the door.

She heard the grate of the chair legs as he got up from the table, and watched as he made his way to the dining room cabinet and withdrew the Colt from the drawer next to the good silverware. He tucked the gun in the back of the Wranglers her mother had bought him at Walmart.

She saw her mother back slowly into the kitchen.

It was cold by the window. The rain tapped like fingers against the glass. The man was still pounding on the door. She felt something in her hand, a hard square inch of wood, and was startled to see the *K* tile clutched between her fingers. She didn't remember grabbing it.

Her father scooped her quilt up off the floor and carried it over to her. He draped it around her shoulders, and to her immediate shame she hid the Scrabble tile in her fist, not wanting him to be disappointed in her thievery. He fixed his eyes on hers and put his face so close that she could smell the spaghetti sauce on his breath, the cooked ground beef. "Stay where you are for now," he whispered, his voice cracking. A glint of flame reflected off his eyeballs in the dark. She tightened her fist around the Scrabble tile, its corners digging into her flesh.

As her father crossed the living room toward the door, she saw him touch the butt of the gun at the small of his spine, like he was making sure it was still there. He was wearing the beaded moccasins that he had bought the summer they lived in Oklahoma, the ones made by real Comanche. The soles were animal hide, soft and soundless.

He didn't look back at her as he went through the door to the front hall, but he left the door open a crack. She heard the front door open and the slap and squeak of the aluminum screen slam shut. She heard her father's voice, fake-friendly, and she heard the stomp of Johnson's boots on the welcome mat as he apologized again for being a bother.

Her body relaxed, and she let her grip on the quilt around her shoulders loosen.

She did not have to run.

Their neighbor would use the phone. They would finish their Scrabble game. She leaned against the wall, fingering the Scrabble tile, wondering how long she was supposed to stay there while the men stood around talking about the storm. The flicker of her own reflection caught her attention. She studied it in the wavy farmhouse glass. Her dark hair disappeared until she was just a face in the window, a glint of eyes and teeth. She got closer until her nose was so close to the glass she could feel the air get colder. This close, she could make out her eyes in detail. Every eyelash. Until the images reflecting back at her began to merge together and overlap.

That's when she saw the light.

She stepped back, startled, and blinked hard. But when she opened her eyes, she still saw it. This wasn't firelight. It wasn't a reflection. She stared at the single blurry dot of brightness down the hill, across the lake, trying to puzzle it out even as her heart fluttered. A light. They had a few lights like that on their property, affixed to the top corners of outbuildings. Those lights had motion detectors that sometimes got set off by passing cats or raccoons. Her father had taken the bulb out of one on their property, because it kept coming on outside her window and waking her up at night.

Their neighbor was lying. He still had electricity.

She needed to tell someone. But her father had told her to stay where she was. She looked back at the kitchen door, but there was no sign of her mother. The men's voices still boomed from the front hall—her father laughing a little too loudly.

She could hear the screen door banging in the wind. Johnson hadn't pulled it closed all the way. The screen would rip in the storm. She felt like a knot that someone was pulling tight, her whole self contracting, the air squeezing out of her lungs.

The screen door banged.

The sound was like an openhanded slap. Her lungs expanded, taking in air, lifting her to the balls of her feet. The Scrabble tile dropped from her hand onto the floor.

And she ran. She scurried across the dark living room, the quilt flapping behind her like a cape, and wrenched open the door to the front hall. Her father looked at her, eyebrows lifted, mouth open. He was so tall—he could lift her up to touch the ceiling. Mr. Johnson's back was to her, just a normal-size man. His wet boots sat neatly together just inside the door. His wet raincoat was on the coat tree. He was standing on the rug, drying himself off with the towel her father kept by the door.

"I saw a light," she said, out of breath.

Her father went gray.

The screen door banged again, and the front door burst open like a thunderclap. Her father stumbled back as the men forced their way into the house. They didn't bother to take off their boots or dark jackets. Water flew off of them, spattering her.

They were shouting, barking orders at her father, who cowered in front of them. Someone was trying to pull her backward, away from him. She yelled to be let go and saw her father reach for his gun. But the men had guns, too, and they saw him and yelled "Gun!" and their guns were at eye height, so that everywhere she looked she saw the barrel of one pointed at where her father shrank at the base of the stairs, his Colt trembling in his hand. His eyes were frantic, glistening with tears. She'd never seen him cry before.

It was loud and quiet at the same time, everyone still, the crackle and honk of walkie-talkies, the adults breathing heavily, the rain, the front door.

One of the men stepped in front of her. He was the first one who moved, which meant he was in charge. They were FBI. The letters were printed in white across the backs of their jackets. Federal Bureau of Investigation. State police, local police, DHS, DEA, Interpol, ATF. Her father had taught her to identify them, and which ones to fear most. The FBI, he'd said, was the scariest of all of them. She had imagined them having eyes like goats and angry faces.

But this FBI agent didn't look like that. He was younger and shorter than her father, with a freckled face, reddish beard, and shaggy hair. His wire-rimmed glasses were beaded with water. He didn't look mean, but he didn't look nice either. He was speaking sternly to her father in a voice that she'd never heard anyone use with him before. His words sliced through the air. "FBI." "Search warrant." "Arrest." "Probation violation."

"I've done nothing wrong," her father sputtered, and the redheaded agent inched toward him, blocking her view, so that all she could see now were those three letters on his back, *FBI*, and one of her father's moccasins.

"Easy, Mel," the redheaded agent said. "You don't want the little girl to get hurt."

Her toes curled, gripping the hardwood.

"Put your hands behind your head," the redheaded agent said, and then he stepped to the side, and she was surprised to see her father lifting his elbows and threading his fingers behind his head like he'd done it before. Her father's Colt was in the redheaded agent's hand. She saw the agent give it to one of the other men. She didn't understand. Her father needed to stand up, to show these men how strong he was.

The redheaded agent cleared his throat. "I've got a warrant to search your property," he said to her father.

Her father didn't respond. His hunched frame quivered.

"How many people are in the house?" the agent demanded.

She willed her father to look up, to give her some instruction, but his eyes were darting around so fast, it was like his focus couldn't alight on anything long enough.

One of the other agents lifted her father roughly

to his feet and handcuffed his hands behind his back. "You better start talking, Mel," he said to her father. "You know what they do to people like you in prison." He grinned when he said it, like it was something worth looking forward to.

"Not in front of the girl," the redheaded agent said.

Tiny dots of red and black peppered the floor, beads from her father's moccasins. Her skin felt like it was shimmering, like she was flickering on and off, a dying lightbulb.

Another man was leading her father toward the kitchen. "Let's find someplace to talk," he said, giving her father a shove.

She tried to speak, to call out to her father, but her body couldn't remember how to make words. He was shuffling away from her, moccasins scuffing against the floor, beads trailing him.

"Find the wife," someone said.

Mother. The word stuck in her throat. She couldn't choke it up. Inside her head, she was screaming, but outside, she was motionless, feet rooted to the floor. She watched as the three other men with guns followed his instructions, moving into the house with the guns raised.

The redheaded agent was talking into a walkie-talkie. "We're on the scene," he said. "Things went down early. Still waiting for backup." He stole another worried glance at her and mopped his brow with a freckled hand. "We've got a kid here," he added.

She made herself swallow. Mr. Johnson cowered just inside the door, eyeing her warily,
still in his socks. Her parents had been careful
about letting the neighbors see her. If a neighbor stopped by for some reason, she hid. Strangers were never allowed in the house. She pressed
the back of her skull into the wall behind her,
listening for her father's voice. But the noise of
the storm and the static from the walkie-talkie
drowned everything out. The harder she listened,
the more she couldn't tell one noise from the
other. She wondered if her mother had made it
out the back door.

The redheaded agent's gun was holstered under
his shoulder. He bent his knees and lowered himself to her height. "I'm a police officer," he said.
"But you can call me Frank."

Her father was right. Adults lied. "You're an FBI
agent," she corrected him.

His eyes flickered with surprise. "O-kay," he
said. "You know something about law enforcement.
That's good. Good. You can help me." He looked
her in the eye. "I need you to tell me your name."

"I told you there was a kid here," Mr. Johnson
said.

This was all because of her. He'd seen her. The
back of her head hurt. She missed her parents. She
moved her hand out of the quilt and up the leg of
the hallway cabinet next to her.

The agent named Frank reached out like he
wanted to put his hand on her shoulder, but

dragged it through his wet hair instead. "Are there any other kids here?" he asked.

She wasn't supposed to answer questions like that. He was trying to trick her, to get her in trouble.

"You're safe now," Frank said.

She found the metal drawer pull with her fingers. Top left.

Then she let the quilt drop. Both Frank's and Mr. Johnson's eyes followed it as it puddled to the floor. The gun was in her hands by the time they looked up.

"Holy hell," she heard Mr. Johnson say.

She planted her feet apart the way her father had taught her and aimed the gun at Frank.

There was a stillness to him, but he didn't look afraid.

"You're safe now," he said again.

She was breathing hard. It made it difficult to keep the gun steady. But the gun gave her courage. She pulled words from her throat. "I want my parents," she said.

"We're going to take you to them," Frank said.

She shook her head back and forth. He didn't understand. "I want my mother and father."

Frank's gun was still holstered. He made a small gesture with his head in the direction of Mr. Johnson. "Step outside, sir," he said.

Mr. Johnson didn't move. She could feel his fear filling up the room, taking up all the oxygen. "Go," she told him. He wasn't supposed to be in the house anyway. Mr. Johnson nodded and then pulled on his boots and went out the front door without his raincoat.

Even for the .22, her hands were small, and she had to use a special grip, and two fingers around the trigger.

"What's your name, honey?" Frank asked her.

"Beth Riley," she said. She could hear footsteps overhead as the agents stomped around her parents' bedroom upstairs.

"What's your *real* name?" he asked.

Her skin prickled. "Beth Riley," she said again.

A sudden sound made her jump, a crack like the screen door slamming, only louder. A sudden bolt of terror stiffened her spine. She knew that sound from target shooting with her father. It was a gunshot.

It sounded like it had come from behind the house.

"Mother," she said.

Frank lifted the walkie-talkie to his mouth, and she didn't protest, didn't tell him not to move.

"I need a report on that gunshot now," he said into the walkie-talkie.

"The mother just blew her brains out," a voice responded through static.

The storm rattled the windows and the whole house shuddered.

She felt something begin to uncoil inside her and flood her insides with feelings. But the emotions were mixed-up, out of order. She tried to push them all away, but they screamed and twisted to get out.

Frank was looking at her. She wanted him to stop looking at her.

She thought the windows might break. The wind was so loud, she could hear it whistling through the walls. Thunder boomed above them. But this wasn't like other thunder. It was rhythmic. It was getting louder and closer. The hall light fixture trembled.

"Those are helicopters," Frank said above the noise. "The guys from the main office like to make an entrance. Can I have the gun now?"

She was splitting in two. She wanted to give the man named Frank the gun. She wanted to let go.

Then the living room door opened and her father appeared. All her muddy emotions evaporated at the sight of him. He had come to rescue her. He would be so proud of her, remembering where to find the gun. She would shoot Frank for him. She would do exactly what he wanted. She had always done exactly what he wanted. All she needed was a nod and she would pull the trigger and kill Frank and her father would take her away from this.

Frank had his hands in the air. She glanced at her father, waiting for his signal to kill, but her father's eyes were downcast. Then she saw the FBI agent over her father's shoulder. The agent went an angry pink when he saw her gun pointed at his friend. He elbowed her father hard in the back and he fell to the ground.

Terror snaked in her belly. "Daddy?" she said. But he didn't answer.

The agent leveled his gun at her, the black barrel pointing at her. He was yelling, calling out to the others, the men upstairs. Her father was on his stomach, his cheek on the floor, his face turned away from her.

"Lower your weapon, Agent," the agent named Frank growled.

Her eyes darted to her father, but the .22 didn't waver. The helicopters were so loud now, she couldn't think. They sounded like they were landing all around the house.

She could hear the other men coming down the stairs. Everyone was inching closer to her.

"She's just a kid," Frank said. "I've got this."

She had to shoot. She had to shoot them all.

"Daddy?" she asked desperately.

This time her father lifted his chin. His face was sweaty and red, and his wrists were still handcuffed behind his back. But his eyes were sharp and dangerous. "They killed your mother, Beth!" he hollered over the noise. "Autonuke! Now!"

It was like a switch being thrown. All those drills they had practiced. She let her body take over. She flew down the hall, toward the back of the house, slipped into the closet under the stairs, went through the secret wall panel, pulled up the trapdoor on the floor, and scampered down the ladder one-handed, the gun still clutched in the other. She could feel the vibrations of the men chasing her, their boots pounding on the floor, as she descended into darkness. She jumped from the fifth rung, her bare feet landing on the carpet, and spun around to the desk where the computer screen's aquarium screen saver was the only light in the room. She sat down with the gun in her lap and felt around the desk drawer for the thumb drive. A lionfish swam by. She inserted the thumb drive into the computer like her father had shown her. Then she hit the space bar on the keyboard. In a blink all the fish were gone and a blue window appeared on the screen. She had never seen the blue box before, but she knew what to do. A white cursor blinked at the bottom of it. She typed in one word: "autonuke."

Then she sat back in the desk chair, brought her knees to her chest, and waited.

She could hear the FBI agents arguing above her and she knew that they would come down the ladder soon and lock her up forever, but she didn't care. She had done what she was supposed to do.

Finally, the trapdoor opened, and she glanced up to see Frank peering down at her. She put her hand on the gun.

"Can I come down, Beth?" he called.

She saw other faces behind his, crowding into the rectangle of light, looking at her. New people. The people from the helicopters.

"I still have the gun," she called up.

"I just want to talk to you," Frank said. He said something to one of the new people and then swung his body over the edge and started down the ladder.

She turned to the blue computer screen. "It's done," she said. "You can't stop it."

Frank's feet landed with a thud. She hoped his shoes weren't too muddy. Her mother didn't like the carpet to get dirty. Frank stepped beside her and peered at the computer screen, his hands on his hips. She saw the words "autonuke complete" reflected in his glasses.

"You deleted the files?" Frank asked. She could tell he was trying not to sound angry.

She made herself small in the chair. The white of her nightgown looked blue in the light from the computer, and the giraffes were faded. It hadn't fit for years. She stretched the hem over her knees.

"Do you have any idea what you've just done?" Frank muttered. He moved so suddenly she thought he might hit her, but he was just reaching for the light switch.

Their basement movie studio lit up. Four sets: a princess bedroom, a classroom, a doctor's office, and a scary dungeon. Beth's father took each set apart into pieces and packed it every time they moved. She wasn't allowed to touch the cameras. She had to be careful not to trip on all the black cords that snaked across the floor.

Frank spun slowly back to her. Her father had said that people would look at her differently if they knew. He said that it would make grown-ups angry. But Frank didn't look mad. He looked a little scared, like she was a bomb that might explode if he didn't figure out which wire to cut.

"Agent Moony?" a man hollered from above them. "You okay down there?"

Frank took a moment to answer. He probably hadn't seen movie sets before.

"Frank?" hollered the man.

"We'll be up in a minute," Frank called. His eyes moved from one set to the next. "Then you'll want to see this," he added.

The basement air tasted like mildew. The basements always tasted like that.

Frank wasn't saying anything anymore. He was just rubbing the back of his neck.

"Is my mother alive?" she asked.

He took his glasses off and cleaned them on his shirt. "I don't know who your mother is," he said gently.

"Linda," she reminded him. She twisted the hem of her nightgown around her fingers. "She shot herself." She knew about caliber size. The faster and heavier a bullet was, the more damage it caused. Some people survived gunshots to the head. "I'll know if you're lying," she said.

Frank hooked his glasses back over his ears and stared at her for another moment. His eyes were wide. His red eyebrows and beard were streaked with blond, like he'd spent time in the sun. Even his ears had freckles. "She's dead, Beth."

She pulled at the nightgown, stretching the giraffes. "Oh," she said. Hot snot filled her nose, and her eyes burned, but she didn't cry. "She was nice. She couldn't have kids, you know."

"Is that what they told you?" Frank said.

"They took care of me," she said.

Frank knelt beside her chair so that they were eye to eye. "I need to know: Were there any other kids?"

His glasses were octagons, not ovals. His shaggy curls were still wet from the storm; his beard sprouted wildly in all directions. Men were supposed to shave every day. It was a sign of discipline. "I want to stay with him," she said.

Frank looked pained. "I'm sure that your family has never stopped looking for you," he said.

She wondered if that was true.

Frank hadn't done a very good job cleaning his glasses. She could see his fingerprints on the lenses. But his eyes seemed nice enough.

A dog was barking outside. Not theirs. They didn't have any dogs. She wasn't allowed.

"How old are you now, Beth?" Frank asked her.

"Ten." She hesitated. Her chest hurt. It felt like someone was squeezing it. "But . . ."

He raised his sun-bleached eyebrows at her.

She could still hear the barking. Or maybe it was just the screen door banging. She didn't know. Her skin felt hot.

"I had a dog once," she said, remembering.

Frank was motionless. "What was its name?" he asked.

"Monster." She felt warm tears slide down her cheeks. She was shaking. The memories were coming up her throat. She had worked so hard for so long to swallow them down. It was a relief. "My old birthday was in April," she added, wiping her nose with her hand. "Mel changed it. So I guess I'm actually eleven."

Frank squinted at her and tilted his head. He was close, but not too close. "How long have you lived with Mel?"

She thought for a moment, trying to piece the details together. "Monster used to run away. I was in the front yard looking for him, and Mel said he could help me find him. He said he'd drive me around the neighborhood. I was in first grade."

"What's your name?" Frank asked, and she heard the crack in his voice.

Her name. She *knew* it. She could feel it under her collarbone. It was like having a word at the tip of your tongue, when you can see it, the shape of it, but you can't quite remember what it is. She concentrated. "Kick?" she guessed.

He tilted his head more and leaned forward a little. "What did you say it was?"

"Kick?" she tried again. But that wasn't it. Something close to that . . .

"Kit?" Frank said. "Do you mean Kit Lannigan?"

It was like she had touched an electric fence, that feeling of all your cells crying out at once. She scrambled backward in the chair. "We're not supposed to say that name," she whispered.

Frank's eyes ran over her features. "It *is* you," he said.

She was seeing faces, images, flashes of color. She couldn't breathe. Everything was unraveling. "I didn't mean to let Monster out," she said quickly, the words tumbling out. "I opened the door to get something off the porch and he just slid out before I could stop him." She swallowed a wet hiccup and put her hand over her mouth. "It's my fault," she said between her fingers.

"Hey, hey, hey," Frank said. He looked like he wanted to pat her hand but he didn't. "Easy," he said. "It's over. It's over now. No one's mad at you about the dog, I promise you. You're not in trouble." He dug something out of his pocket. "Here," he said, extending his hand, palm up. "I think you dropped this." Her father's Scrabble tile lay in his palm. Kick reached tentatively for it.

"It's okay," Frank said. "Take it."

She plucked the tile from his hand and squeezed it in her fist until her hand hurt.

Frank rocked back on his heels. "Kit Lannigan," he said. "Holy shit." He was blinking at her, mouth open. "You've been away a long time."

Behind Frank, she could see the canopy princess bed, pink and frilly. She was shaking. She couldn't stop. "It's over?" she asked.

Frank nodded. "The worst part is, kiddo." And he smiled at her, and she knew she was supposed to smile back, to be happy, but she couldn't find the right feelings inside.

It was like dying. That's what Mel had said. *Kit is dead*, he'd told her. *Now you are Beth.* But now Beth was dead too. And if Kit was dead, and Beth was dead, then she was someone new, someone who didn't even have a name.

"So what happens now?" she asked numbly.

"Now I take you home," Frank said.

1

KICK LANNIGAN AIMED THE sights of her Glock, lined up the shot, and squeezed the trigger. The paper target shuddered. Kick inhaled the satisfying smell of gunpowder and concrete and squeezed the trigger again. And again. She emptied the magazine. The gun barely moved in her hand. She had learned to shoot with a .22, but she'd been firing a .45 since she turned fourteen and first started coming to the shooting range. Even at fourteen, she'd known she wanted something that could bring down a bigger target.

She laid the gun on the counter, pressed the button to reel in the target, and watched it flutter toward her. Half the targets they sold at the range now were zombies—everyone loved shooting zombies—but Kick preferred the old-fashioned black-and-white image of a square-jawed guy in a black watch cap. The target arrived and she inspected her handiwork. Bullet holes collected at the heart, groin, and center of the forehead.

A blush of pleasure burned her cheeks.

For the last seven years she had only been allowed to fire range rental weapons. Now, finally, she was firing her own gun. Some people went out and got drunk when they came of age; Kick had picked out a Glock with a ten-round magazine and applied for a concealed-weapons permit.

The Glock 37 had all the performance of a .45 ACP, but with a shorter grip. It was a big gun sized for small hands. The beveled slide and sleek black finish, the finger grooves and thumb rests—Kick loved every millimeter of that pistol. Her knuckles were raw and the blue polish on her fingernails was chipped, but that Glock still looked beautiful in her hand.

She glanced up from the gun and listened.

The range was too quiet.

The skin on Kick's arms prickled. She set the Glock back on the counter and tilted her head, straining to hear through her noise-reduction headphones.

The muffled crack of gunshots had been steady around her. There were only three people using the range that morning, and Kick had taken note of them all. Her martial arts sensei called it being mindful. Kick called it being vigilant. Now she listened to the muted shots around her and tried to pinpoint what had changed.

The woman a lane over from Kick had stopped firing. Kick had seen the woman's weapon when she crossed behind her, a pretty Beretta Stampede with a nickel finish and a revolving six-bullet chamber. The Stampede was a replica of an Old West gunslinger's weapon, a big gun. Fire it at a car, and the bullet would pierce the body panel and crack the engine block. It was too much gun for that woman. Which was why Kick had noted it.

The woman had fired all six rounds, reloaded, and then fired just three.

Kick could feel her heartbeat instantly quicken. Her muscles tensed. Her calves itched. Fight or flight. That's how the shrinks explained it. For a few years after she'd first come home, the feeling would overcome her and she'd just take off, pell-mell, on foot. Once her mother found her nearly five miles away in a Safeway parking lot. Her mother and sister had to force her into the car, screaming.

Biofeedback. Meditation. Talk therapy. Drug therapy. Scream therapy. Sensory deprivation tanks. Yoga. Tai chi. Chinese herbs. Equine therapy. None of it had helped.

It had been Frank who suggested letting her take kung fu when she was eleven. The FBI had transferred him to Portland to help get her ready to testify, and he told her mother that martial arts would give Kick confidence, help her get through the trial. But he probably knew she just needed to hit something. There was no getting her into the sensory deprivation tank after that. She started martial arts, boxing, target shooting, archery, and even knife throwing. Her parents thought she did it all to feel safe, and in a way they were right. She wanted to make sure that no one—not even her mother—would ever be able to force her into a car again. After her father left, she took on more: rock climbing, mountaineering, flying lessons—anything to keep her busy and out of the house.

Kick scanned the floor for spent shell casings. Now when she felt the itch in her calves, she didn't think about running; she thought about how to thrust her right arm forward so that the meaty part of her hand between her thumb and index finger connected with her opponent's throat. She eyed a casing on the concrete and gave it a nudge with the steel toe of her boot and watched the brass cartridge rattle out of her shooting stall. Then she followed it. The woman from the next lane over was leaning up against a back wall, texting someone. Kick had her sweatshirt hood up, covering her hair, headphones on top of the hood; she was wearing protective goggles, black jeans, boots, and a sweatshirt zipped up to her neck. She could have robbed a bank and gotten away unidentified. But this woman? She recognized Kick. She wasn't even subtle about it; she inhaled so sharply, she almost dropped her phone. Kick instinctively turned her head to hide her face, reached for the shell casing on the floor, and stepped quickly back into her stall.

Kick had not been a good witness in court. The prosecution had called her four times over the three months Mel was on trial. They wanted to know what she remembered about other people who had come to the house, other children, what she'd seen or heard, where they'd traveled. But there was so much that had faded into darkness.

She had spent the last decade training herself to notice details.

Tightening her fist around the still-warm spent cartridge in her hand, Kick conjured a picture in her head. The woman was in her mid-fifties and expensively maintained. She was in full makeup at nine a.m., and her black hair around her hot-pink noise-canceling headphones had been teased perfectly, which had to have required fifteen minutes and a mirror. Kick dropped the spent cartridge into a plastic tub with the rest of her shell casings. But she was at the gun range at nine a.m. on a Tuesday, so she didn't work banker's hours. No wedding ring. Some people took them off to shoot, but Kick guessed the woman didn't know that. Kick glanced across the open lanes but couldn't see the woman's target. A middle-aged woman picks up shooting for self-defense, after a violent incident or a change of circumstance, like a divorce. The woman hadn't been looking for Kick. She'd stumbled upon her. Now she was texting . . . whom? The hair and makeup could mean TV reporter. Kick didn't recognize her, but then, Kick's interest in the news was very subject-specific.

Kick ejected the empty magazine of her Glock and reloaded it with nine .45 GAP rounds.

The ten-year anniversary of her rescue was coming up. They always came looking for her before the anniversaries. *Where was she now? How was she coping?* Her mother was probably already angling for another *Good Morning America* appearance.

Kick lifted her backpack over her shoulder, stowed her Glock in her sweatshirt pocket, lowered her head, and left her stall. She was not going to run.

Even with her head down, Kick could see that the woman was still there. She had positioned herself in Kick's path. She said something, but Kick just tapped her headphones and went to step around her. The woman moved in front of her again, but Kick was agile and slid between the woman and the wall. The woman didn't give up. Kick could feel her behind her, just a foot or two back. When Kick opened the glass door from the range to the lobby gun shop, the woman caught it before it swung closed.

Kick spun around. "What?" she demanded. She could execute a front kick to the woman's chin, crushing her larynx, shattering her teeth, and breaking her jaw.

The woman smiled brightly and said something that Kick couldn't hear.

Kick took her headphones off.

The woman did the same.

Kick's grip tightened around the Glock in her pocket.

"I just wanted to say . . ." the woman said. She pressed her lips together and her eyes filled with tears. "We were all so happy you made it home."

Kick took her hand off the gun.

A gold pendant set with four different gems hung around the woman's neck, and she worried it with a nervous hand. Four gems—the birth-stones of each of her children. The woman was Kick's mother's age, which meant that she'd probably had kids about Kick's age when Kick had disappeared.

The woman wasn't a reporter. She was a mother.

Glass display cases full of weapons lined the gun shop walls below paper targets for sale: Osama bin Laden, a woman with a beret and an AK-47, zombies, a man with a watch cap and a bag full of cash.

"I prayed for you," the woman said.

Kick saw the ex-cop working behind the counter glance up from the page of *Guns & Ammo* magazine he was reading and then go back to his article.

A lot of people had told Kick that they'd prayed for her. It was like they wanted credit, to be counted. Kick was never sure how she should respond. *I guess God wasn't listening the first five years?* "Thank you," Kick muttered.

The woman put her hand on Kick's shoulders, and Kick flinched. People always wanted to touch her, especially the mothers.

"You were rescued for a reason," the woman said, and Kick groaned internally. She knew the reason she'd been rescued. Mel's IP address had turned up in an investigation into online child pornography trading. According to Frank, the entire operation was a series of botched calls and inter-agency drama. They hadn't even known she was there. The reason she was rescued was dumb luck. "If you ask me," the woman continued, "that bastard deserves what's coming to him. The devil gets his due, one way or another."

"Excuse me," Kick said politely. "I have to buy a Taser." She stepped backward, out of the woman's reach.

"We all thought you were dead," the woman called. She was gazing at Kick with a sort of glassy-eyed reverence, like she'd just found the face of Jesus on her toast. On the wall behind her, the bank robber was aiming the barrel of his gun at her back. "It's like a resurrection," the woman said, beaming. She pointed upward, at the gun shop's drop-panel ceiling. "There's a plan for you," she said. Her tongue was out a little bit, the tiny pink tip. If Kick connected with her chin, the woman would bite it right off.

The woman took a step toward Kick. "Trust yourself, Kit," she said.

Kick winced at the sound of her old name. "*Kick*," she corrected her.

There was no comprehension in the woman's face.

"I go by *Kick*," Kick said, feeling her center harden. "Not Kit. Not anymore." She hadn't been able to get used to her old name after she came home. It made her feel like an impersonator.

"Well," the woman said, touching the pendant again, "time heals all wounds."

"Your gun's too big," Kick said. "It's got too much recoil; that's why you're not hitting the target. Start with something smaller, like a .22. And aim for the head."

The woman gave the corner of her mouth a tiny scratch. "Thank you."

They looked at each other in silence for a moment. Kick felt an urge to run like she had not felt in a long time. "I have to pee," Kick said, tilting her head toward the restroom sign. The woman let her go. Kick hurried through the bathroom door and locked it behind her. The outline of the Glock was visible in her sweatshirt pocket. She had red lines on her face where her safety goggles had made an impression on her forehead and cheeks. She pulled back her hood and examined her reflection. People knew her from the Missing Child posters. Her first-grade school photograph, bangs and braids, a forced smile. She had been famous in her absence—on billboards, national news, the subject of talk shows and newspaper stories. She'd been on the covers of magazines. The first photo of her, after she was saved, went global. But she wasn't the girl people remembered—eleven years old, angry-eyed, a tangle of long dark hair down her back. Kick's mother cut her bangs and braided her hair and the family released another photograph: Kick reunited with her sister, their arms around one another. That one had been on the cover of *People*. Her mother sold pictures every year after that, on the anniversary, until Kick left home. They owed it to the public, her mother said, to let them see Kick grow up.

Kick turned the cold water on in the sink, pushed up her sleeves, and started washing her hands. Ammo left lead residue on everything. She cupped her hands under the faucet and lowered her face into the water. After she dried herself, she inspected herself in the mirror again.

She undid her ponytail and let her hair fall loose. It came down to her elbows. She didn't get haircuts. Not anymore.

Her phone buzzed in her pants pocket and she dug it out with cold fingers.

She reread the message three times. It made her stomach hurt.

An Amber Alert had just been issued by Washington State police looking for a five-year-old girl abducted by a stranger and last seen in a white SUV with Washington State plates, heading down I-5 toward Oregon.

Kick hesitated. She knew how this went.

But she couldn't stop herself.

Kick opened the police scanner app on her phone, picked up her backpack off the bathroom floor, and headed for the door, the loaded Glock still in her sweatshirt. Whenever they had traveled, Mel put her under a blanket on the floor of the backseat and switched the vehicle plates out for fake dealer ones. The dealer plates were harder to read, and produced little information, so patrol cops often didn't bother running them.

It's not like she thought she'd find the car. This was something that none of her shrinks ever seemed to understand. Kick knew exactly how futile it was. She knew she'd drive up and down the interstate until she was exhausted, and stay up half the night refreshing her browser, sorting through every detail, hunting for anything familiar. She knew that the kid was probably already dead and that when the police did find the body, it would feel like a part of Kick had died too.

That's how this went.

How it always went.

Penance wasn't supposed to be fun.

2

KICK WAS FOUR HOURS late by the time she let herself into her brother's southeast Portland apartment. Her sweatshirt was dampened with rain. She shook off the hood, took a few steps, and accidentally knocked over one of the bags of recyclables that James had been collecting inside his front door for the last month. Plastic water bottles, empty split pea soup cans, and drained Mountain Dew bottles rolled off in all directions. Kick trudged down the hall after a can. She was always chasing after something.

"You're late," James's voice called from the living room.

Her brother's apartment was two stories below her own, and the layouts were identical. The main part of the space consisted of a living room, dining room, and kitchen, all with an open floor plan, high ceilings, and oppressively large windows. The private spaces—the bathroom and bedroom—were cramped, with ugly carpeting. Kick thought there was a metaphor there somewhere.

"You better not bring that gun in here," James called.

Kick crammed the last plastic water bottle back into the bag. "Fine," she said. She took the Glock from her sweatshirt pocket and tucked it into her backpack. Then she slung the backpack over one shoulder, made her way past the rest of the recycling, and followed the hallway to the living room.

James was sitting at his computer as usual, his headphones around his neck. All three monitors were on. Programming books lined the shelf above his desk, along with coffee cups and science fiction paperbacks and Mountain Dew bottles with an inch or two of flat soda at the bottom. His desk was pushed up against a floor-to-ceiling window that was covered with inspirational posters that he had Scotch-taped to the glass. *Try to be like the turtle—at ease in your own shell. Change your thoughts and you change your world.*

"You were supposed to be here at eleven," he said without turning around. "And when I said you couldn't bring the gun in here, I didn't mean you could bring it in here if you put it in your backpack."

Kick scrutinized her backpack. James hadn't even turned around. She didn't know how he did that. Still, she ignored him, retrieved a piece of cheese pizza from a grease-stained pizza box that she had almost stepped on, and flopped down on his sofa and set the backpack at her feet. The interior wall of the living room was a collage of travel posters. Not the vintage painted kind with the art deco lettering, but the travel agency kind, the ones with a photograph of the Eiffel Tower and the words *Visit Paris!* scrawled across the corner in a cursive font. James had never been out of the country. Kick spotted a water bill on top of an issue of *Macworld* that was open on the sofa next to her, and she stuffed the bill in her sweatshirt to pay later.

"Did you see the Amber Alert?" she asked.

Her brother was still pretending to type something on his keyboard. "Is this going to be like Adam Rice?" he asked.

Adam Rice had disappeared three weeks ago from the yard of his mother's apartment building in Tacoma. It's what had set Kick off. She didn't know why—she never did. Maybe it was because Tacoma wasn't that far away. But from the first moment she saw Adam's picture, she felt a connection with him.

The pizza was cold and stale. Kick took a bite anyway. "I have it under control," she said. She got a pack of throwing stars out of her backpack and stowed them in her sweatshirt pocket. She could relax better if she had weapons immediately handy.

James spun his chair around to face her. His *Doctor Who* TARDIS T-shirt had a green crusty stain on the neck. Split pea soup, Kick hoped.

He pushed his brown hair out of his eyes and adjusted his glasses. "So the app worked?" he asked. He had recently started trying to grow a mustache. Kick didn't have the heart to tell him that he still looked fifteen. Most people were surprised to learn that he was two years older than she was.

"You designed it," Kick said. "Of course it worked."

"What did you do?" he asked heavily. "Drive up and down I-5 all morning, looking for white SUVs?"

He made it sound so ineffectual.

"It's not healthy," he said. "You know that." He pointed at the pizza in her hand. "That's five days old," he said.

She took another bite of the pizza and chewed it slowly right at him with her mouth open.

"That is so unnecessary," James said, rolling his eyes as he turned his chair back toward his desk.

He made a show of being absorbed in something on his computer screen.

Kick didn't take the bait.

Finally, James said, "Want to see what I've been doing?"

He was supposed to be getting an online certification in some new programming language. Kick craned forward, noticing that her brother's monitors weren't filled with their usual coding gibberish. She got up off the couch and joined him at the desk. It was spread with clutter, except for the area in front of his keyboard where James kept his talisman, a little man made of twisted wire. His largest screen, the center one, was checkered with video thumbnails. Kick reached across James for his computer mouse, but he swatted her hand away. "I'll do it," he said, and guided the cursor to one of the thumbnails and clicked to expand it.

The window enlarged to reveal a video feed of cars on the interstate. Kick scanned the other thumbnails. They were all similar. "What are those?" she asked.

The corner of James's mouth turned up into a satisfied smile. "Traffic cameras," he said. "I have a program that takes a screen shot of any vehicle I specify. For instance, white SUVs." His fingers grazed his keyboard and a window opened on another monitor. "Look here," he said. At least a hundred screen shots of white SUVs filled the screen.

Kick's eyes hurt trying to tell one from the next. "That's a fuckload of white SUVs," she said.

"I've crowdsourced the images," James explained. "So I've got volunteers all over the world looking at all these live as they come in. If any of them spot a vehicle with a matching plate, or dealer plates, I'll know immediately. It's faster than whatever the police are doing."

Kick wrapped her arms around her brother's neck and kissed him. His T-shirt smelled like he'd been wearing it for days. "You're brilliant," she said.

James's face reddened. She could tell he was pleased. He hadn't exactly been Mr. Sunshine lately, so it felt like a good sign. Kick sat down on the arm of his chair and leaned against him as they both watched his monitor. All the video was in black-and-white and every car appeared to be a shade of gray. Every few moments James would minimize one video and enlarge another one. There were so many cars, and so much water on the road, that the license plates were passing blurs.

Kick glanced away from the monitor and noticed a new poster on the window. It had a picture of a baseball and a Babe Ruth quote: *Don't let the fear of striking out hold you back.*

"That's two stranger abductions in the last month," Kick said.

James didn't say anything. He reached for the little wire man. The scars on his wrists were faint white stripes. She'd never asked about them. The wire man was an inch tall, small enough to hold in your hand. But James didn't let Kick touch it.

"You know what that could mean," Kick said.

James pushed his glasses up his nose. "You called the police again, didn't you?"

He knew her too well. "They said that they still don't need my help and suggested I call my therapist," she said.

"You want to help?" James asked. "Use some of your settlement money to buy them a better computer system." Then he smirked and set the talisman back in its place. "Or cuter uniforms."

Kick opened her mouth to say something smart-ass, but she forgot what she was going to say as her eyes fell on James's monitor. "Motherfucker," she said.

"What?" James asked. She felt him tense. "Oh."

A local news site was streaming live on the screen below the traffic cam footage. Kick sat up and rocked forward. A female news anchor was speaking from behind a desk. She was in her mid-fifties, with coiffed black hair and a familiar pendant. A graphic took up much of the screen next to her: a photograph of Kick, hood up, just beginning to reach for the spent cartridge at the gun range. "She *was* a reporter," Kick said. She hadn't been texting; she'd been taking a photo with her phone. "She was at the range this morning," Kick explained to James. She scowled at the screen and balled her hands into fists. "I knew I should have kicked her teeth in."

"Do you want me to turn it up?" James asked hesitantly.

"No," Kick said, eyes still glued to the silent images on the monitor. A teaser below the image read: *Kit Lannigan Update! From Kidnap Victim to Ace Shot.* She'd never be able to go to that gun range again.

Kick's photograph dissolved and another photograph appeared. Kick recognized it right away as the author photo from a book called *My Story: Lessons I Learned from My Daughter's Abduction.* Her mother had written that one. It had been the last straw before Kick filed for emancipation. *Tonight at five, interview with kidnap mom Paula Lannigan!*

Kick's stomach twisted. It was a constant struggle—not strangling her mother. "Kidnap mom." Who knew that was a career?

Then the screen went to video footage of a thickened, bearded man in a suit trying to climb the wide concrete stairs to an office building while a reporter shouted questions at him. This was the only time Kick saw Frank: when he popped up on the news, a boom mic stuck in his ruddy face. James turned up the volume. "Any comment on Mel Riley's health, Agent Moony?" the reporter hollered. "Are you glad he's dying?" Frank glowered at the camera and shoved his way past the reporter.

He'd never given an interview.

"Turn it off," Kick said quietly.

James tapped a button and the video window vanished from the screen. Kick's pulse throbbed in her ears.

"You want to talk about it?" her brother asked with a nervous glance.

A poster of a frog, caught mid-hop, was taped above the printer. *Leap, and the net will appear.*

"No," Kick said. She slid the pack of throwing stars out of her pocket, extracted one, pinched it between her thumb and forefinger, and zinged it hard at a dartboard James had hung on the opposite wall. It sank into the center target and the dartboard clattered to the floor.

"Yeah," James said drily. "You're fine."

"Sorry," Kick said, under her breath. She kissed

her brother on the cheek and stood up. "I smell like gunpowder. I need a shower." She put two fingers in her mouth and blew out an earsplitting whistle.

James cringed. "I wish you wouldn't do that," he said.

"It's the only thing he can hear," Kick said. She waited, her eyes fixed on the hall, and a moment later her dog came shuffling from James's bedroom. His muzzle was white and his gait was arthritic and he was nearly blind and almost entirely deaf, but he could still hear her whistle.

"He would have been fine by himself at your place," James said.

Kick watched as her dog limped across the living room, wagging his shaggy tail. He was part border terrier and part Australian shepherd, with a few other breeds thrown in that no one could identify. "He likes to be with family," she said. He came right to her, a big grin on his face, panting, and pressed his black snout against her knee.

"Your mail's on the counter," her brother said, turning his gaze to his monitor. "You got another letter from the court."

The federal victim notification system spit out a form letter every time Kick's image showed up in a child pornography prosecution. Because she had been the star of one of the most collected series the industry had seen, her image showed up on a lot of hard drives. They were referred to as "the Beth

Movies," and there was, incredibly, no way to get them off the Internet.

Kick scratched under Monster's hairy chin and looked into his milky eyes. She didn't care what the vet said: sometimes she could swear that dog could see her.

"Hey, Monster," she said. "Did you miss me?"

3

THE LETTER FROM THE court went with the others, unopened, into a cardboard file box in Kick's bedroom closet. The boxes took up half the closet now, three rows, four boxes high. Before she filed for emancipation at seventeen, the letters had come addressed to her mother. Kick hadn't known anything about them. A few weeks after she moved into her apartment, the first letter showed up, addressed to Kathleen Lannigan, Kick's legal name.

She had opened that one.

A man named Randall Albert Murphy was being prosecuted in Houston, the letter stated, for trading nearly three thousand child pornography photos and videos online. Sixty-seven of the images were of her.

After that, Kick stopped opening the envelopes. She kept track of the numbers for a while, adding to the running tally every time one arrived. After five hundred, she stopped counting.

Kick turned her back on her closet. Monster was staring blankly out the bedroom door, down the hall, with his head cocked.

She went over and scratched him on the top of his skull as she studied the map.

The Rand McNally pull-down classroom map of the United States hung from a bar mounted near the ceiling on the south wall of her bedroom. The map was as tall as she was, and wider than she could reach. It had come out of a classroom in Wisconsin—at least, that's what the people on eBay had said—and it had those cheery elementary school colors: lemon-yellow landmasses, tangerine-orange mountain ranges, cerulean-blue oceans and lakes. Florida was a little wrinkled, there was a tear near Delaware, and at some point in the map's life someone had circled Death Valley with a black Sharpie.

Kick had done much more damage since then. Pushpins marked the locations of kids who had been taken since Adam Rice had disappeared three weeks earlier. Oakland, Riverside, Chicago, Columbus, Richmond, Baltimore, San Antonio, and on and on. Red pushpins meant a stranger abduction; blue pushpins meant a runaway; white pushpins meant custodial interference. The system was imperfect. Runaways might leave out of free will but get abducted off the street. Custodial interference might result in the abductor parent panicking and harming or abandoning the child.

Kick ran her fingers over the surface of the map, feeling the tiny holes where pushpins had pierced the map and then been removed. A hole meant a kid had been found—dead or alive. The small perforations were hard to see with the naked eye, but under Kick's fingers the map felt like it had been peppered with buckshot.

Monster nudged her leg with his snout and Kick lowered her hand back to his head.

Printouts of Adam Rice papered the wall around the map. They'd released two Missing Child posters, and Kick had found several more pictures of him online. She had Google Street View images of the apartment building where he was taken, and a street map of the area with Post-it notes marking the locations of witnesses. Not that anyone had seen anything particularly useful. Adam's mother had been inside her first-floor apartment, twenty feet from the yard he was playing in. A utility worker installing new cable line at the corner had seen Adam still in the yard. A neighbor had seen Adam as she left to run an errand. He was there. And then he wasn't.

Monster slipped away from under her hand and a moment later dropped a ball at Kick's feet. She picked it up and tossed it behind her through the bedroom door, down the hall, and Monster went loping after it.

A newspaper photograph of Adam's mother making a statement to the press a few days after his abduction was taped next to the Pacific Ocean. Her expression was raw with grief, her eyes so swollen she could barely open them. She hugged a stuffed elephant in her arms. She told the press that she was keeping the elephant company until her son came home.

Kick reached for the box of red pushpins, took one out, and pushed it into Seattle with enough force that it left an imprint on her thumb. Tacoma was just a half hour south of Seattle, so close that the two red pushpins touched.

Monster didn't come back with the ball. Kick noticed it, vaguely, but Monster was old and he was easily distracted, so she didn't think much of it. She still hadn't showered. She peeled off her sweatshirt and walked to the bathroom, anxious to smell like something other than gunpowder.

• • •

Kick used showers as an opportunity to conduct injury checks. She started at her feet. Her blackened big toenail was progressing nicely. The nail was already starting to separate as the skin beneath it healed. She beamed at it proudly, wiggling the toe on the wet shower floor. She'd driven that toe into another student's thigh at the dojo, and his femur had been way worse off than her toenail. Kick twisted around to catalog the bruises on her legs. She'd been working on learning how to take a fall, throwing herself forward on the mat at the gym again and again until she knew how to reflexively roll. She ran her hands over the sore spots on her ribs where she'd taken hits sparring at the boxing gym, and over a scrape on her shoulder from when she spontaneously decided to take a fall on concrete just to see if she could do it. She examined the scabs on her knuckles from practicing breaking boards with her latest karate move. Each injury made her feel stronger. Not young. Not soft. Safe.

Satisfied, she turned the water off, opened the glass door, grabbed a towel, and stepped out of the shower, her skin instantly pebbling with goose bumps. She could have retreated back into the warm shower stall to dry off, but she was working on making herself tougher. She rubbed herself dry, trying to ignore the slow sucking sound the water made as it fought its way down the shower drain. This was the price of having elbow-length hair: it had a way of collecting in pipes, of forming dams and obstructions. It seemed to have an agenda all its own.

Kick wrapped herself in the towel. The condensation was clearing off the mirror. She was never as badass-looking as she imagined herself.

As she combed out her hair, the last of the shower water wheezed down the drain. The quiet only lasted a moment before she heard a faint dripping sound: *bthmmp, bthmmp*. Kick ignored it, pulling at a snarl. Her phone was on the counter. She checked it. There were no developments in the Amber Alert case. She looked back at her image in the mirror. A puddle of water was forming at her feet where runoff from her hair had pooled. *Maybe I should get a Mohawk,* she thought.

The words hung in the silence. And then: *bthmmp, bthmmp*.

Kick opened the shower door and tightened both of the knobs. She stared up at the shower-head. She didn't see any drops of water hanging from it. She stepped back and let the shower door close.

Bthmmp, bthmmp.

She spun around. It wasn't coming from the shower; it had to be coming from another source. As she surveyed the bathroom, she realized something else.

Monster wasn't there.

Her dog usually curled up on the rug in front of the sink while she was showering, and then, as soon as she got out, he'd follow her around, licking up the water she left in her wake. She didn't know why he did it. James thought it was because the water tasted like her. Eau de Kick, he called it.

Kick opened the bathroom door. The comb was still in her hair, stuck in a snarl over her ear, but she just left it there. She didn't see Monster in the hall.

She whistled.

He didn't come.

A tiny thread of fear tightened around her throat. Monster was old. He had habits. He knew his way easily around her apartment; she never moved any of the furniture and was careful not to leave things on the floor where he might run into them. But he stuck close. In the past few months he had gotten confused a few times and settled down in a room without her. When she found him, he seemed surprised, like he hadn't known she was even home. Mild dementia, the vet said. Then the vet started talking about quality-of-life issues, and Kick scooped Monster up and got out of there before they gave her another brochure on euthanasia.

She wasn't in denial, no matter what the vet said. Kick knew Monster would die one day. *Just please don't let it be today,* she pleaded silently to the universe. She walked barefoot to her bedroom, leaving a trail of wet footprints, the comb still stuck in her hair. Monster slept in her bed, and when his body finally failed him, she knew that's where he'd go.

Her feet hit the bedroom carpet and she switched on the light. The map loomed over everything: her green desk, her dresser, her bedside table, her bed. Her heart sank. Under her twisted bedding, she could see a dog-shaped lump at the end of the bed where Monster always slept.

She was certain, then, that her dog was dead. She felt his loss like a physical pressure on her chest. She had imagined this so many times. Monster was so old. He'd been dying for the last year. She wanted to let him go, to let him die in his sleep, but she wasn't ready.

Not today, she thought. *Please, just don't die today.*

Her gut tightened. She approached the bed slowly, arm extended, forcing each foot forward, the muscles in her face drawn into a grimace. She put a hand on the duvet, summoned all her courage, and snatched back the bedding like she was ripping off a Band-Aid.

The air rushed out of her lungs in a sob of relief.

It wasn't Monster, just a balled-up sheet. The dog hair that she'd disturbed when she pulled back the bedding hung in the air.

So where was he?

Kick spun around and whistled again, so hard it hurt, so hard that James probably heard her two floors below. But Monster didn't come. She had never realized before how much her apartment smelled like dog, how much dog hair there was.

She heard it again: *bthmmp, bthmmp.*

It was coming from the living room.

Kick snatched Monster's favorite bacon-flavored tennis ball off the floor and started down the hall with it. She was halfway to the living room when she noticed that her backpack had been moved.

She stopped in her tracks.

At first glance, the backpack looked like it was exactly where she had left it, on the floor inside the door to the apartment, propped against the wall. It was where she always left it when she went to punch the security code into the alarm pad. The backpack was facing the same direction it always did, shoulder straps against the wall. The zippers were still zipped. Except something was just a tiny bit off. It wasn't the kind of thing anyone else would ever notice. But she had a blind dog, and she had places for things, and the place for that backpack was three inches over.

Bthmmp, bthmmp.

Kick squinted down the hallway. The living room lights were off. The Realtor had talked up the floor-to-ceiling living room windows as a selling point when Kick had bought the building. They let in so much light, the Realtor said over and over again. Kick installed blinds before she even finished unpacking: seeing out meant that other people could see in, and the last thing she wanted were telephoto-lens photographs of her in her living room ending up in *Us Weekly*. Now, when the blinds were closed, daylight barely penetrated.

Kick squeaked the bacon tennis ball. "Monster," she hissed, even though she knew he couldn't hear her.

She checked the alarm pad on the wall. She hadn't even wanted the stupid thing; her mother had insisted on it. Kick could protect herself. Most of the time, she didn't even set the alarm. But it was on now, the green light blinking contentedly. Then, as she was looking at it, it stopped blinking. The light went out. Kick drew her towel tighter around her chest. The pad's digital screen was dark. She pushed the panic button and held it for four seconds. Nothing happened. She pushed "police" and "medical" and "fire." They depressed silently, uselessly.

Kick put her back to the wall.

She knew she should get out of the apartment. It was Self-defense 101: *Awareness is the best self-defense. Escape is the second.* But she couldn't leave without

Monster. It was a promise she'd made to herself the first time they were separated: she would not leave without her dog.

With a cautious glance toward the dark living room, Kick moved quickly to the backpack, knelt, and pulled the zipper open. The Glock was still there. She put her hand around the grip and removed it tenderly from the backpack. Mel had taught her how to shoot a .22, but it had been Frank who taught her how to shoot a .45. Kick held the Glock in one hand and the bacon ball in the other.

Pfttnk, bthnnk. The hair on the back of her neck stood up. It was the same sound, but now she could hear it more clearly.

Kick peered down the hallway. She knew that sound. She rolled the bacon ball around in her palm and then bounced it hard on the floor so it rebounded off the wall and back into her hand. *Pfttnk, bthnnk.*

A ball bouncing.

She let the ball drop from her hand, secured her towel, lifted the Glock, and started moving forward along the wall.

Her bare feet were silent on the wood floor. She took slow, deep breaths through her nose, letting her diaphragm do the work instead of her lungs. She made herself quiet.

Pfttnk, bthnnk.

As she got closer, the darkness took on shape and texture. She could see only part of the living room from her vantage point, and none of the dining room or kitchen areas. But she could make out the geometry of the modern furniture that her mother's decorator had picked out. One of the blinds was cranked slightly open and slivers of light penetrated between the slats, drawing bright stripes across the floor. Kick leaned around the corner, trying to see more, and followed a blade of light across the silhouette of her Eames-style chair.

Something moved.

Kick drew back and flattened herself against the wall.

She had seen a foot, she was sure of it—as if someone were sitting in the chair and had shifted a foot back out of the light.

She closed her eyes.

She was not young. She was not soft. She was safe. She knew how to take out someone's eye using her finger as a fishhook. She could shoot, and take a fall, and break someone's trachea with a snap of her elbow.

She opened her eyes, felt around the corner for the light switch, flipped it, raised the Glock, and entered the room.

The man sitting in her living room smiled at her.

If Kick had not been so startled, she would have shot him.

He didn't look like a meth head out to steal her TV. She guessed he was in his mid-thirties. His dark hair was short and sculpted with a sharp part on the side. He was clean-shaven. But there was something about him that seemed off, something dead about his eyes. His face was gaunt and his features were all hard angles, light and shadow. His hawkish features made the smile seem menacing.

He was wearing jeans, a T-shirt, and the sort of fashionable sneakers you aren't supposed to exercise in. The shoes looked new, never worn. A black blazer was draped over the arm of the chair, folded neatly. He didn't have the comportment of someone in the midst of committing a crime. He was fit and long limbed, his body draped in the chair like he sat there all the time, like she was the one who'd barged in on *him*. One of his elbows was propped on the arm of the chair, and in that hand he held a purple tennis ball.

He seemed to be expecting her.

Monster was sitting at his feet, quivering with anticipation, his tail wagging.

The man held up the tennis ball, then bounced it off the floor, against the wall, and caught it without looking. Monster followed the motion of the ball with his head.

Kick moved her finger over the Glock's trigger and aimed the sights at the man's head. "Get away from my fucking dog," she said.

4

THE MAN DIDN'T MOVE. Kick didn't move. A trickle of cold water dripped between her shoulder blades.

Then he let the ball go again.

Again it hit the floor, bounced off the wall, and back into his hand. Again, Monster tracked it with his frosted corneas. Kick didn't know if her dog could somehow hear that ball, make out a blur of color, or if he was just smelling it, but he was mesmerized.

Kick inched closer, her eyes moving between her dog and the man. Her small steps were meant to keep the towel up as much as they were out of any sort of caution. She felt hyperaware of her body: the bottoms of her feet pressing against the floor, the air in her lungs, the way her eyelids stuck for a fraction of a second when she blinked. The Glock remained perfectly steady in her hands. Out of the corner of her left eye, she could see the orange plastic handle of the comb, still stuck in her hair. It was the same color as the man's shoes.

Now the room seemed too bright, too colorful, like spilled candy.

Monster whined and nosed at the ball.

"I guess Frank and I have something in common," the man said smoothly.

Kick hesitated at the mention of Frank's name. Her eyes flicked to the end-table drawer by the man's elbow. She never responded to Frank's Christmas cards, but she read them, and displayed them, and then saved them, in a stack with a rubber band around it, in that drawer. "What are you talking about?" Kick demanded.

The man's irises were dark gray, like stones. "Now you've pointed a gun at both of us," the man said. He smiled some more. But his eyes remained empty.

Kick didn't like the way he looked at her. His gaze pulled at the roots of her hair. She took another step toward him, steadying the Glock. Her fingers were still wrinkled from the shower. "Who are you?" she demanded, trying to keep her voice calm.

Monster's ears perked up.

"You can call me Bishop," the man said, turning the ball in his hand.

The way he said it made her wonder if it was really his name. Kick narrowed her eyes at him. Maybe if she shot him in the kneecap, he'd tell her something true.

"Frank recommended you for a job," Bishop continued. He let the ball go again, and it hit the same two points and then landed neatly in his palm.

Monster barked for him to do it again.

Kick eyed Bishop warily. There was something coiled about him, as if he were holding in something dangerous that he wasn't ready to let out. "I don't want a job," she said.

"Frank said you'd say that," Bishop said.

Kick didn't like it when he said Frank's name. It made her bite her tongue a little. "I haven't seen Frank in years," she said.

"Well, he remembers you," Bishop said. He tossed the ball up in the air with a flick of his wrist and caught it. Kick was getting tired of that ball; she was thinking about shooting it. Monster's tail thumped rapturously on the floor.

Kick let out a sharp whistle.

Monster's ears lifted and angled toward her. He leaned forward, but something was preventing him from moving. He pawed lightly at the floor, his nails scratching noisily against the wood, and Kick realized that he was straining against a short tether. Bishop had used it to secure Monster to the base of the chair.

She crossed the rest of the room in three steps, stood in front of Bishop, and pointed the Glock squarely at his forehead. Monster scratched at the floor some more and strained to touch her knee with his wet snout. She inhaled his dog smell: flea soap and fur and old-dog stink.

Bishop's eyes darkened. He let the purple tennis ball drop from his hand. It bounced twice and then rolled under the red couch.

"I told you to get away from my dog," Kick said.

"You don't want to shoot me," Bishop said. "You'll ruin that lovely new gun. Firing an empty Glock puts tension on the firing pin. Pin could come loose. You know that."

Kick glanced at the Glock uncertainly. She had been so relieved to find it still in the backpack, she hadn't thought to check to see if it was still loaded.

Bishop's face was absolutely, unnervingly still. Monster whined and pulled at the tether. "Personally, I'm not a fan of guns," he said. "They make it too easy to hurt someone."

Kick's brain was racing. A loaded gun and an unloaded gun felt exactly the same. There was only one way to know for sure. Kick ejected the magazine and her fingers went cold. The magazine was empty. She pulled the Glock's beveled slide back and checked the chamber. Nothing. "Shit," she said.

Bishop reached up and took hold of the Glock's barrel. "Want to know an interesting fact?" he asked. "People who keep guns in their homes have a 2.7 times greater chance of being murdered." He moved his hand along the barrel toward the grip. Kick flinched as his fingers grazed hers, but she didn't let go of the Glock.

Bishop sighed. "Fine," he said. "Let me try another tack." His gray eyes settled on her. "Adam Rice," he said.

Kick stared at him, stunned.

Bishop's fingers moved over hers. She could barely feel the gun anymore. She couldn't tell where her flesh stopped and the gunmetal started. He continued to try to pry the Glock from her grip, and she continued to cling to it. She thought about using it to bludgeon him.

His eyes showed a flicker of impatience. One of his fingers moved to the inside of her wrist. "Mia Turner," he said.

Blood pounded in Kick's ears.

"Think they're connected?" Bishop drew a small circle on her wrist with his fingertip. It sent shudders up her arms. Her hand opened, and he lifted the Glock from her palm and set it on the end table next to his chair. She couldn't stop it.

"Who are you?" Kick asked him.

"An interested party," Bishop said with a faint, dark smile. He reached into the pocket of the blazer and removed a handful of .45 GAP bullets and set all nine, one by one, on the end table next to the gun. "I wanted to make sure you wouldn't shoot me," he said. "Before we had a chance to talk."

Kick glanced at Monster. Monster growled.

Bishop leaned back in the chair and regarded her with his dead eyes.

Kick inched her right foot forward on the floor, between his orange sneakers, and softened her knee.

Bishop's eyes traveled slowly down the towel that covered her. He didn't leer, but there was something about the attentiveness of his gaze that made her skin crawl. His eyes weren't the color of stone, she realized. They were more the color of concrete. "I'll wait," he said. "If you want to change."

Kick brought her knee up, aimed, and snapped her lower leg forward. The ball of her foot connected with the crotch of his jeans. She could feel the give of soft tissue underneath the denim. He doubled forward and coughed hard like he was choking on something and then slid off the chair onto his knees on the floor. His hands cradled his midsection. His head was down, dark hair in his face, but she could see that his forehead was flushed and lined with pain. She adjusted her towel and waited for him to collapse fully. When he didn't, she put her hand lightly on his shoulder and gave him a small push, and he fell over on his side on the floor into a fetal position. She knelt and hurriedly untied Monster's tether.

Bishop moaned, his knees clenched together, and rolled onto on his back. He looked like he was trying to talk, but he couldn't stop grimacing long enough to get the words out. Pulling Monster protectively behind her, Kick snatched Bishop's jacket from the back of the chair and started going through the pockets. She found a black leather wallet and flipped it open and shuffled through the contents, keeping one eye on Bishop as he struggled to get a breath.

A Washington State driver's license said his name was John Bishop. She pulled out other cards: a black American Express card with the same name on it, insurance cards, a private banking card.

Bishop squirmed, his eyes following her.

Kick put the wallet back into his jacket and felt around for anything else, her fingers landing on a folded piece of paper that was tucked in an inside pocket. She pulled it out and quickly unfolded it.

It was a satellite photo of a house. The house had a rectangular roof, a second-story deck, and a large fenced-in backyard. There were neighbors on either side, but neither close enough to ask too many questions. A white SUV was parked in the driveway.

Kick glanced down at Bishop, who was still on the floor. "Is this the car from the Mia Turner Amber Alert?" she asked.

Bishop nodded at her, his face still tense with pain.

"Why do you have this?" Kick demanded.

"I wanted to show it to you," Bishop said, gasping between each word.

Kick studied the photograph. She needed to get this to the police. They could identify the people who lived in this house. They could identify the owners of the car.

She sensed movement an instant too late.

Before she had time to react, Bishop was off the ground and had one arm hooked around her waist, the other around her neck, the crook of his elbow pressed under her chin. The photograph fluttered to the floor. Kick tried to twist free of him, but he just tightened his grip. She flailed her arms around her sides, fingers curled to scratch, but he just moved with her, his body against hers, reading her, anticipating her movements. Monster was growling at the air, hackles raised, disoriented. Kick jabbed her elbow back, expecting to make contact with Bishop's gut, but he just shifted sideways so that her elbow cut through the air, wrenching her shoulder. The towel loosened as she struggled, like she was sloughing off an extra skin, until the arm he had around her waist was all that was keeping it up. She was out of breath, panting and grunting. She managed to get a handful of Bishop's T-shirt and heard a satisfying rip as the cloth tore before she lost her grip. She kicked at him, and he heaved her up off the ground so that she was flailing, unmoored, with no leverage, her blackened toe skimming the floorboards.

She hated him.

Monster was trembling now, ears flat against his head, tail tucked under. Kick could feel saliva on her chin. Threads of it snapped in her throat as she breathed. "It's okay, boy," Kick called. But Monster kept pacing.

Kick's hair was stuck to her face. The towel was around her waist, exposing her breasts. She couldn't get Bishop off her by brute force. The pressure of his arms was unrelenting. He was stronger. He knew how to do this. But she was smarter. And she knew something he didn't: she knew that she would not be forced to do anything against her will, ever again. She let herself go limp, to make her body heavy. Five years of yoga and progressive relaxation had been good for something. As her muscles softened she felt his grapple start to give, and then he slowly lowered her feet back to the floor.

The gun was still on the end table, several arm's lengths away, the bullets a neat line of brass soldiers beside it.

Bishop hooked his left foot around her leg and then placed his orange sneaker on the floor between her feet, forcing her knees apart and securing her to the spot. Their embrace was so tight, she could feel his rib cage expanding against her as he breathed. His arm around her neck was like a choke collar, tightening if she made even a micromovement from where he wanted her to be. She could smell him, a faint clean odor like lime. She felt his arm unwind from her waist, and braced herself. Without his arm to hold it up, the towel dropped to the floor and Kick felt the air like cold hands on her naked body. Her stomach muscles went rigid. She tried to bring her thighs together, but it was impossible with the hold that Bishop had on her. He wanted her afraid? Well, screw him. She wouldn't give him the satisfaction. Monster nosed around her feet at the towel. Kick held on to the arm Bishop had around her throat. Goose bumps covered her skin; every hair was on end. But she didn't try to cover herself, and her body didn't give an inch.

"We're ready," Bishop said quietly.

Kick craned her head around. Bishop was on his phone. Another voice was saying something in response to his, but she couldn't make out the words. In her peripheral vision she saw him lower the phone and then felt him tuck it back in a pants pocket. Her pulse throbbed against the inside of his elbow. Some of her hair was caught under his arm, and her scalp stung where it was being pulled. Bishop's lower leg was still hooked around hers, keeping her legs open. Monster licked her ankles, like he was comforting her. Her nakedness felt like another person in the room. When she got the chance, she'd go for Bishop's eyes.

She felt the sound in her skin first. It flushed across her body like a fever. The faraway thrum of helicopter blades. The vibration of the engine came through the floorboards, up through the soles of her feet, and echoed inside her hips. Even Monster looked up. Kick's body went stiff. Bishop clenched her tighter.

"That's our ride," Bishop said, his breath hot in her ear.

She couldn't stop it this time. Her fear crept up her legs, through her stomach and her spine, and finally settled in her heart. "I'm not going with you," Kick said.

Bishop gave her neck a wrench, and Kick's vision went momentarily black. She dropped her arms to her sides and let her body go slack. "If you don't," he said, "two kids will die." Kick was motionless. Bishop's lips were inches from her temple. "So hear me out."

His voice was chilling in its matter-of-factness. She

felt it: a physical cold. Monster, too, seemed to sense it, and he began to whine, his anxious whimpers muffled by the steady churning of the helicopter blades. Bishop unhooked his leg from hers. She remained perfectly still, waiting for his next move. Then, slowly, like a man releasing a feral animal in the woods, he cautiously removed his arm from her neck.

The helicopter was louder, closer.

She turned and stepped back from him, naked, panting, the towel a circle of yellow around her feet. She didn't look at the nine bullets on the end table. She didn't calculate the time it would take to load the magazine. She didn't want to be distracted. She didn't cross her arms over her bare breasts, or move to pick up the towel to cover herself. She kept her eyes on Bishop's, brought her index and middle finger together, bent them slightly in case she hit bone, and shifted her weight back onto her left foot.

"Before you try to blind me, look at the sat photo again," Bishop said. He didn't sound particularly concerned about the blinding bit. He didn't even make a defensive move, which irritated her. *Try* to blind him? She could jab her fingers knuckle deep into his cornea before he could lift a hand to stop her. "I need you to look at the sat photo again," he said, a little more urgently.

She noticed then that he had barely broken a sweat. He knew how to do this: how to subdue someone, how to break into an apartment.

How long had he been waiting there, biding

time until she stepped out of the shower? He'd known to ambush her at her most vulnerable.

The windows of the apartment rattled in their frames, and the vibration under Kick's feet made her think of Beth, of that last night on the farm. She let her hand relax.

The satellite photograph was on the floor. She crossed to it and knelt, and Monster was immediately at her side, pressing against her, like he was shielding her naked body with his own. Kick reached for the yellow towel and brought it under her armpits and around her chest. She kept one hand on her dog as she reached for the photo, scratching his muzzle, and moving her fingers over the soft velvet of his triangular ears, trying to reassure him with her touch. By the time she turned back to Bishop, she had the towel secured and a hand coated with dog hair.

Kick's eyes searched the photograph, stalling, battling for equilibrium. House. Car in the driveway. Plants on the deck. Backyard. What was she supposed to see?

The whir of the chopper was directly above them. She glanced up. It sounded like it was landing on the roof. Kick could hear it inside her head like a memory. She stole a peek at the Glock on the end table, useless to her. Bishop stood nearby, too close, his coiled calm an implied threat. Monster was limping in circles around them, gazing occasionally at the ceiling. Even her deaf dog could hear that racket.

The helicopter rotors were slowing, the sound becoming a dull throb. The chopper had landed and was cycling down. Whoever was up there, time was running out.

House. Car in the driveway. Plants on the deck. Backyard.

Wait. House.

She squinted at the photograph, at the second-floor window at the front of the house. The glass looked dark at first glance, but if you really looked you could see a shape, like a small face, like a child looking out. Kick snapped her head up at Bishop. He had his hands in his pockets, eyebrows raised. *Shit*. The photograph was trembling in her hands. She was doing it again, going down the maze. She could feel her skin start to tingle with excitement, the thrill of possibility, of hope. She lifted the photograph and peered at it closer, to convince herself that it was true, that her mind wasn't playing tricks on her. Because she knew that face. It was on her bedroom wall; it stared at her as she slept. She had studied it, committing it to memory, burning it into her brain, so she would always know that image, no matter how many years passed. There was no doubt in Kick's mind that she was looking at Adam Rice. He was alive.

She didn't know if Bishop was good or bad, trustworthy or not. Maybe it didn't matter.

This was what she had been waiting for.

Her brain was already going a mile a minute. The white SUV in the driveway connected this house to Mia Turner's abduction, so this was possible proof that Mia Turner and Adam Rice had been abducted by the same people.

She looked up from the photo. "What are you?" she asked Bishop.

Bishop stepped forward and lifted the photograph from her hands. "I used to sell weapons," he said.

"As in guns?"

"Among other things," he said.

"'Other things'?"

Bishop shrugged. "I made a lot of money." He held the satellite photograph up. "And a lot of friends with access to expensive toys."

"I've never heard of you," Kick said.

"That's funny," Bishop said with a faint smile. "Because I've heard of you."

Kick didn't know what to make of him at all. "You should have opened with that," Kick said, indicating the photograph.

"I was planning on getting around to it," Bishop said, walking back to the chair and picking up his jacket.

She noticed that he moved a little gingerly. "Did I hurt you?" she asked.

Bishop shrugged the blazer on. "Only a little," he said.

"Next time I'll know to do it harder," Kick said.

"Next time I won't give you the chance," Bishop said.

Kick considered hitting him in the nuts again,

right then and there. Instead, she did the next most aggressive thing that occurred to her: she peeled off the damp yellow towel, held it out at arm's length, and let it drop.

Bishop didn't react; he didn't even avert his eyes.

Flummoxed, Kick stepped directly in front of him, stark naked; all hair and breasts and pubic hair, scrapes, bruises, and strained muscles. She drew herself up taller, shoulders back, feet apart. Except for the sound of Monster pawing frantically under the couch for something, it was quiet. No rotor noise. Which meant that the chopper was parked, waiting, on the roof above them.

Bishop regarded her thoughtfully. "You have some intimacy issues, don't you?"

She had wanted to see what he'd do. Now it felt more like he was testing *her*.

"We're wasting time," he said, glancing upward.

"I haven't said I'm going with you," Kick said.

"Yeah," Bishop said. "And I haven't told you that my nut sack hurts so much I can barely stand." He grimaced and adjusted himself. "But we both know it's true."

Kick felt a satisfying pride in that.

Bishop slipped the photo back into his blazer. "You're coming with me, and I'll tell you why," he said. He had lowered his voice, so that she had to lean in to hear him. "In not very long, Mel Riley is going to die in prison of kidney failure."

He said it like it was nothing. Like it was a given.

Kick was afraid to move, afraid that the smallest gesture might give away more than she wanted to.

"He's done ten years' hard time," Bishop continued, "and he hasn't given up a single detail about his network of associates."

Bishop moved closer, and she wanted to lean back, to step away, but she made herself stand her ground. "His *contacts*," Bishop said, and the word sounded vulgar. "Child pornographers, pedophiles, the scum off the sole of humanity's shoe, the people who aided and abetted your abductors, sheltered them in some cases—they are still at it, exploiting children with impunity."

"Stop it," she said. Her body hurt. It was like she had more nerve endings; suddenly she could feel the perimeter of each and every bruise.

"You could have stopped it ten years ago," Bishop said. "All you had to do was *nothing*."

And there it was. He knew about the database. No one was supposed to know. That testimony had been sealed. It didn't fit the narrative. The rescue story worked for everyone: the FBI, Kick's family, the media. It made for feel-good television. The fact that Kick had autonuked Mel's database of contacts and blown the FBI's shot at taking down hundreds or thousands of criminals? That was an inconvenient truth that no one wanted to talk about. The floor felt like it was softening under Kick's feet.

"I get why it eats at you," Bishop said. "Why you have that map, with the pushpins, on your wall; why you paper your bedroom with abduction stories. You must think: How many Amber Alerts could have been prevented if you'd done nothing that night?"

How many? "So?" she said.

"So that's why you'll come with me," Bishop said. "Not because any of that shit I just said is true, because it's not, and you know that—you were a kid, and you'd been manipulated—but because you blame yourself anyway. And you know that sticking pushpins in a map isn't going to change anything. But coming with me to the house in that sat photo, using your background to see things I can't—that's at least in the ballpark."

God, he was maddening. It wasn't that he was wrong; it was his complete confidence that he was right that really irritated her. "How's your nut sack now?" she asked.

"Maybe it's not too late to get someone else," Bishop said.

"I'm in," Kick said. She wanted him to look at least a little surprised, but he didn't, which only made it worse. "Not because of your speech," she added. She didn't need him. She had spent most of her life training for this. She was an escape artist, a warrior. She couldn't walk away from an opportunity like this. Because while saving a kid wouldn't make up for what she'd done, it would be a start. "I guess I'll get dressed," she said.

Monster yelped with pleasure and a purple tennis ball rolled out from under the couch and across the room. Monster hustled after it as fast as a hobbled, arthritic, blind canine can.

Bishop shifted painfully, reached into his pocket, and extracted his phone. "Can I get some ice, maybe?" he asked.

Kick stared at him in disbelief. He was already busy typing a text and didn't look up. "Get it yourself," Kick said, turning away. "Asshole," she added, under her breath. She stalked off, naked, toward her bedroom. Monster followed her, tail wagging, the tennis ball in his mouth.

"Welcome to the team," she heard Bishop call after her. "I think we're really going to enjoy working together."

5

KICK HAD A WORRY list. She added to it every day. By keeping track of each worry, she could put off worrying in the moment and instead do it all at once during the designated worry period she set aside before dinner. The so-called list now was five composition books long. Adam Rice's name was on it, and recently there had been a lot of entries about Monster's health and Kick's dwindling savings. The helicopter banked sharply, and Kick bent over her notebook and scribbled another item on the list.

Vomiting.

Her handwriting was barely legible. She clutched the airsickness bag that the helicopter pilot had given her. She could still see James standing in his apartment doorway, holding Monster's leash. He'd pointed out that the image of Adam Rice had been enlarged, grainy; the license plate on the SUV had been too fuzzy to read. James was James. Logical. Careful. Neurotic. Kick was only one of those things.

The helicopter dipped and banked again. The pilot looked like Thor, or at least like a low-rent, steroid-fueled version of him. Kick was sure she was green. Bishop didn't look airsick at all. He was up in front next to Thor, with his phone out and his orange sneakers on the chopper's dash. The windshield was streaked with rain. They were flying low, below the cloud cover. If Kick looked down, she could see rush-hour traffic crawling along the Banfield. But mostly she avoided looking down.

She added *Helicopter crash* to the list.

The helicopter swooped earthward and Kick's insides took a second to catch up. She braced a hand on the back of the pilot's seat, lowered her head, and watched as her long braid swung between her knees. *I will not vomit. I will not vomit. I will not vomit.* Thor's blond hair was tied back with a leather strap. The back of his bomber jacket had a lightning-bolt insignia embroidered on it and something else that Kick couldn't make out. She snuck a peek at Bishop. His expression was vague, or maybe bored, or maybe that's just what assholes looked like. She tried to see what he was reading on his phone in the reflection of his sunglasses, but they weren't polarized enough. *Reading.* Even thinking about reading made Kick's mouth fill with warm saliva. She swallowed it down. *I will not vomit.* Bishop hadn't said a word to her since they'd climbed aboard the helicopter on her roof, even though all of them, including Thor, were wearing headsets with microphones. The headsets were supposed to reduce the noise, but as far as Kick could tell, hers wasn't working.

She was relieved when she recognized landmarks that indicated they were close to the airport. That huge sign, four yellow letters on blue, all capitals: *IKEA*. Wasn't there an IKEA near every airport in the world?

Thor tilted the helicopter toward the ground. Kick shut her eyes.

She knew the instant the chopper touched down. Her body was still, settled, once again her own. The engine changed in pitch as the pilot shut down the engine and rotors.

Kick opened her eyes. The passenger-side door was open and Bishop was gone. Kick unlatched her seat belt, threw off her headset, heaved her heavy pack off the floor, put her worry book under her arm, and pushed open the chopper's back door. Rain spit in her eyes, and her braid lashed around like a whip.

This was not a part of Portland International Airport that she had ever been to before. Sleek small planes dotted the runway. She spotted Bishop headed toward one. She didn't have the address of the house in the satellite photo. If he left without her, she realized, she'd have nothing.

Technically, you're not supposed to exit a helicopter until the blades stop rotating. But if the chopper is on level ground, the main rotor blades are going to be above your head. Kick knew this, and she also knew that most people who got chopped up by helicopters trudged right into the tail rotor. She took hold of her hair, hunched under the main rotor blades, and cleared the tail rotor by fifty feet, her black boots slapping against the wet runway.

Bishop was halfway up the stairs to one of the larger private planes. Emblazoned on the fuselage, glistening in the wet slick of rain, Kick noticed a logo, a black *W* in a circle. It probably stood for "Weasel." A flight attendant was waiting at the top of the stairs with a huge black umbrella. Kick knew she was a flight attendant because she was dressed like some sort of caricature of a flight attendant, like Flight Attendant Barbie. Kick called Bishop's name but he didn't turn. Kick considered shooting him to get his attention but decided it would take too long to draw her weapon. Bishop disappeared through the plane door just as Kick reached the bottom of the stairs. Flight Attendant Barbie was at the door folding the umbrella. Kick stomped up the steps. Flight Attendant Barbie looked up, seemingly flummoxed by Kick's arrival, or maybe by the complex mechanism of the umbrella. Her sky-blue uniform was spotted with raindrops. Her white blouse showed a lot of freckled cleavage. She was wearing nude pantyhose and stilettos that could take out someone's eye.

"Excuse me," Kick said, shoving past her, out of the rain and into the cabin.

The interior of the plane was all light wood and creamy leather. It smelled like an expensive car, like it had just been Armor All'd. No industrial blue carpeting. No foldout trays. No fighting for space in an overhead bin. Six enormous cushioned seats sat on either side of the plane.

Kick stood motionless, dripping onto the carpet.

"Take a seat anywhere," Bishop said. He had settled into one of the chairs at the back of the plane and had his nose in his smartphone again. He didn't look up. She wasn't sure how he even knew she'd come on board.

Flight Attendant Barbie had managed to fold the umbrella and had wriggled around Kick through the door. She pulled the door closed behind her and locked it.

Kick tightened her grip on her backpack strap and considered her seating options. Then she plunked down in a chair a few chairs back from Bishop. She put the worry book on her lap and the damp backpack at her feet. The chair swiveled. She pushed off the floor and spun around. Flight Attendant Barbie dropped a towel in Kick's lap, then moved on to Bishop.

"Would you like a drink, sir?" Flight Attendant Barbie asked him. Kick watched her, fascinated. Her face was somehow both pretty and indistinct, and she had the curves of one of those girls from the mud flaps of eighteen-wheelers.

"No, thanks," Bishop said. He looked back at Kick and smiled. It was a reptilian smile, thin-lipped and hard to read. "But I'd love a bag of ice," he said.

"Certainly, sir," said Flight Attendant Barbie, and she appeared authentically delighted at the task. She wiggled past Kick on her way to the galley, eyes fixed with purpose. She didn't ask Kick if she wanted a drink.

Kick's phone buzzed in her lap, startling her. It was a text from James. YOU STILL OKAY? it read. When she'd dropped Monster off she had agreed to text James every two hours. YES, Kick typed back.

Then she crossed *Vomiting* off the list.

Flight Attendant Barbie tottered back with the ice. Kick turned off her phone for the flight. When she looked back up, Flight Attendant Barbie was hovering over Bishop with ice in a ziplock bag and towel. Her blouse was tight. She'd lost the jacket somewhere between the main cabin and the galley.

"Where would you like it, Mr. Bishop?" she asked.

Bishop was checking texts again. The neck of his shirt flopped down in a triangle where Kick had ripped it. He swiped at his phone's touch screen, opened his knees, and gestured to his lap.

Flight Attendant Barbie bent at the waist, all rounded buttocks and toned calves, and pressed the bag of ice against Bishop's groin. "How does that feel, Mr. Bishop?" she asked.

Unbelievable.

Bishop's eyes lifted from his phone.

So that's what it took to get his attention.

Kick would sooner shoot him in the back.

Kick coughed to remind them she was there.

Bishop leaned his head back. "A little to the left,"

he said, and Kick thought she saw him look at her again, but she couldn't be sure.

Flight Attendant Barbie shifted the ice.

"Much better," Bishop said.

"I have a gun," Kick said.

Both the flight attendant and Bishop turned and looked at her. The flight attendant's hand was still cupped against Bishop's groin. She had lipstick on her front teeth that hadn't been there before.

"A Glock 37," Kick said, liking the way the name of the weapon made the flight attendant flinch. Kick also had pepper spray, a Leatherman, a Taser, two extra magazines of .45 GAP ammo, and a box of Winchester jacketed hollow points in her backpack. "I have a permit," Kick added. "But I need to check it, right?" Firearms had to be declared, unloaded, stowed in a hard-sided locked container, and checked. Everyone knew that. She didn't want the Glock confiscated while she made her way through a month of TSA paperwork.

Bishop was back on his phone. "This isn't commercial air travel," he said. Then he seemed to suddenly remember the woman whose hand was on his cock. "I want wings up in five," he told her.

Flight Attendant Barbie straightened up with a disappointed sigh. "Yes, sir," she said. Duty called. "Anything else?"

Kick resisted asking for a glass of water.

Bishop pulled his ripped T-shirt off over his head. Kick was so startled, she forgot to look away. He was muscular, she had to admit, lean but toned, with enough definition to catch the light. He tossed Flight Attendant Barbie the shirt. She cradled it, along with the ice.

"Can you get me a new shirt?" Bishop asked.

As Flight Attendant Barbie slunk off through a door at the back of the plane, Kick leaned forward over the side of her chair and could just make out what looked like the corner of a king-size mattress.

"Is that a bedroom?" Kick asked. She didn't even want to think about what went on in there. "Seriously?"

The plane started taxiing, and Kick put on her seat belt.

"Check your phone," Bishop said.

Kick studiously avoided looking at his abs. "For what?"

Bishop held up his own phone and wiggled it. "I sent you something," he said.

"I turned it off," Kick said.

"Again," Bishop said, "not commercial air travel."

"Right," Kick said. She retrieved her phone, enabled her browser, and checked her email. She had a new message from jBishop@Bishop.com. No subject line. She clicked on the email. There was no message, only an attached PDF. She opened it and found a sixty-five-page series of documents. Most of it consisted of documentation regarding the abduction of Adam Rice. Interviews, photographs, forensics.

"Is this a police report?" she asked. The plane

was going faster. The runway flashed by out the window.

"I told you I have friends in the government," Bishop said.

Actually, he'd said he had friends with expensive toys, but Kick decided not to quibble. Instead, she pretended to scan the attachment while she surreptitiously forwarded it to James.

"How do you know my email address?" she asked Bishop.

He swiveled his chair around so that he was no longer facing her. There was a logo on the back, stitched into the flap of cream-colored leather that draped over the headrest: a *W* with a circle around it, like the one on the outside of the plane. "I told you," Bishop said.

"I know," she said. "You have friends in the government."

The plane lifted into the air and began its steady incline into the sky. There was no getting off now, no turning back. Kick hoped it was a smoother ride than on the chopper. She studied the photo of Adam Rice looking earnestly up from the digital file. The flight attendant came back with a new shirt for Bishop that looked exactly like the old one. Kick peeked up as he put it on. Then she flipped to the back of the worry book, where she kept a list of self-destructive behaviors she needed to work on, and wrote, *Getting into vehicles with strangers.* She underlined it.

6

KICK KNEW A LOT about cars. She knew how to execute a hairpin turn, she knew to always cross her palms over her chest before jumping from a speeding vehicle, and she knew that every American car made after 2002 had an emergency release lever inside the trunk should you happen to find yourself in need of one. She knew that the car Bishop retrieved from a hangar at Seattle's Boeing Field was a Tesla Model S. She knew that it had cost a hundred grand, standard, and that—judging by the abundance of leather and the car's all-glass panoramic roof—Bishop had gone with some add-ons. The touch screen on the dash was bigger than her home computer monitor.

They were headed south on I-5, technically still in Seattle, though all the good parts of Seattle were behind them. The interstate sliced through California, Oregon, and Washington, and extended all the way from Mexico to Canada, and nothing good ever happened on it. Kick had a theory that 30 percent of the drivers on it at any given time were actively committing a crime.

"I thought you'd have a driver," Kick said to

Bishop, hitting "send" on the text she'd just sent James.

Bishop smirked. "I'm trying to remain inconspicuous," he said. He whipped the Tesla around a Saab.

The road was dry, but the Seattle sky was veiled with low cloud cover. Portland got a few more inches of actual rainfall, but Seattle had Portland beat when it came to smothering gloom. It was cloudy 201 days out of the year, and partly cloudy 93 days. Kick knew a lot about weather too. She liked forecasts, almanacs, tide charts. She liked to know what was coming. It was a safety precaution not enough people took.

"How fast does this thing go?" she asked Bishop.

"One-thirty-two," Bishop said with a grin.

He could drive. Kick saw how he shifted his attention between the vehicle in front of theirs and the ones six or eight ahead, anticipating traffic. He used the accelerator smoothly, and when he braked, he squeezed the pedal before he put his foot down and then tapered off so that the motion of the car was always fluid.

Bishop gave the wheel a sharp turn and veered around a van into the carpool lane. He didn't turn the wheel too soon like most people did, so he didn't have to let up on the throttle. Most drivers merged too slowly, making the engine work harder than it needed to.

They were at the southern edge of the city. Thick trees formed a hedge on either side of the interstate, protecting drivers from the sight of auto dealerships and office parks. The slate-colored sky was darkening. Not so much a sunset as a progressive dimming of light.

"Is anyone meeting us there?" she asked.

"Like who?" Bishop asked, merging right, across two lanes.

"The cops? Your bodyguards? Blackwater mercenaries? Your royal footmen?"

"It's not called Blackwater anymore," Bishop said.

That wasn't the point. "It's just us?" Kick asked. Her throat constricted slightly. "We're going to a house that might be connected to two child abductions, and it's just us?"

"That's the point." Bishop veered right and exited the interstate. He didn't lift his foot off the gas. Accelerating is the hardest thing a car can do; the more you kept your foot on the gas, the better. "I just need you," Bishop said.

Was that supposed to make her feel better? Kick unzipped her backpack, moved her Glock to her lap, got out her worry book, and opened it.

Bishop looked at her sideways. "What's that for?" he asked.

"It's a worry book," Kick said. "If I have a worry, I—"

"I meant the Glock," Bishop said.

"Shooting the kidnappers." Obviously.

"No guns," Bishop said firmly. "I don't like guns."

Everything about this guy made Kick's head hurt. "I thought you were a weapons dealer," she said.

"I used to be," he said.

Bishop was paying a lot of attention to the road behind them. His eyes darted between his rearview and side mirrors. "Keep a lookout," he said.

Kick twisted around so she could see out the back window. The street was quiet. She didn't see any headlights behind them. She didn't see anything. "For what exactly?"

"We're almost there," Bishop said.

Kick wiped the palm of her trigger hand on her thigh and then rewrapped it around the grip of the Glock.

When people thought of Seattle, they thought of Craftsman houses and coffee shops and grunge guitar chords and sensible rain gear and guys throwing fish around at Pike Place Market. But Seattle had crappy neighborhoods, like anywhere. This was one of them. Split-level ranch homes with ugly yards, one after the next. There was nothing to walk to and no sidewalks to walk on. The only business Kick spotted was a burned-out low-rent motel surrounded by a chain-link fence and No Trespassing signs. Bishop took a left down a dark residential street. Televisions flickered in the windows. RVs sat in the driveways. The houses were big and cheap and indistinguishable. The road they were on snaked alongside the edge of the hillside and a No Dumping sign warned that there was a $5,000 fine for tossing trash below. A hundred feet later they came to a Dead End sign to the left of a fifteen-foot laurel hedge.

It was the kind of neighborhood where people didn't ask too many questions.

Bishop pulled the car around the hedge, past a For Rent sign that promised 3+ bedrooms for $1,300, and up a gravel driveway. Kick's body tensed and she inched down in her seat and tightened her grip on the Glock. This was not how she had imagined this going. Where were the helicopters? Where were the friends in the government? The gravel grinding under the tires seemed unbelievably loud. She peeked over the dash, which radiated a violet glow from the touch screen. The sky had faded to a bleak twilight and the house was dark except for a porchlight, but Kick recognized it from the satellite photo, a split-level ranch like all the rest, except more isolated. Bishop pulled to a stop. He braked so expertly the gravel barely crackled. Then he opened the driver's-side door, stepped out of the car, and left her. Kick hesitated for a second before she followed. Then she strapped on her backpack, tossed the worry book aside, and went after him. She raised the Glock as she exited the car, using the Tesla for cover. The smell of fresh paint fumes lingered in the air.

Bishop was in the front yard, waiting in the shadows, looking up at the house.

Somewhere, a dog started barking. Kick gazed at the cheerless house.

Something wasn't right.

There was no white SUV to be seen. In the photo there had been a bamboo wind chime hanging from the porch overhang. Now it was gone. Kick squinted up at the second story. The railing was empty. In the photo, there had been plants.

A Realtor's lockbox hung from the doorknob.

Kick lowered the Glock.

No one lived in this house. "When was the photo really taken?" she demanded.

"I told you you wouldn't need a gun," Bishop said.

Heat rose in Kick's cheeks. She raised her weapon and aimed at the front of the Tesla. "I wonder what would happen if I put a bullet through the 1,000 pounds of battery under your hood," she said.

It was the first time she'd seen Bishop flinch. "The sat photo was taken ten days ago," he said, eyes on the gun. "I didn't get it until early this afternoon. I sent my people here immediately, but the place had already been cleared out."

His *people*? He hadn't mentioned any people. What else wasn't he telling her?

She raised an eyebrow. The Tesla was twenty feet away. Even in the low light, the hood practically gleamed. It would be like hitting the broad side of a barn.

Bishop directed a worried look at his car and then reached into his blazer, withdrew a small spiral-bound black notebook, and opened it. "According to the landlord," he read, "the occupant moved out ten days ago. Josie Reed, in her fifties. Worked at home. No kids living at the residence, neighbors think she might have had a boyfriend, but no one got a good look at him. She drove a decade-old Outback. Packed a U-Haul trailer and moved out in the middle of the night, no forwarding address." He closed the notebook with a flick of his wrist and looked at Kick. "Josie Reed isn't her real name," he said. "She used a fake social, and the landlord never ran a background check. He owns several properties in the neighborhood but isn't very hands on due to the fact that he is currently living in an assisted-living facility. He says he's keeping her deposit." Bishop scratched his temple. "Anything else you want to know?"

"Why did you bring me here?" Kick asked warily. The dog was barking its head off now. No one yelled at it to shut up.

"I wanted to know what you thought of the house," Bishop said.

"The rent seems a little high."

His gray eyes didn't leave her. "Tell me about the house, Kick. Does it look right?"

She knew what he meant. She had lost track of how many houses she had been moved to during her life with Mel. Forty? Fifty? They never stayed anywhere long. The houses changed, but their attributes remained the same. Each was ideally suited for one purpose: hiding a child.

Kick took a tiny step back and slowly lowered the Glock. The bottoms of her feet itched. She tried to focus, to push back the tide of fractured images she was so practiced at keeping at bay. "You said she drove a Subaru?" she asked.

Bishop nodded.

Then it wasn't her white SUV. "What did the boyfriend drive?" she asked.

"No one noticed."

Kick scrutinized the house. The ranch style allowed for a big footprint, and a big footprint meant a big basement. "If I wanted to hide a kid," she said, "I'd want a sizable basement like this one." She peered at the basement windows closest to them. Both had been blocked from the inside with dark cloth. She cleared her throat. "I'd want a rental, month to month, ideally. Streets with no sidewalks means no foot traffic, few unplanned interactions with neighbors. I'd want a hedge around the property, or a tall fence." She turned and looked behind them down the driveway. "I didn't see any bikes in the yards we passed. I'd look for that too. I'd want a neighborhood without too many kids. Kids notice other kids in a way that adults don't. And they talk to one another. So if a new kid moves into the neighborhood, all the kids know." She snuck a glance at Bishop. He was studying her. Not the way that people usually did. She didn't see any of the usual sorrow-tinged pity. But the weight of his attention still made her uncomfortable. She slipped the gun into the pocket of her jacket. "So, yeah," she said, "the house looks right."

"What else?" Bishop asked.

He was still testing her. Kick didn't like it. It made her feel like a child. "I don't trust you," Kick said. "I don't even like you."

Bishop did not appear overly devastated by this news. "I don't care," he said. "What *else?*"

"The chalk," Kick said. "There's a piece of light-blue sidewalk chalk on the porch steps."

"Good girl," Bishop said.

Good girl. The words sucked the air out of Kick's lungs. Some words were like that: they circled her head like flies. She didn't know why.

When she was a kid, the shrinks told her she had anger issues. But she didn't have anger issues, at least not the way that they meant. She was just angry.

She had learned to redirect her anger since then, and to reduce triggers that led to aggression. She had used that last bit of pop psych to get out of her mother's house during the emancipation hearing, because her mother—she was one giant walking rage-trigger. But redirecting was the most useful, and it was the only thing stopping her from body-slamming Bishop to the ground, because she wanted to, she really, really did.

Instead, she stalked past him, over to the steps,

and picked up the blue chalk. *Take a time-out*—that was always the first step on the anger management lists. Kick concentrated on the chalk. The edges were smooth where it had been dragged over rough concrete, used by a kid to draw pictures on the sidewalk. Kick's fingers were blue with chalk dust. She smiled. *What was the second redirection strategy? Identify possible solutions.* She had to get inside the house and see for herself what was going on. Bishop was clearly some sort of unreliable psychopath. Kick snuck a peek at him, then looked away when their eyes met. She returned her attention to the chalk, rolling it between her hands until her palms were entirely blue.

"Catch," she said, and she tossed the chalk to Bishop—or, more accurately, tossed it *at* him.

He snatched it easily out of the air.

Kick nudged the heel of one boot off with the toe of the other.

"That's a bad idea," Bishop said.

She didn't like that, how he seemed to know what she was going to do almost as soon as she did. What was the third redirection strategy? *Think before you speak.* Now, there was a lesson that had been drilled into her as a kid. She was thinking Bishop was a fuckwad, so she didn't say anything. She got one boot off and then the other, and set it beside the first. Then she tucked the Glock in her backpack, strapped it on her back, and started walking the perimeter of the house, looking for her way in.

"You don't take constructive criticism very well, do you?" Bishop asked.

Kick kept her eyes skyward. Even with the sun gone, light pollution from the city kept the clouds bright. For her purposes, it was better than a full moon.

The second-story deck was her best shot. She visually backtracked down the side of the house, identifying her route: water meter, windowsill, gutter bracket, cable box, railing. What was the fourth redirection strategy? *Get some exercise.* She put the toe of her socked foot on the water meter, hooked a chalked hand around the window frame, and lifted herself upward.

The barking started almost instantaneously, a steady yap yap yap, like artillery fire. It sounded like the same dog as before, close, but not too close, just some neighborhood K-9 wannabe who didn't know how to mind his own business.

She had to ignore it, to focus.

Scaling the side of a house is a lot like rock climbing: it's all about adequate handholds and footholds. The chalk helped with traction. Kick kept her center of gravity over her feet and pushed up with her legs, her braid smacking against her shoulder blades. The fading light was a challenge. She groped for another handhold, using the chalk for traction, and managed to find a cable box, then she found another foothold. The dog was going ballistic. The noise it made was crawling under her skin, made it hard to concentrate. She willed the dog to shut up. Climbing was all about solving one problem at a time. Power was relative to body size. Balance and flexibility were paramount. As long as you had three points of body in contact with the wall and you didn't panic, you were fine. Having a high percentage of Lycra in your pants didn't hurt either.

She was almost there. But the dog was rattling her. She wished she had her worry book so she could add the dog to the list and worry about it later, but the book was in the car, so she had no choice but to do the worrying now. She craned her head over her left shoulder, in the direction it sounded like the noise was coming from. The laurel hedge that separated the house she was attempting to climb from the house next door had a dead spot where the leaves had shriveled, and it made a kind of window. There was light coming from the other side, and Kick swore she saw a flash of movement. She snapped her head forward. Sometimes it was better not to see the things that go bump in the night. Don't look. Eyes forward. She managed to get a toehold on the cable box and was in the process of shifting her weight to it, when a sudden blast of pain shot through her foot. She caught herself as she cried out, biting her tongue so that her shriek came out more like a startled turkey gobble. It didn't matter. The dog went bonkers. Kick lost her footing and barely managed to catch herself with her hands, clinging to the slats of the upper-deck railing as her feet scrambled

in midair, searching for solid ground. The dog
sounded like Cujo now, like it was horse-size and
rabid. But one problem at a time. Kick knew she'd
lost a toenail. She'd felt the pop as it caught. She
found the cable box again with her foot, pushed
off it with a grunt, and, using all her arm strength,
pulled herself up just enough that she was able to
hook her foot between the railing slats. She clung
horizontally to the railing, twenty feet off the
ground, and hoped that Bishop could see this. Not
the slipping part but the awesome, badass recovery.
The idea gave her strength as she clawed her way
slowly over the side of the railing. She had to take a
moment to catch her breath. Her big toe throbbed.
Cujo was howling even louder than before. Kick
moved onto her knees and crawled across the patio
deck, to the railing nearest the dog. The house
was dark but an outdoor fixture had been left on,
and Kick could make out the general geography
of the yard and the movement of a manic, barking
shadow in the grass. There was an ancient cherry
tree in the yard, massive and gnarled, and the dog
was circling it. No, he was tied to it, or at least to a
stake near the base of the trunk. From up here, the
dog looked small and hobbled, pacing along with a
weird hopping limp. As it moved closer to the light,
its silhouette sharpened, and Kick recognized the
distinctive shape of its long snout and pointed ears.
Not Cujo. Lassie. Kick realized then, as it rounded
the tree, why it moved so strangely. Her nemesis
was a three-legged collie.

Her fury at the dog was momentarily supplanted by her fury for its owner. What kind of jackass tied a dog up outside all night like that? The backyard was fenced in. It didn't even need to be tethered.

Then the dog's howl went up a decibel and her sympathy for it instantly faded. Lassie was clearly on a mission, intent to wake up the whole block.

Kick crawled along the balcony deck over to the sliding glass door and gave the handle a try. It was locked. She sat down, shrugged her backpack into her lap, and unzipped it.

It was the sound that tipped her off, the bright, familiar, everyday *zwippp* of all those zipper teeth parting. The barking had stopped. Had Lassie thrown in the towel? Kick looked back over her shoulder. The twisted black branches of the neighbor's cherry tree seemed to reach for her. Kick was tempted to peek back over the railing, to check on the beast, but she didn't want to risk setting it off again.

Focus on a task.

That was the fifth redirection strategy.

Mel had given her her first padlock the Christmas she turned eight. A Kwikset. He showed her how to pick the lock with a bobby pin. By New Year's she could get it open in under ten seconds. Anyone could get into any lock. He brought her home a new lock every few weeks, each one heavier and shinier than the last. She kept them on a shelf in her bedroom and displayed them like dolls. By Presidents' Day she could get into an Abloy Protec padlock in under five minutes. After that, Mel said she was ready for doors.

Sliding glass doors were the easiest.

Some people used crowbars to pop the handle off, but Mel had taught Kick how to leverage her body weight and push down at just the right angle. She leaned into it, using both hands, pushing so hard she wasn't even breathing, and after ten seconds of pressure the handle snapped off cleanly into one hand.

Kick was sweating now. But the handle was perfect. It had popped right off its screws like it was supposed to. She put the handle in her jacket pocket, and then took off the jacket and laid it on the deck. She dug the Leatherman out of her backpack, along with a penlight, folded out the flathead screwdriver, put the penlight between her teeth, and knelt down in front of the now-exposed lock mechanism. She had honed her lock-picking skills by practicing on the sliding glass door at her mother's house. Out the front door in the middle of the night, around the side yard, and back inside through the sliding doors that her mother had paid for with *Today Show* money. Ten times a night sometimes. Her mother never had a clue.

The mechanism on this door looked standard. The threaded shanks of the two screws that had held the handle in place were now exposed, as were two holes that hid the screwheads that operated the lock. Kick inserted the flathead screwdriver into each of the holes and turned the screwhead inside clockwise. This unsprung the lock. It was that easy. A clean entry, Mel had called it. When you left, all you had to do was use the screwdriver again to relock the door from the outside, then screw the handle back on, and there'd be no trace you were ever there. Any junkie with a brick could break into a house, but it took some skill to break in and out again without someone noticing.

Kick returned the Leatherman and penlight to her backpack, shrugged the shoulder straps back on, and slid open the door. Venetian blinds were a bitch. They were ugly and loud and you could get tangled up in them if you weren't careful. Kick took her time, inching sideways around the blinds. The room was dark and smelled overwhelmingly like bleach. Kick's skin prickled. She could make out the general shape of the room, a box spring on the floor. A bedroom. The blinds shuddered in the wind behind her. The fumes from the bleach made her eyes water. Kick stepped forward, her socked feet padding silently on carpet.

"It took you long enough," a voice said. The room filled with light. Kick aimed the Glock in the direction of the voice, finger on the trigger. It was Bishop. He stood in the doorway, across the room from her. Between them were the remnants of a child's bedroom: circus wallpaper, purple carpeting, broken toys strewn in the corner. She looked to Bishop for an explanation. The ugly expression on his face made her insides go cold. He was as still as ever, but now Kick recognized the stillness for what it was: contained violence. He held a dog collar out, jangling its tags.

"I had the code to the lockbox," he said. He tossed the dog collar at her feet. "If we'd done it my way, I wouldn't have had to kill the dog."

7

VISUALIZE A RELAXING EXPERIENCE. Close your eyes and travel there in your mind.

Kick is in her backyard. It is before Mel, before everything. She still has only one father, her real one, and he still loves her. The grass is thick and green and thatched with clover. She is on a tire swing, and she is swinging back and forth, and she is so high she can almost touch the clouds.

"We don't have time for this," Bishop said.

Kick opened her eyes. Sometimes she could convince herself that the backyard was real, but not tonight.

"Smell that?" Bishop asked. He hadn't moved from the door.

The faint, harsh odor of bleach burned slightly at Kick's nostrils.

Bishop sniffed the air. "They cleaned up," he said.

"I'm calling 911," Kick said, reaching for her phone. If he came near her, she would punch him in the throat.

"What are the police going to do?" Bishop asked.

"Collect trace evidence," Kick said. "See if it matches Adam Rice or Mia Turner."

"They bathed the place in industrial bleach," Bishop said. He pointed at the carpet. "It's new," he said. "The place is clean. There *is* no trace evidence."

The corner of his mouth twitched up in a smile. "But the cops will certainly be interested in the blue handprints leading up the side of the house."

Kick looked down at the phone in her hand. It was powdered with blue chalk dust. She wiped it on her shirt and then rubbed her palms against her thighs.

"I told you I had my people here," Bishop said.

His people, again. But Kick had other things to worry about. The chalk dust was everywhere. On her pants. All over her shirt. She looked like she'd fallen into a vat of 1980s eye shadow. It had mixed with her hand sweat and formed a kind of Smurf epoxy.

Bishop held a white handkerchief out.

Who even carried handkerchiefs anymore?

She snatched the handkerchief from his hand and blew her nose. Her snot came out blue.

"Keep it," Bishop said.

She glared at him.

He'd positioned himself well. She wouldn't be able to get back through the sliding doors easily without getting past him. She could make a run for the door, but clearly he knew the house better than she did. The cops had her fingerprints on file. They were part of her missing-person file.

"This wasn't a setup," Bishop said. "I didn't

know that you'd coat your hands with blue dust and climb the outside of a house."

He had a point.

"Here's my problem," Bishop said. "The satellite photos aren't admissible because they were illegally acquired. Having a kid's room when you don't have a kid is weird, but it is not probable cause to search a house. Adam was here. The car from the Mia Turner Amber Alert was here. This house is somehow connected to their abductions."

Bishop didn't have the microexpressions other people did. He didn't give anything away with gestures or posture. He had learned that somewhere, which meant that he had also learned how to read microexpressions and body language in other people. Maybe he was reading her right now. Kick straightened up and tried to relax the muscles in her face.

How had he done it? she wondered. How had he killed the dog? He said he didn't like guns. Had he strangled it?

"I need your help," Bishop said.

He was taller than she was, and this close the angle of his face changed. She could see the shadow of his lower eyelashes, the million light-brown dots of facial hair pressing against the surface of his chin and jaw. The color didn't match the black of his hair.

"I have a gun," she said. "I will shoot you if you come closer."

"You have a gun," Bishop said, *"in your backpack."*

"I can get to it in under four seconds," Kick said. "Try me."

"You should keep your hands free," Bishop said. "You're more dangerous with your hands free."

"I will shoot you," Kick said. "I swear I will."

"I believe you," Bishop said.

Something changed in his eyes, in the way that he was looking at her, and he blinked and looked away. "I shouldn't have brought you here," he said. "This was a mistake." He backed away from her and then turned and headed for the door like he was going to leave her there, alone, in that terrible room with its circus trains, its rows of elephants marched trunk to tail, its girls standing on horses, its poodles walking on their hind legs, and its men brandishing whips at lions.

"The houses we stayed in," Kick called. "There was always a box. A place to hide if anyone ever came looking." Her stomach twisted as the words left her mouth.

Bishop appeared back in the doorway. "Put the gun away," he said.

She looked down to see her hand inside her backpack, fingers already curling around the grip of the Glock. She hadn't reached for it consciously.

"You carry that thing around enough, you'll end up shooting someone," Bishop said. "And I don't want it to be me."

Kick didn't need the gun. She knew 571 ways

to take someone to the ground with her left hand alone. She left the weapon in the backpack. "Fine," she said, securing the backpack straps over her shoulders.

Bishop lifted his eyes from his phone and turned the screen toward her. It was displaying some sort of architectural blueprints. Kick peered at it. "That's here," she said. She didn't bother asking how he'd managed to acquire them so quickly.

He scrolled through several pages of the prints and then tapped his finger over a faded line of blue ink. "Let's start here," he said. "Stay behind me."

Kick followed him. Plan B was to punch him in the kidney and make a quick exit back through the sliding doors and down the side of the house. Plans C through F were variations of Plan B, and Plan G involved the Glock.

She walked a few steps behind him, through the bedroom door into the hallway, where the lilac carpet continued. The white walls still had nails where pictures had hung a week before. Bishop had left a trail of lights on when he'd come upstairs, and now they retraced his steps downstairs. All that empty space and lilac carpeting made the house seem especially desolate.

The smell of bleach wasn't as strong on the first floor, or maybe Kick was just getting used to it. She was a good adapter. Wasn't that what the shrinks said?

Bishop's eyes moved back and forth between the walls and his phone, like he was comparing every spec. Kick kept her distance, a good arm's length back. Bishop led her down another lilac hall past a closed door, then stopped at a second one. He stepped past the door before he opened it, she noticed, so that he pushed it in from the doorknob side. It was how you opened a door if you wanted to lessen the chance that someone would shoot you through it. Frank had taught Kick that. Bishop seemed to know it by rote. This room was bigger than the bedroom, with a small double-paned window and a louvered closet. The walls had recently gotten a sloppy coat of white paint. A bulletin board still hung at desk height on one wall. Kick wandered over to it. All of the pushpins were lined up along one edge of the board, separated into rows by color.

What did it say about her, Kick wondered, that when she saw pushpins she thought, *Missing kids*?

"That's not right," Bishop muttered.

Kick glanced back at him. He was scrutinizing the louvered closet. It was a standard-enough-looking closet, the kind of thing that you can buy in a kit from Home Depot and install yourself. Standard enough that it didn't attract attention.

Bishop was already crossing the room to the closet. "That's not right," he said, again.

He slid open the closet door and Kick heard the click of a chain light being pulled. She stepped beside him. The closet was double-wide and empty except for a few abandoned wire hangers. He gave her a sideways look and then stepped inside the closet, hunched under the clothing bar, and began running his hands over the closet's back wall like he was trying to crack a safe. Kick did her own survey. It was a good drywall job, professional-looking, without lumps or cracks. A lot of attention to give the back of a closet. Bishop got tangled in the wire hangers and they jangled as he slid them away from him. He dropped to his hands and knees and started inspecting the line where the wall met the floor.

"You won't find it," Kick said.

"It's here," Bishop said, moving his hands over the carpet. "The blueprints show the room should be bigger. This closet—this whole wall—shouldn't be here."

"It's there," Kick said. "But you won't find it."

Bishop sat back on his haunches and looked at her.

She dropped her backpack at her feet and tucked a loose piece of hair behind her ear. "Do you want me to find it?"

"Yes, please."

"If I find the box, we're done. I fly home tonight on the fancy jet. And you find someone else to play *Charlie's Angels* with."

Bishop stood up, wrestled with one of the wire hangers that got caught on his shirt, and then stepped out of the closet. Lilac carpet fuzz stuck to his jeans.

"Deal?" Kick said.

"Show me the box," Bishop said simply.

"Fine," Kick said. She stepped past him into the closet and pulled the light chain. "I need dark," she said, closing the louvered door behind her.

The slats of the louvered door let in light from the office, so it wasn't really dark, just shadowed, but that was fine. It wasn't the dark Kick needed; it was the solitude.

She approached the wall.

Funny how stuff comes back to you.

Sometimes, when they moved into a new house, the box was already there, and sometimes they had to build one, framing it out, wiring it, putting up drywall. Mel was handy. Sometimes he would let Kick help build the spring loading for the door while he built the mechanically controlled lock. You could do a lot with a tiny speaker, a gear reduction motor, some PVC pipe, a few suction cups, and an open-source prototyping platform. You could hide a door in plain sight.

Kick put her hand in the lower right corner of the closet where the wall met the carpet and then walked her fingers up five steps and over to the left five steps.

"Well?" Bishop asked through the louvered door.

"Go away," Kick said. She made a fist against the wall where her finger had been, and knocked.

Shave and a haircut. One knock, followed by four quick knocks, followed by one knock.

The back of the closet popped open an inch.

That sound. She had forgotten the sound the doors made when the spring released.

Kick gave the wall a push and it swung open.

The louvered door started to rattle open behind her. She glanced over her shoulder at Bishop.

Lit from behind, he was a faceless, dark shape.

The edge of the bright rectangle of light touched Kick's knee.

She scrambled forward, through the door, into the box, slamming the trick panel shut behind her. She moved on her hands and knees in the dark, feeling ahead of her, until she found a corner to sit in.

She could hear Bishop pounding and hollering her name on the other side of the wall. She didn't respond. She heard the sound of the wire hangers being ripped from the clothing bar and thrown against a wall.

Kick didn't have a plan. Before, when she was a kid, she'd spent so much time in dark cubbies like these that she had learned to let go of time.

She hugged her knees to her chest.

The bleach smell was stronger in here, and there was some other smell, too, something more rancid. Kick could taste the stench, feel it settling in her lungs along with the dust and cobwebs. The walls weren't framed out, so her back was pressed against an exposed two-by-four.

"You're contaminating evidence," Bishop called. She could hear him knocking. *Shave and a haircut.* He'd figured out that much. He was working his way along the wall.

There was always an override just inside the door. She just had to reach it and she could lock the chamber from the inside. The knock wouldn't open the panel then.

She crawled forward.

Her socked toe caught on something in the dark. She cried out. With the nail torn off, the nail bed was so sensitive that any contact felt like a dropped anvil. She didn't know what she'd hit. But it had felt hard. She went after it, thinking it might be the override.

"Open the goddamn door!" Bishop hollered.

"I'm not coming out," Kick called, poking at the air with her foot. She got to stay in the box as long as she wanted. That was Mel's rule. She didn't have to come out until she wanted to.

Her toe made contact with something again. She twisted around and reached for the spot with her hands. There was something there, on the floor. Too large to be the override lever. Her fingers touched plastic. She explored the surface, following it to the wall, against which it appeared to be propped. Thick plastic, and under it something cool to the touch, and solid. The plastic crinkled under her touch. Some places felt softer and gave when she pushed; others were hard. She gave it another nudge. . . .

She knew an instant before it fell. Something shifted in the dark.

She squawked and jumped out of the way. She felt the air move as it went by. The thing hit the floor with a sickening thunk and the floor vibrated.

"What's going on there?" Bishop called, a new urgency to his voice.

Kick stayed frozen, trying to orient herself. Whatever was in there with her was big. The sound it made when it hit the floor, that solid thud, it sounded like meat.

Bishop was swearing up a storm. Kick could hear him banging around on the other side of the wall, like he might put his elbow through the dry-wall.

Kick eased her phone from her pocket, hit the "home" button with her thumb, and aimed the blue light of the screen toward the thing on the floor.

She absorbed it in a series of mental snapshots, a head, a hip, the curve of a knee. The shape forming a word in Kick's brain: *body*. The body was wrapped in Visqueen, and blood pooled underneath the plastic. The head was inches away from Kick's toes, faceup, or more like the suggestion of a face, pale and lumpy, like unformed clay. Underneath the plastic Kick could see a blond swath of shoulder-length hair. There was something else, too, something packed around the lower part of the body. The phone was shaking, so it was hard to make out much in the jumpy blue light. Kick held the phone closer and trained the screen on the corpse's face. Someone had scrawled capital letters in black Sharpie on top of the Visqueen over the thing's forehead. Kick's mouth silently made the word.

"Boom."

Boom?

"Do you smell that?" a small voice asked from the darkness.

Kick spun the light around.

The little girl was standing perfectly still. Barefoot, hair a long tangle of brown. Her skin was pale. Kick could tell it had been a long time since she'd been let out of the box.

"Go away, Beth," Kick hissed. "It's not safe here."

"Who are you talking to?" Bishop called. "Is someone in there with you?"

"You can't stay here," the girl said.

Kick heard the soft *boing* of the panel's spring mechanism again and turned her head. Bishop had done it. Light spilled into the box. They were never as nice lit up, just dirty glorified crawl spaces, hidey-holes. The girl was gone. The body was still there.

The stomp of Bishop's feet vibrated the plywood flooring under her knees. And then he stopped. She glanced at him, his long neck, his stricken gaze fixed on the corpse, the scrawl across its face. Bishop wasn't supposed to be in there.

"Go away," Kick said.

Bishop squatted next to the thing, head turning back and forth, taking in every detail. Then he said, "Shit." He pivoted and lunged at Kick.

He caught her off guard and managed to get his hand around her elbow before she could react. Kick felt a stab of pain from her shoulder to her wrist as he stood, pulling her up roughly with him. He was dragging her back, out of the box. She clawed at his clamp-like grip on her arm, and managed to free his pinkie and bend it back as she pulled and twisted the joint. She got away, and tried to get back to the corner of the box. But he got her by the waist, his arms hooked around her hips. She tried to stamp on his feet, but without shoes she was at a disadvantage. He was grunting and swearing, hauling her toward the closet, out of the box. He was hurting her. She screamed and scratched at his arms, but he wouldn't let go.

He was saying something to her, in her ear, over and over again. He wrestled her through the secret door, back onto the lilac carpet. She tried to slam her heels into his knees, but couldn't make contact. She was gulping air, adrenaline on overdrive. He didn't understand. She couldn't leave Beth. She was just a little girl. They couldn't leave her alone in the dark with that thing. Kick's socked heels bounced on the carpet as they cleared the closet threshold and moved through the office.

Kick struggled, but it was like her mind and body had gone out of sync. Bishop got one of his arms over hers so that he had her from behind by the waist and had her forearms pinned to her chest. Then he spun her around and lifted her off the ground.

He never stopped moving, never missed a step. He had her out of the office and was carrying her down the hall. He sounded like an animal, straining and grunting.

It occurred to her that he was going to kill her, like he'd killed the dog.

She caught sight of the front door ahead. Teslas were made in America; if he put her in the trunk, all she had to do was find the emergency release lever. Bishop shifted his hold on her as he turned the doorknob and used a foot to throw open the door and they stepped outside and onto the stoop.

A blast of heat hit them from behind and they were thrust forward, and for a moment Kick felt her body lifted from Bishop's arms, and they were both sailing through the air, bathed in bright light. A deep, hollow sound reverberated behind them, deafening everything. Kick didn't have time to correct her fall: she hit the dirt face-first, skidding several feet before stopping. Debris rained down on her—she didn't know what kind. She covered her head with her hands and waited. She lifted her head slightly to see where Bishop had landed and saw him a few feet away on the singed grass. The house was ablaze in orange. Black smoke billowed into the gray sky. Even where she'd landed, thirty feet from the stoop, Kick could feel the heat from the fire.

Boom.

"Remember that smell?" Beth had asked.

Sulfur.

Sometimes Kick had helped Mel make the bombs.

Bleach.

They had used it every time they moved. Leave

no trace, Mel would say. It was the way of the Comanche.

Kick lifted herself painfully to her hands and knees, her eyes fixed on the inferno that now engulfed the house. Beth was still in there. She was still in the box. Kick had to save her. She rocked back onto her feet and tried to stand, but her limbs felt foreign and the ground kept moving out from under her. She slid forward and her face hit the mud. *I'm going to lose consciousness now,* she thought.

8

AFTER A WHILE, KIT *got used to the dark. It was her own little world. She had her own sleeping bag, and a nightgown, and a hairbrush, and a bucket to do her business in. She knew the room with her hands: the rough wood, the heads of nails, the soft padding on the walls. The man who called her Beth came every day. Each day he took the bucket, and each day when he brought it back it smelled like bubble gum. When he was there, Kit was as still and quiet as a mouse.*

Sometimes he brought food. Peanut butter sandwiches. Oreos.

Today, when he brought the bucket back, he turned on a light.

The brightness almost knocked her over. She was a bug under a rock, scrambling for some kind of cover.

"It's okay," the man said.

She was wrapped in a little ball. She was a potato bug. She was a pebble.

"Look," he said, "I brought you cherries."

Kit looked up, trying to get her eyes used to the stinging light. The man was sitting on the floor, at the light's center. He had already lied to her. He had not helped her find her dog. But now he was holding out a white bowl.

He tipped it forward, and it was full of cherries, and she had been in the dark so long that the red was extra red and the white was extra white.

"Look what else," he said. He set the cherries down on the floor and pulled a rectangular board game from behind his back, and a book. The book had a drawing of rabbits on the cover. "It's one of my favorites," he said. "It's called Watership Down. *I'm going to read it to you." Then he tapped the board game. "And I'm going to teach you how to play this game. It says ages eight and up on it, but you're a smart girl, aren't you, Beth?"*

"You said you'd find my dog," Kit said.

"Your dog is safe, Beth," the man said. "He's home. You don't have to worry about him."

Kit nodded and was grateful. If anything had happened to Monster, it would have been her fault.

"But this is your home now," the man continued. "With me and Linda." He set the game on the floor and opened the lid. His blond hair was fine, like a baby's. "Are you good at following directions, Beth?"

Kit's stomach growled and she snuck a peek at the cherries in the bowl.

He unfolded the board from the game. It was covered with colored squares. "Draw seven tiles," he said, "and I'll teach you how to play."

She hesitated for only a second before she scooted forward across the wood floor, just close enough to reach into the bag. She took a handful of what was inside and eyed him across the game board as he drew his own letters and placed them one by one on a wooden rack. She looked around for her own rack and found one in the box and put it on her edge of the board and started setting up her wooden letters too. As she counted them from her fist to the rack, she realized that she'd drawn one too many. She should have put it back in the bag, but she didn't. Instead, heart pounding, she hid it in her hand.

"See if you can arrange your letters to make a word," he said. He held her gaze. She was not used to grown-ups doing that, and her face got hot, and she wanted to let go of the tile, put it back, but she was afraid that she would get in trouble. The man smiled and picked up the bowl of cherries and held them out to her. "It's your turn, Beth."

9

KICK WOKE UP COUGHING, gasping for air. Something was pressed against her face, covering her mouth. She clawed at it, but something was in the way.

"Easy," a woman's voice soothed. "It's an oxygen mask. Deep breaths now, hon."

An oxygen mask?

Where was she? Kick's eyes stung. Her ears were ringing. The sky was dark and full of fireflies. She was on her back. Everything hurt. The smallest movement echoed through her skull. She felt grass under her fingertips.

She blinked. There were sirens. She could feel people running past, their footfalls reverberating through the ground. Embers floated and whirled, hundreds of thousands of them, tiny stars. A dry heat puckered her skin. The house was on fire. The sound of the blaze was punctuated by exploding glass. Her eyes burned with grit; she could taste smoke. She strained to turn her head toward the orange glow, but the woman holding the oxygen mask to Kick's mouth was taking up too much of her visual field.

"Breathe," the woman said. Kick could do that. That was easy. She'd had a therapist once—all they'd done was breathe; they'd breathed for hours. Kick inhaled. Kick exhaled. *Breathe. Check.* The woman had a ponytail and a gold paramedic's badge on her left pocket. A patch on her uniform sleeve read: King County Medic One. *Exhale. Inhale. Check.* The oxygen was making Kick a little light-headed. She felt the paramedic's fingers find the inside of her wrist, between her bone and tendon, looking for a pulse. Her face flashed blue and red.

The paramedic lifted the oxygen mask from Kick's mouth. She leaned close. Her lips moved. She was wearing tiny silver stud earrings shaped like turtles.

Kick heard sirens. Her face hurt. She didn't know why. "What?" she croaked.

The paramedic's head came closer. "Where's Beth?" the paramedic asked. "Is she still in the house?"

Half the sky was orange. The other half was charcoal.

The ponytailed paramedic had the oxygen mask back over Kick's mouth. "It'll be all right," she said. "We've called your mother."

Kick vomited. The paramedic pulled the oxygen mask away and rolled Kick onto her side.

Inhale. Exhale. Check.

Now there was a man squatting in the grass next to her. A fine sheen of sooty sweat gleamed on his olive-colored skin, and the knees of his pants had grass stains on them. A gold detective's badge hung around his neck. Kick stared at him, trying to make him come into focus. His black hair was flecked with white.

The detective smiled at Kick and then gave his head a shake, and the white flecks fell out of his hair.

"Ash," he said.

She watched as the white flecks floated away behind him.

The fire made a sizzling sound, like frying flesh. Even from across the yard, she could feel the heat on her face. Through the flames that engulfed the house, she could see that the entire second floor was already skeletal, burned down to the studs. Water from the fire hoses turned to steam.

"They're letting her burn herself out," the detective explained. *"Her?"* He pointed to another part of the yard. "That's where you landed," he said. "Blast threw you almost thirty feet. I'd say you got out of there without a second to spare."

She was thirsty. Her head felt funny.

"Bishop saved your life," the detective said.

"No," Kick said through her fog.

"He told us everything," the detective said. "The *body*," he continued. "The hidden room. The fact that someone was using the house to hide abducted kids."

Kick made a noncommittal noise.

"Unfortunately," the detective continued, "any

evidence, including the corpse, is now charcoal. But we can name the people who lived in this house as persons of interest. The media will pick it up. Might lead somewhere."

A thought formed in Kick's rubbery brain, and she pushed it to the surface. "The dog," she said.

The detective's eyebrows knitted.

"Bishop . . . killed . . . Lassie." No, that wasn't right. Her head throbbed. "A collie. He killed a collie."

"A three-legged collie?" the detective asked.

Kick looked at him uncertainly.

"Turn around," the detective said.

Kick looked over her shoulder. A three-legged collie sat at the edge of the yard, nose in the air, alert and definitely alive.

"First responders found her loose in the yard," the detective said, "barking at the fire. Looks like she busted loose from her collar. The people across the street say she lives there." He nodded at the house next door. "But they're not at home. Animal Control is around here somewhere. They haven't been able to catch her yet. She's fast for an amputee."

This didn't make sense. "Maybe he killed a different three-legged collie," Kick said.

The detective scratched the back of his neck and looked at her funny. "Sometimes," he said, "a blow to the head can cause this kind of stuff."

She had not imagined it. She did not imagine dead dogs. She tried to stand.

"I'm not sure you should be doing that," the detective said.

Kick braced herself on his shoulder and forced three words through her gritted teeth. "Where. Is. He?"

• • •

The detective was gone. The ponytailed paramedic was back. Kick, fueled by adrenaline, weaved around patrol cars and in between fire hoses, searching in the direction the detective had pointed her in, as the paramedic tripped along behind her. She could see the satellite dishes of news vans over the other side of the front hedge. But no cameras. The press was being kept at a distance. She found Bishop perched on the back bumper of an ambulance, shirtless, and bathed in the headlights of a nearby fire truck. Kick stomped toward him in her socks, wondering if he'd even bothered to check on her or if he'd just left her there, unconscious in the yard. He had the nerve to smile when he saw her, half his face blackened with soot, blood in his ear.

Kick slapped him across the face as hard as she could.

The force of the blow knocked Bishop sideways, revealing a startled paramedic behind him, a blood-tipped scalpel in her latex-gloved hand. A suturing kit was open at her side: a syringe, a hemostat, forceps, gauze, sutures, and all the bloody slivers of wood that the paramedic had already extracted from Bishop's back. "Oh," Kick said.

Bishop grimaced and sat back up.

Someone grabbed Kick from behind, pinning her arms, which was okay with Kick because she wasn't sure she could stand much longer on her own.

"I'm fine," Bishop said. "Let her go."

Kick barely managed to stay upright when the ponytailed paramedic released her. "We've been pulling wood out of him for an hour," the paramedic said. Kick could see his wounds now, a dozen of them, many already cleaned and sutured. A few splinters, the size of toothpicks, were still visible under his skin.

Bishop's paramedic used a gauze pad to wipe up the blood from the wound her scalpel had unexpectedly inflicted. "Sorry," she said.

"My fault," Bishop said, with a look at Kick that said otherwise. "I shouldn't have moved when you had a scalpel in my back."

"When I want you stabbed, you'll know it," Kick told him.

"You have some anger issues," Bishop said. "You know that, right?" His forearms had scratches on them, like he'd fought a cat and lost.

The ponytailed paramedic was still hovering next to Kick. Too close. Crowding her.

"She's suffered a concussion," the paramedic said to Bishop. "She's agitated."

"She's always like that," Bishop said. His abdominal muscles tensed and the paramedic in the ambulance dropped a four-inch splinter on the tray.

Kick refused to be distracted. She jabbed a finger in Bishop's face accusingly. "You didn't kill the dog," she said.

Bishop's cheek was red where she'd slapped him. He looked at her with bewilderment. "You're angry I didn't kill a dog?" he asked.

She saw the paramedics exchange a look, like she might need to be subdued.

"I don't like being lied to," Kick said, clarifying.

She caught a sudden, strong whiff of vomit and had the vague sense that it was in her hair. She didn't remember throwing up. She needed a shower. "Where's my backpack?" she asked Bishop, searching the ground around his feet.

Bishop took a moment to answer. Then, with what she thought might be just a hint of merriment, he directed her gaze to the burning house.

Kick pivoted toward the two stories of flames. She shook her head emphatically, refusing to believe it. He'd picked the backpack up after she dropped it. She remembered. "No," she insisted. Emotion welled in her throat. She had to choke it back to keep it down. She looked at Bishop pleadingly. "You had it."

The paramedic behind Bishop threaded a black suture through his skin like she was sewing up a Thanksgiving turkey. He barely registered it. "I must have dropped it while I was trying to save our lives," he said evenly. He turned his forearm up, displaying the cat scratches. "Thanks for these, by the way."

Kick looked at her hands. One of her nails was broken. Those last minutes in the house were hazy, but whatever she had done, he had it coming. She turned her face back to the flames. Part of the skeletal second floor had caved in on itself. *They're letting her burn herself out.* By morning "she" would be reduced to ten feet of cremated rubble. Kick could feel the grit of ash in her eyes, on her eyelashes. Her beautiful Glock. No gun could survive that kind of sustained heat. It was lost.

"Are you crying?" Bishop asked incredulously. "Because that very expensive automobile we drove here in is now a burned-out metal husk, so if anyone should be crying, it's me."

"It's the smoke," Kick snapped at him. It took a moment for what he'd said to sink in. The Tesla? She had left her composition book in the Tesla. "My worry book," she whispered. She wouldn't know what to worry about now.

"Seriously?" Bishop said.

Kick wiped the ash out of her eyes with the blanket. She was going down the worry maze, letting herself get overcome by negative thinking.

"Am I free to go?" she asked the ponytailed paramedic. "Or do I need to give a statement first?"

"You already gave a statement," the paramedic said hesitantly. "To Detective Alva."

"Good," Kick said, trying to seem as if she remembered that. "Then can someone call me a cab?"

The ponytailed paramedic was starting to look a little alarmed. "Your mother's coming. I called her. Remember?"

Kick coughed and vomit burned the back of her throat. The paramedic was talking to Bishop now, a hand worrying one of her turtle earrings. "We always look for 'Mom' in the person's cell phone contacts in a situation like this," she was saying. "I've already explained this to her," she said. "She keeps forgetting. It's the concussion."

Not her mother. Anyone but her mother. "No," Kick said.

"She needs to be monitored through the night," the paramedic continued. Maybe the earrings weren't turtles. Maybe they were tortoises. Kick didn't know the difference. The other paramedic's elbow went up and down as she threaded another suture into Bishop's shoulder blade. Kick must have looked stricken, because the paramedic with the ponytail gave Kick's arm a reassuring pat. "Your mother will be here within the hour," she said.

"No," Kick said again. Her brain felt soft and thick, like ice cream.

"It's either that or we admit you to the hospital," the paramedic said.

"I said no hospital," Bishop said. "No media. No paperwork."

The ponytailed paramedic gave Kick a nervous glance and leaned a few inches closer toward Bishop. "Do you know who 'Beth' is?" she asked him.

Kick didn't know why the paramedic kept bringing Beth up. Beth was dead.

"She kept asking for her when she was coming to," the paramedic continued.

Everything was wavy, like Kick was looking at it from the surface of a rippling pond.

Bishop rubbed his face with his hands and sighed. His gray eyes looked blurry. The paramedic behind him tied off a suture. "Fuck," Bishop said to no one in particular. He looked at Kick, studying her again, like he was trying to get to the bottom of her. She'd seen that look on cops and therapists. His eyebrow lifted. "You're crazier than I thought," he said.

"I have dirt in my mouth." It was the last thing Kick remembered saying before losing consciousness.

10

THE CEILING WAS FAR away, with exposed wooden beams that came together at unnatural angles. Kick started to sit up, but a pair of hands on her shoulders stopped her. Bishop was standing over her, wearing a red robe.

What the hell?

"Don't freak out," he said.

"Where am I?" Kick asked.

"At my house," Bishop said.

She was in a bed. Kick started to sit up again.

"In the *guest room*," he clarified. His hands were on her shoulders again. "You suffered a concussion. I'm supposed to wake you up every hour to make sure you're not dead. You're not dead, are you?"

"No."

"I'm going to shine this light in your eyes," Bishop said. "The last time I did this you tried to kick me in the teeth, and I'd rather you didn't do that again because I'm tired and my reflexes are slow."

He held a penlight up and hesitated. "Okay?" he said.

"Okay," Kick whispered hoarsely.

Bishop turned on the light and Kick winced as he shined it in each of her eyes.

"Your pupils look good," he said, switching off the light. He dropped the penlight in his robe pocket, sat down in a chair next to her bed, and picked up a book that was open on the armrest. "Go to sleep," he said, not looking up from the book. "I'll see you in a few hours."

• • •

"Where am I?" Kick asked.

"My house, in a guest room," Bishop said. "You suffered a concussion. I'm supposed to wake you up every few hours to make sure you're lucid. Are you lucid, Kick?"

"No," she said.

Bishop held up a thick silver pen. "This is a penlight," he said. "I'm going to turn it on and shine it in both your eyes. Don't kick me."

"Why would I—" Kick winced as the light met her pupils.

"Good," Bishop said. "I'll see you in a few hours."

• • •

Kick opened her eyes and looked around.

"You're at my house," Bishop said. "You suffered a concussion. How do you feel?"

"Like some asshole keeps waking me up," Kick said.

"Look at me," Bishop said. He held up a penlight. "This is a—"

"I know," Kick said.

Bishop shined the light in both her pupils.

"Okay," Bishop said, clicking the light off. He turned around and started walking away, and Kick sat up on her elbows.

"Where are you going?" she asked.

"It's morning," Bishop said over his shoulder. "Congratulations, you lived through the night."

The moment Bishop closed the door, Kick sat up and threw off the covers. She was wearing pajamas. They were white with tiny yellow flowers—pants and a short-sleeved top with a scalloped neckline. They were not hers. Waking up in someone else's clothes was not definitely an item for the Worry Book, but at the moment Kick was more concerned with the fact that she had found herself in someone else's house. She touched a tender spot over her forehead and winced. She remembered the feeling of heat, waking up in the grass, faces, fragments. The knot on her head was the size of a grape. The last thing she remembered was . . . She grabbed a handful of her hair and smelled it. No vomit. Just a musky-scented shampoo. She looked at her hands. They were clean. No blue powder. No dirt. Even the remnants of her blue nail polish were gone. She wiggled her fingers. Her right hand felt stiff.

She did not remember bathing. She did not remember changing her clothes.

But she couldn't go down that road. That road led to the Worry Maze.

Kick wished she had a throwing star, a fishing knife, anything.

"Ha!" Kick said.

She sounded like a lunatic, but sometimes if she made herself laugh it would calm her down. Laughing lowered cortisol levels, released endorphins, and boosted oxygen levels in the blood. It was science.

She tried again. "Ha!"

It wasn't working. Her cortisol levels felt about the same. She swung her legs off the bed, got on the floor, and did a hundred sit-ups.

Her head felt like it was going to explode, but her brain was better. Her heart rate was up. She felt the warm burn of her muscles working.

She was ready.

Bishop had said she was in a guest room. Looking around, it made sense. The king-size bed and clinical design screamed expensive hotel room. She spotted her phone on the bedside table and reached for it. The screen was dark, the battery dead. She didn't see a charger. There was no landline in the room.

She hadn't talked to James since the night before. He was probably frantic by now. She had to find a phone.

Kick tucked her own phone into the waistband

of her pajama pants and crossed to the door. It was unlocked. She cracked it and listened. She could hear what sounded like the faint cry of seagulls.

The door opened onto a hallway that extended in both directions. No sign of Bishop. The floors were wood, no rugs. Kick flexed her knees deeply, sank into them, and followed the hall left, breathing along with her movement. With no weapon, silence was her main advantage. It was Bishop's turn to be startled by *her*. She passed closed doors, focusing on staying in the open hall, where she could see what was in front of her. She stepped with her toes first and rolled her weight back to her heels, ready to adjust to any floor creak.

The hallway led to a light-filled room roughly the size of a high school gymnasium and decorated with mission-style furniture. One wall was almost entirely glass. Beyond it, Kick saw a wedge of stone shoreline and an expanse of dark-blue water with white gulls circling above it. Morning mist cloaked the opposite shore of evergreens, tiny homes, and docks.

Kick recognized the silhouette of a Washington State ferry in the distance, about the size of a shoe box. Across the water, to the north, a faint city skyline was visible, the red light on top of the Space Needle blinking bleakly in the mist.

She was on an island in Puget Sound.

Kick twirled around, certain that she'd heard a noise behind her. But she was alone. The glass wall made her feel like a bug in a jar. She quickened her steps as she circled the perimeter, looking for a phone somewhere in all that gleaming wood, leather, and strong, masculine lines. Folded Pendleton blankets draped the backs of all the chairs. It was all very put together, like the guest room. There were fresh flowers, in three bouquets so big that they looked like they'd be more at home in a hotel lobby. Nothing was out of place. It gave Kick the creeps. She had as much chance of finding a landline here as she did finding a stain on the carpet. She didn't see any personal touches. Even the art on the walls felt like some interior designer's bulk order. She scanned outlets, hoping for a phone charger, but saw none. A blocky oak cabinet with hammered bronze pulls looked promising, but every drawer she checked was empty. Not just empty—clean, as if each drawer had been recently wiped out by a diligent housekeeper.

There were no books in the room, no magazines, no half-empty glasses sitting on the coffee table, no coasters, or upholstery stains or any other indications of actual habitation.

It was like a set, like it was all staged.

The light changed—maybe the mist shifted. Kick's attention returned to a series of framed images she'd just passed. They were so uniform and evenly hung, each matted and framed, that she had assumed they were more designer-bought art. She hadn't even looked at the images themselves. But now the glare off the glass was gone, and she was drawn back to them.

The dozen or so images looked to actually be enlarged snapshots. Kick glanced from one image to the next. Most of the photographs appeared to be of the same two dark-haired boys, at the beach, posing with a birthday cake, at a park.

They had the same narrow gray eyes and large ears: brothers. One was older by a year or two. He smiled more than the other. The photographs went along more or less chronologically, the boys aging until they were roughly eight and ten years old. Then the younger boy dropped off. He disappeared. It was just the older boy after that, pictured alone, at age twelve, at age fourteen, going about the business of growing up.

What had happened to the other boy?

"The kid's alive," Bishop said from behind her. Kick spun around, bringing her elbows in and planting her feet, ready to defend herself. Bishop strolled barefoot toward her, wearing black jeans and a black T-shirt with a stretched-out neck, his dark hair wet from a shower, his arms marked with her scratches. Kick expected him to question her, but he barely gave her a glance. He certainly didn't look surprised to find her out of bed, wearing a stranger's pajamas, standing in his living room. He swept a remote off an end table, aimed it at the sofa, and pressed a button. Kick let her fight stance ease as an enormous flat-screen TV elevated from behind the sofa. She was about to question *him* when a KING-TV breaking news logo appeared on the screen, followed by a photograph of Mia Turner. Stamped diagonally across the photo was a single word: *Found*.

Found?

Kick didn't understand.

"She turned up in a motel room in Tacoma," Bishop said. "The room was rented yesterday afternoon by a fiftyish blond female. Housekeeping found the child alone in the room at checkout about thirty minutes ago."

The TV news went to a live shot of a motel. It looked drab but clean. The marquee touted free HBO and in-room coffeemakers.

"She doesn't appear to have been hurt," Bishop added.

Fiftyish. Blond. The description fit. "Josie Reed," Kick said.

"She checked in under the name Elinore Martinez," Bishop said.

Kick rocked forward on the balls of her feet. The hair on the body she had seen in the box had looked blond too. Adam Rice, Josie Reed, Mia Turner, the house explosion—they were all connected. If Mia had been saved, maybe Adam still had a chance. "We have to go there," Kick said as the TV news feed went back to the studio.

"Shh," Bishop said. He put a finger to his lips and his eyes went to the ceiling. Kick listened. She could just hear the faint steady chop of helicopter blades.

"That's your ride home," Bishop said.

He had a lot of gall, dragging her up there, almost getting her killed, and then sending her packing. He couldn't just make her come and go as he pleased. "What about Adam?" Kick asked.

Bishop turned off the TV and tossed the remote aside. He looked drained, like he hadn't slept at all. "He's been gone four weeks," he said. "That photo is ten days old. You and I both know what his odds are."

He didn't care at all. Not really. She had been right about him. "Sure," she said. "No one lasts longer than that."

The chopper was louder now, getting closer.

"Your clothes have been cleaned," Bishop said, "and are in the top drawer of the dresser in your room. You should probably get changed."

"Excuse me," a woman's voice said, and Kick and Bishop turned in unison toward the door.

The woman fumbled to close the red robe she was wearing. She was not quick enough that Kick didn't notice she was naked underneath it.

"Sorry," the woman giggled to Bishop. "I was looking for coffee."

"Try the kitchen," Bishop said. "Through the door to your left."

"You two want anything?" The woman tucked her blond hair behind her ear and glanced at Kick, and as their gaze met Kick recognized her doe-like features, even without the ponytail. She was prettier without her uniform, or maybe that was just postcoital glow.

"No, thanks, I only drink kava," Kick said. "For anxiety."

The blonde disappeared down the hall, the robe fluttering open behind her.

Kick leveled an incredulous look at Bishop. "The paramedic?"

Bishop gave her a sort of half shrug.

So he had not spent the whole night in a chair in the guest room after all. Kick felt like a fool for supposing that he had. "Thanks for pausing your one-night stand every few hours to make sure I was still alive," she said.

Bishop tapped his forehead. "You should get that looked at," he said. "But if anyone asks, you fell. We were never in Renton. Our names aren't in any of the police reports."

"Is that why you brought me to your house: so we could get our stories straight?"

"I brought you to my house because you didn't seem to want to go with your mother. I brought the paramedic here to help take care of you . . . and," he conceded, "because I wanted to have sex with her. Now, go home to your dog."

He started walking away in the direction of the coffee and the naked woman wearing his robe.

Kick had a hundred questions, so many that she didn't even know where to begin, which was probably why the one she settled on seemed so random.

"Whose pajamas am I wearing?" Kick asked.

Bishop stopped, his back to Kick, and shook his head with a chuckle.

Kick didn't see what was so funny.

The wall of windows rattled in their casements. Outside, branches bent in the wind and leaves swirled. Inside the room, everything was still. Kick could smell coffee brewing.

Bishop looked back at her, over his shoulder. He was still smiling, but there was something about the smile that struck Kick as particularly joyless. "My wife's," he said.

11

SOMETIMES, KICK COULD MAKE herself disappear.
It was a trick, like magic, based on gimmicks and
artifice. Don't make eye contact. It invites people
to look at you. Don't smile, don't frown; it attracts
attention. Keep your face still. Keep your head
down. Never initiate conversation, but if someone
talks to you, answer as briefly as possible. If everyone else is eating, eat; if everyone else is reading,
read. Blend in.

Toward the end, Mel could take her to air
shows, to the community pool, to the mall. No one
gave her a second glance. The most famous missing
girl in America went unnoticed.

It's all she had wanted ever since. A hiding place.

It was harder now. Especially with the headache. Kick stood outside the charter terminal
at PDX, hunched against a brick wall, far away
from doorways and trash cans, waiting for James.
There had been no kava on the flight back, not
even Flight Attendant Barbie and her come-hither
scowl. The bright sky made Kick's eyes ache, and
the roar of planes passing overhead was unrelenting. She stayed in the shade and tried to keep track

of her surroundings. Eight other people loitered out front, most of them with roller bags, probably waiting to be picked up. They were all staring at their smartphones, so Kick had hers out, too, even though the screen was black. *Hiding in plain sight,* Mel called it.

She didn't have luggage, wasn't wearing shoes, and was sporting a blunt-force injury to her forehead, but so far no one seemed to care. Such were the benefits of private air travel.

By the time James pulled up in Kick's car at the charter terminal at PDX, it was almost three p.m. Kick saw him coming a mile away, inching along, his right-turn signal blinking for no reason. He drove in the least gas-efficient way possible, alternating between paranoid caution and reckless endangerment. She stepped out of the shade and waved, and the car accelerated, swerved toward her, and jumped the curb with one wheel.

James didn't even acknowledge Kick as she climbed into the passenger seat, so she knew he was pissed. He didn't like to leave his apartment, much less drive. He stared straight ahead out the dirty windshield, fingers twitching on the steering wheel. He was still wearing the TARDIS T-shirt.

"Your turn signal's on," Kick said quietly.

James gave her a withering look.

Someone behind them honked.

"Do you want me to drive?" Kick asked hopefully.

"I thought you were dead," James said, his hands fidgeting on the wheel. "I was up all night trolling police reports, calling hospitals." His eyes darted to the rearview mirror.

She had seen him like this before. But it didn't usually come on this fast.

"They're following me again," James said.

"James?" Kick asked. "Did you take your medicine this morning?"

Another jackass behind them laid on his horn, and James practically jumped out of his skin. Kick held her middle finger up over her shoulder.

"I don't feel well," James murmured.

Kick put a hand on his cheek. He felt clammy. His breathing sounded labored. His knuckles had gone white around the steering wheel. "I'm here," she told him. She reached across his lap and unrolled the driver's-side window, then settled her arm lightly around his slender shoulders. "Anxiety is a normal emotion," she reminded him. "You're safe. You are relaxed and calm."

James took a shaky breath, squeezed his eyes shut, and nodded.

"You enjoy leaving the house," Kick continued. "You enjoy open spaces." They had done this so many times before, the affirmations rolled off her tongue like state capitals. "Say it," she said.

"I enjoy leaving the house," James said, nodding.

Kick took his hand, threading her fingers through his. The scars across his wrist quivered with his pulse. "Take a minute," Kick said soothingly. "Breathe deeply." She took a few long slow breaths to demonstrate. "Ready?"

James nodded again.

"Okay," she said.

She squeezed his hand and closed her eyes, and they inhaled together and started to scream—full-throated, openmouthed, at-the-top-of-your-lungs screaming. It felt like the car was vibrating, like the windshield might break. Primal therapy had never really worked for Kick. Screaming your head off was supposed to eliminate the hold of your childhood trauma. Mostly it just made Kick's throat hurt. But James had taken to it right away. He could scream like his life depended on it.

"Miss?" a voice demanded.

Kick opened one eye and squeezed James's hand, and they both went silent.

An airport cop was crouched by the window. "You okay?" he asked Kick.

She glanced at James. His fingers had loosened around the wheel. His breathing had slowed. The panic attack had subsided.

Kick felt a rush of relief. "We're fine," she said.

The cop was real, not TSA. He had a silver Portland Police Department badge and a Glock in his holster. It was probably a Glock 17. Short recoil, standard magazine capacity of seventeen rounds. A respectable 9mm.

Kick let her hair fall forward to cover the bruise on her forehead. "I thought I saw a snake," she said.

She heard James stifle a giggle.

The cop leaned forward and for a moment Kick thought he'd recognized her. But a call came over his walkie-talkie and he glanced at it, distracted. "You need to move along, son," he said to James.

"Yes, sir," James said.

James pulled sharply into traffic, causing a gray Taurus to slam on its brakes behind them. Kick reflexively braced for impact, but the two bumpers missed each other by an inch. She smelled burnt rubber from the Taurus's tires. James didn't seem to even notice. She could hear the tick-tick of his right-turn signal, still on.

She put on her seat belt. "Are you sure you don't want me to drive?" she asked.

"I'm okay," James said, glancing in the rearview mirror.

At this point Kick wasn't worried about James. She was worried about her paint job. "Your turn signal's still on," Kick said.

James rolled his eyes and flipped the signal off, accidentally turning the windshield wipers on first. "They found Mia Turner," he said.

Kick reached over to plug her phone into the car charger. "I heard." She glanced in the backseat, a nest of fur-coated pillows and dog toys. "Where's Monster?" she asked.

"I told him you'd been murdered," James said. "I told him you must have been murdered because you'd promised that you'd text every two hours and I hadn't heard from you in eight."

"I called," Kick protested.

"Twenty minutes ago," James said. "From the airport. Because you needed a ride."

Kick resented his tone. She *had* needed a ride. But she had also called the first moment she could so he'd know she was okay. "I told you, my phone's dead," Kick said. "And I lost my charger when my backpack blew up." She really did feel bad about making him worry. "I'm sorry you had to come get me. My wallet blew up, too, or I would have called a cab."

She opened the glove box and dug through half a dozen survival knives and a box's worth of loose bullets until she found a pair of sunglasses.

James looked like he was concentrating. "Your wallet and charger blew up in your backpack?"

It had seemed too complicated to get into over the airport pay phone.

"My *backpack* didn't blow up," Kick said. The sunglasses didn't help: it was still too bright, like her pupils were a millimeter overdilated. "The *house* blew up," she explained. "My backpack happened to be in it."

By the time James steered them onto I-84, Kick had told him everything, sparing no detail and indulging in some pretty vivid ones having to do with her current opinion of John Bishop.

"The house had a box," James repeated.

He was going forty miles per hour in the passing lane. It was the kind of thing that Kick might usually mention, but she knew he wouldn't take it well right now.

"Are you sure?"

"I was in it," Kick said. She hadn't told James everything. She hadn't told him about Beth.

The loose bullets in the glove box jangled. "What was it like?" James asked.

Kick could hear Beth's voice in the dark, an echo of her own. "It was kind of nice," she said. It sounded crazy. But she knew James would understand. She glanced over at him. "Except for the dead body and the bomb," she added.

"Is that what happened to your head?" James asked.

"Can you see it?" Kick asked. "Is it bad?" She flipped down the sun visor and adjusted the mirror.

"It's hideous," James said.

Kick studied her reflection and beamed. The lump on top of her forehead was developing a faint purplish hue. Her face shimmered in and out of focus. Kick blinked.

For a moment she thought it was the mirror, that it needed cleaning or was warped and refracting poorly. But when she moved her eyes away from her reflection, she noticed that everything in her view seemed to have a halo, a ghost of itself.

"By the way, your friend John Bishop doesn't exist," James said. "You'd know that if you checked your messages." He gave her a knowing smirk. "I know how to find people online. The guy doesn't show up on any networking sites, he doesn't have a PayPal account, he's not on mailing lists, he doesn't show up on any of the people-finding sites, he's not on alumni lists."

Kick was dubious. "You're telling me there's no one named John Bishop with a PayPal account?"

"There are half a million John Bishops with Pay-Pal accounts. None of them him." James took a deep breath. "This involves data mining automated agents," he explained, "and a custom-designed neural network filtering algorithm, and my ingenious hack of the Amazon Elastic Computer Cloud. Still interested?"

"Sorry, I spaced out," Kick said. "What were you saying?"

"The point is, the results came back empty," James said.

Kick was puzzling over that when she saw James do a double take in the rearview mirror. She turned her head just in time to see a gray Taurus slip out of sight behind a bus in the next lane. It looked like the car that James had cut off at the airport.

James's breathing had quickened. He took a hand off the wheel and wiped the sweat off his palm onto the thigh of his pants.

"It doesn't mean we're being followed," Kick said. James had paranoid tendencies under ordinary circumstances. She needed him undistracted, reliable, so she could be the crazy one.

"I know," James said. But she saw his eyes dart back to the rearview mirror.

12

"THE HOUSE WAS ON Vashon Island," Kick said. She sat cross-legged, Monster's head in her lap.

James typed on his keyboard, staring at his center monitor. "He's not listed on any property deeds for Vashon, or any of the surrounding islands," he said.

"What about the Tesla?"

"We did that already," James said. "He doesn't match any listings for the Washington DMV. There are only three hundred Teslas registered in Washington, none of them under his name. Look, the filtering algorithm would have found this stuff." He paused. "You could call Frank."

"I'm not calling Frank," Kick said. The front of her head hurt. She reached up for the ibuprofen on James's desk, rattled a few into her hand, and knocked them back with a swallow of flat Mountain Dew. "I thought it wasn't possible to delete someone from the Internet," she said.

"It shouldn't be," James said. "Not like this."

But if it *were*. Kick knew not to get her hopes up, but she couldn't help it. If John Bishop could wipe his own identity off the Internet, then . . .

James read her face. "The Beth Movies are in a whole different category," he said. "They're hosted on file-sharing services. They're traded between individuals. There are millions of copies." He shrugged miserably. "If there was a way to get them down, I'd know about it. I'd have done it already."

Kick knew he'd already spent thousands of hours trying. "Yeah," she said, unable to keep the disappointment from her voice.

Something shook loose from Kick's brain. "The boys," she said.

"What?"

"He had photographs in his house, of two boys," Kick said excitedly. "I think one of them was him. And the other one was maybe his brother. I think something happened to the brother. He disappears. There are all these pictures of the two of them, and then there are a few of Bishop, and he gets older, and the other boy isn't there. Maybe that's why Bishop is so interested in missing kids. Check the website." She didn't have to say which website. There was a time when Kick had spent more hours on the website for the National Center for Missing & Exploited Children than anyone thought was healthy.

Maybe Bishop had found a way to scrub himself from the Internet, but if he had a missing brother, the brother's picture would be in the database.

The homepage was a sea of faces and sad facts. *Missing from . . . Missing since . . .*

"What years?" James asked, opening a search field.

Kick realized she had no idea. The images were in generic locations: the beach, a park. The boys wore commonplace, conventional clothes. "They were color photographs," Kick said, struggling to remember. "But could have been anytime in the last twenty years." She did the math and reconsidered. "Or forty."

"So between 1970 and now," James said. He brought up the results, and sighed. "That's 2,700 kids. Almost three hundred missing in Oregon alone."

"Can you sort them? Like by gender and hair color?"

"Not on this website," James said. "You know who can do that?" He looked at her pointedly. "*The police.*"

"Can't you use your algorithm?" Kick asked.

"No," James said. "I could write another one. Just give me ten hours and a truck of Mountain Dew."

Kick massaged her throbbing temples. "So we'll skim through them," she said, trying to sound more upbeat than she felt.

There were 295 pages to look at, with nine faces per page. At first it went quickly. Kick moved her eyes from face to face, looking for a match to the image in her mind. Most of the pictures were school photographs. Some were snapshots. The babies looked up from high chairs or the lap of an adult. Some were forensic sketches. Those kids had been found, or at least their bodies had. It was their identities that were missing. Thirty pages in, the faces all started to look the same: babies, teenagers, girls, boys, black, white. "Stop," Kick said, rubbing her eyes. She was so tired, she was starting to see double. She reached, absentmindedly, for James's wire talisman. "Where did you find this thing, anyway?"

James plucked it from her hand. "I'll do it," he said, setting the little wire man back down in his place by the monitor. "I'll sort them."

"How?"

James reached for his Cthulhu mug. "With my brain." He took a sip from the mug, clicked on his mouse, dragged a copy of one of the photographs to his other monitor, and dropped it in an open document. "Go walk the dog," he said.

When Kick and Monster got back from the walk, James was still at it. Kick, woozy and sore, curled up with Monster on the couch and fell asleep.

The mechanical spitting sound of the printer woke her up. Monster was snoring softly with his tongue out, one ear twitching as he dreamed.

"How long was I out?" Kick asked, sitting up.

"Two hours," James said. "Look at this." He scooted back his chair so she could see the computer station. Kick blinked and her head swam a little. All three monitors were tiled with the faces of dark-haired missing boys. "I pulled all the boys who fit your description, between the ages of six and ten," James said. "There are 190. Do you see the boy from Bishop's photographs?"

"Give me a second," Kick said, reaching for the ibuprofen again. She swallowed a pill as she scrutinized the faces on the screen, which seemed especially bright. Kick was struck by how different they all looked. Maybe it was their set of basic similarities that made their uniqueness stand out. Most Kick could dismiss right away. The neck was too long, the head the wrong shape, eyes too far apart, chin too pointed. But some of the faces made her pause. She had to look harder for differences. "No," she said. "I don't see him." She pointed at one of the boys, a thin-armed, floppy-haired boy with a forced class-picture grimace. "But he's close," she said. She cocked her head, and studied another of the boys, also slight and dark, with pale skin and a hesitant expression. "And he kind of looks like him," she said.

James had the self-satisfied smile he got when he'd figured something out. "Check the printer," he said.

Kick reached across the desk and lifted a stack of paper from the printer tray. As she flipped through the still-warm pages, she recognized the two boys she'd pointed out, as well as others from James's screens. Removed from the context of the others, the differences between these boys evaporated. None of these boys matched the boys in Bishop's photographs, but they were indisputably similar. They could have all been brothers.

"I found ten of them," James said, talking fast. "Look at the most recent, on the bottom."

Sometimes James could see patterns that no one else could. Sometimes he could see patterns that weren't even there. Kick riffled through the printouts to the last page.

Her skin goose pimpled. The boy she was looking at was eight years old. Caucasian. Dark hair. Light eyes. But this wasn't the boy from Bishop's wall. This was a picture of Adam Rice.

Kick carried the stack of images to the middle of the room, got down on her knees, and started spreading them in a circle on the floor around her. "Print Adam Rice's investigation report," she said. "Print everything we have: media reports, anything." She studied the boys' faces. She didn't know what it meant or what she was looking for. What stood out, again, were the pieces that didn't fit. Mia Turner. Josie Reed. If Adam Rice's abduction had something to do with all these other boys, what did they have to do with them?

"Synchronicity," Kick said.

"Events that reveal an underlying pattern," James said. "How long did you see the Jungian?"

"Just once," Kick said. "But she talked a lot about synchronicity. She kept trying to get me to see the meaningful coincidences in my life." Kick stood, eyes roving the circle of images she'd made on the floor. "My dad bought me a puppy," she said. "I let the puppy get out." She glanced at Monster, still snoring on the couch. "I went after the puppy, and Mel was there, and he used the lost puppy to get me into his car. All those years later, when I couldn't remember anything from before, I remembered Monster; I remembered enough that Frank was able to figure out who I was and get me home. Is it a meaningful coincidence that Monster was at the center of my abduction and my rescue? Is it a meaningful coincidence that my dad left us just months after I was reunited with the puppy he bought me? Or that I couldn't remember my name but I remembered my dog's?"

"We see what we want to see," James said. "It's called cognitive bias. Synchronicity has potential in fractal geometry; otherwise, it's bunk."

"But what if I'm right?" Kick asked. She hadn't gotten caught up in a missing-child case in over a year. Maybe there was a reason that Adam Rice had broken her streak. She gazed down at the lost boys. "Maybe I'm supposed to save them."

"That's what's called an error of inductive inference," James said.

Kick wasn't so sure. "I've spent the last ten years training myself to be stronger, and smarter—offensively and defensively," she said. "Two kids are abducted a few hours away. John Bishop shows up. He has photographs in his house that send us down a rabbit hole, and we end up back at square one: Adam Rice. And nine other boys who fit the same profile."

James scratched his head. "We're looking at ten boys with recognizably similar features and comportment, abducted over a fifteen-year period, from locations all over the map."

He was doing the math, she could tell, back-tracking.

"I would probably come up with ten other groupings from a sample size this large," he said. "It's compelling, but it doesn't tell us anything. We didn't find the boy from Bishop's photographs, did we?"

"He's dead," Kick said. It seemed like the obvious answer. If she was right, and Bishop's brother had been abducted, then the only reason he would have been taken off the missing-child list was if he had been found. Dead. Or alive. Call it flawed inductive inference, but Bishop had lost someone. Kick had seen Bishop's dead stare. Her mind went back to Adam Rice looking out the window in that satellite photo. It *had* been Adam Rice, hadn't it?

"You're doing it again," James said. "You're obsessing."

"Give me some paper," Kick said, standing up.

James hesitated, then pulled a quarter-inch stack of copy paper off the feed tray of the printer and wheeled backward in his task chair to hand it to her. "There's not enough data to draw any conclusion."

"I'm going to need more paper than that," Kick said.

Two hours later Kick had plastered James's apartment with notes. She'd made bulleted lists, circled words, drawn arrows, underlined, and used all caps—everything she knew about Bishop, about the missing kids, everything he'd told her, everything they'd found out. Some items she'd written in pencil, some in ink, some in purple marker. It was all color coded, though when James had tried to puzzle out her methodology, Kick wasn't able to put it into words. She'd torn the copy paper into jagged pieces in order to make it stretch. They were laid out piecemeal on the floor, were taped on the wall, and covered the sofa cushions. Kick stood up and inspected the images of the boys that she'd arranged over James's travel posters. *See Italy!* a poster of the Leaning Tower of Pisa commanded, over which Kick had taped a photograph of Adam Rice.

"And you think *I'm* messy," James said.

"This isn't a mess," Kick said. "I know where everything is."

"Remind me to talk to you about chaos theory sometime," James said.

Monster lifted his head, yawned, then did a sort of pratfall off the couch onto some notes that Kick had fanned out on the rug. Dog hair floated in the air. Monster circled the notes once, flopped down on them, and closed his eyes. Kick rocked back on her heels. It had all been for nothing. She had thought that getting everything out of her head would help. But sitting in the center of the paper blizzard she'd created, nothing connected. There was no synchronicity.

"I'm going to bed," Kick said. It was almost ten p.m.

"You can sleep on the couch," James said. *Change Your Thoughts and You Change Your World,* advised the poster above his desk. This from a guy who thought the Jungians were full of shit.

Kick rubbed the back of her neck. Her head was throbbing. "No, thank you," she said. She went over and kissed James on the cheek. His skin always tasted a little sour. It was probably from all the medications he took.

"Don't have sex with him," James said.

Kick wasn't sure she'd heard him right. "Excuse me?"

"People like us, it just fucks things up. You know the rule."

Kick did know the rule. She had been the one to come up with it after a particularly traumatic teenage encounter with a boy who burst into tears from the pressure he felt to provide "a positive heteronormative sexual experience." His mother was her shrink.

The rule was: Don't have sex with anyone who knows anything about you. (Also, don't have sex with your shrink's children—but that was more of a personal guideline, and Kick had expanded it to include all shrinks' children.) "I don't even like him," Kick said. He was a smug, horny liar with a stupid-looking house and a wife, and she was beginning to suspect that he'd let her Glock get blown up on purpose.

There was that self-satisfied smile again. James swiveled back to his computer. "But you knew who I meant," he said.

"You're my favorite relative," Kick said.

"Well, obviously," James said.

13

WHEN KICK OPENED HER eyes the next morning, the first thing she saw was the map. For a second she thought it looked blurry, but when she blinked it came into focus, every state boundary and push-pin. She made herself get up. Her head still hurt but was better, she thought, than the night before. She reached for the ibuprofen at her bedside. Monster burrowed out from under the covers and rolled over on his back next to her, and she gave him his morning tummy rub. He stayed in bed when she got up, eyes half open, watching her. She was sore and stiff, and she stretched before she made her way to her dresser. After she changed into her running clothes, she went to her closet and found her sneakers on the closet floor, next to the boxes of letters. Kick touched the lump on her forehead and turned back to the map. Adam Rice, in duplicate, stared back at her from the wall. Kick went to her laptop and turned it on.

The news sites were ablaze with stories of Mia Turner's miraculous recovery. Kick scanned them, but there hadn't been any developments of inter-est since she'd read all the latest last night. Instead, despite herself, she clicked on another story: "Mel Riley: On Death's Door."

Kick read it, then snapped her laptop closed.

She had to force Monster out of bed. The arthritis in his back had made dismounting to the floor a huge production, involving Kick hoisting him in her arms and him going stiff, then panicking, and finally both of them making groaning noises as he was lowered to the floor. Once he was off the bed, Kick brushed the dog hair off her running pants and Monster blinked his milky eyes and panted happily at her, his tail thumping against the floor.

"I'm not facing her without you," Kick said.

Monster followed her to the bathroom. While braiding her hair in the mirror, she noticed that her forehead looked almost normal, which she found vaguely disappointing, especially since she still had the headache.

"Are you ready for our marathon?" Kick asked him, sliding his red harness over his snout.

There had been a time when even the sight of that harness would send Monster bounding about like a hyperactive lamb. They would run ten miles together, and even then Monster only stopped because she did. Now they walked a block to the park and Monster sat tied to the leg of a park bench while Kick exercised.

Today they had the park to themselves. It wasn't much of a park, just a plot of grass with a children's playground set, a water fountain, and five public trash bins all marked with differing categories of recyclables. There was no fencing, so the dog people went elsewhere, up Mount Tabor, or to the trails of Forest Park, or to the local dog parks. Fences didn't much matter with Monster. Kick always kept him on his leash outside anyway. Sometimes her whistle didn't work out in the world, and he was so frail she worried about him getting hurt.

Tae kwon do required focus, strength, and endurance, but mostly it required the ability to deal with looking like an ass in public. It was the opposite of disappearing. Kick could have practiced at home or at the dojo, but going to the park got Monster outside, and there was something about looking like an ass in public that Kick found a little appealing. She had been stared at so much by strangers since her rescue, she liked thinking that some of them were staring now because she looked ridiculous and not for all the other reasons.

She stripped down to her tank top, dropped to the grass, and did leg lifts until her thighs trembled while Monster fixed his glazed eyes at her with his head cocked. Then she got up, brushed the grass off her pants, and did a hundred lunges, followed by fifty step-ups on the bench, with a pat for Monster each time. Squat thrust, single leg squat. They were not pretty, and they were not exercises for the socially insecure. But they were all a necessary foundation so that if Bishop ever showed up again, Kick could use an eagle strike to shatter his pointy jawbone.

Kick focused on that as she lowered herself into horse stance, widening her knees, bending them, and holding it. She bent her elbows, held her hands in loose fists, palms up, on either side of her waist, and visualized directing a tiger claw strike at Bishop's trachea. Sweat began to bead on her neck. Her thighs burned. Kick let her eyes close. *I shall be a champion of freedom and justice*, she repeated in her mind. *I shall build a more peaceful world*.

"In tae kwon do, they say that the elbow is the strongest part of the body," a woman's voice said.

Kick snapped her eyes open but otherwise remained motionless, squatting over the grass like she was peeing in the woods.

Striding toward her, wearing three-hundred-dollar sneakers and all-white exercise clothes, was her mother. "Since when do you know anything about tae kwon do?" Kick asked her, making herself sink lower into the stance even as she could feel her face turn scarlet from the effort.

"They offer it at the MAC club," her mother said breezily. She unzipped the white jacket she was wearing. "After Zumba." She tossed the jacket over the back of the bench, revealing a white halter top that was no bigger than a jogging bra.

Kick was determined not to give up on her stance even as her mother stood there with her hand on her hip like she was waiting for a hug.

To anyone watching, they would have looked like friends meeting up to exercise together. Paula

Lannigan worked hard to maintain her figure and she spent a fortune on laser treatments and blow-outs and eyelash grower and injectables. She said it was for her TV appearances as a spokesperson for the Missing Person Alliance. If a kid went missing, CNN didn't want to have someone ugly on to talk about it, apparently.

"What happened to your head?" Paula asked finally.

"I hit it on something," Kick grunted, inching her feet farther apart. The wider the stance, the stronger the base. "Did you bring it?"

Paula pointedly ignored the question, spun back toward the bench, bent down, and took Monster's face in her hands. "There's my boy," she said in a gooey voice.

Monster snuffled and licked at her, and Kick couldn't help but think: *Traitor.* She resumed her mantra: *I shall be a champion of freedom and justice. I shall build a more peaceful world.* Her pelvis and hamstrings felt like they had gone to war.

Paula sat down on the bench. "You made me look like a fool last night," she said with a glare at Kick. "I left a fund-raising dinner and drove three hours to take care of you after I got the call you'd been hurt. I showed up with the press. The police wouldn't even confirm you had been there."

That was just like Kick's mother, to make it all about her. Sweat trickled down Kick's face. "I'm feeling much better, thank you," she said. She could barely get the words out. Monster had rolled over on his back and was letting Paula stroke his belly with the toe of her sneaker.

"You have to release a statement," Paula said. "I've been fielding calls all day. You know how rare a live rescue is in stranger abductions. People want to know your reaction."

"My reaction?" Kick said. Her legs gave out, but she fell beautifully. She lay in the grass for a long moment, finding strength in the exhaustion she felt, the dilated vessels, the heat, the surrender. When her legs stopped trembling enough that she could manage it, she slowly stood up. Her mother regarded her cautiously from the bench like a nice lady who's raised a chimp as a pet but knows it's only a matter of time before the chimp rips someone's face off.

Kick wiped the sweat off her forehead with the back of her wrist. "I'm *pro*–child rescuing," she said. "That's my reaction."

Her mother held her gaze for a moment. Ever since she'd read Elizabeth Smart's book, she acted like she had some psychological insight into Kick's behavior. "Nothing more complicated than that?" Paula pressed.

Kick launched herself backward toward the ground. Her body hit the grass and she rolled on her shoulder.

"What are you doing?" Paula asked with a look of horror that Kick found immeasurably satisfying.

"Falling," Kick said. She got back to her feet and threw herself backward again, really putting her weight into it. She winced, then got up and did it again.

"Stop it," Paula said.

Kick rolled up into a sitting position. "Did you bring what I asked?"

Paula unzipped a hitherto hidden pocket on the knee of her white workout capris and withdrew a business-size white envelope. "Is this what I think it is?" she asked.

"I'm surprised you didn't open it," Kick said.

Paula held the letter to her heart. "This is disturbed, Kathleen. I know how I feel doesn't matter to you, but if you pursue this, I will seek a conservatorship over you and your affairs, and no judge in the world will deny me." She extended the letter to Kick, and Kick snatched it out of her hand.

The heat from her mother's body had made the envelope warm. Kick gave it a shake and held it up to the sky, inspecting the triangular flap on the back for signs of infiltration. The envelope appeared untampered with, but who the hell could ever know with Paula? Kick flipped the envelope back over and peered through the plastic window at her name printed above her mother's address. Her mother thought that it had come to her house by mistake—a bureaucratic mix-up. The truth was more complicated.

Kick's stomach clenched as her eyes skimmed the official-looking medical seal on the return address, but she was sure her mother hadn't noticed.

"I can take care of myself," Kick said. She folded the envelope in half, then in half again, and tucked it carefully in her pocket.

"You can't take care of yourself," Paula said, crossing her arms. "You can't even take care of Monster."

Monster had managed to wrap his leash around the leg of the park bench four times, and was blinking at Kick balefully. Kick's face burned. "Don't talk about my dog," she said.

"*Your* dog?" Paula said with a look of astonishment. "Who do you think took care of him while you were gone? Who walked him, who house-trained him, who took him to the vet when he was sick? He slept in my bed every night for five years. Look at him." Monster had stretched out sideways on the grass with his mouth open and his tongue out. "He's almost sixteen years old. He can barely walk. You want to be a grown-up? Being a grown-up means making tough decisions and living with them."

Kick clenched her teeth. Tough decisions? She'd made decisions tougher than her mother could even begin to imagine. If that's what made a grown-up, Kick was middle-aged. Paula was the teenager. "He slept in a crate in Marnie's room," Kick said.

Paula's mouth twisted.

"Monster slept in Marnie's room," Kick repeated, enjoying the rising color in her mother's cheeks. Kick had known all along. Her sister had thrown it in her face enough times. "In her room, not with you."

"Your father is allergic," Paula sputtered.

Kick's father had bailed on them almost ten years ago. At some point they'd have to start referring to him in the past tense.

Kick rolled her eyes and gave Monster's harness a tug so he'd stand up. "I have to go." She wanted to make a breezy exit, but it took some doing to unwind Monster's leash from the bench.

"Burn the letter," her mother ordered. She looked pointedly at Monster. "Or I will take control of your affairs."

Had Paula really just threatened to euthanize her dog? "You wouldn't," Kick said.

"I'm not afraid of you hating me, Kit," Paula said. "You decided to hate me a long time ago."

"You don't get it," Kick said, pulling Monster closer to her. His white eyes were half closed. His ear twitched. He had been such a sweet puppy. When Mel appeared out of nowhere and told her he'd help find him, Kick had been so grateful, she hadn't even questioned it. "I lost him once," she said. "I'm not losing him again."

"That was fifteen years ago," Paula said. "You've been back with us for ten." She tried to put her hand on Kick's arm, but Kick backed away. "A *decade*," her mother said, as if that were any sort of length of time at all.

Ten years to the day, but who was counting?

"I have to give you credit," Kick said to her

mother. "I thought you'd make a bigger deal about wanting some bogus family photo op today."

Paula took a step closer to Kick and cupped Kick's face in her hands. "Long lens, kitten," she said. She brushed a stray piece of hair off of Kick's forehead and frowned at the faint contusion there. "It's more flattering anyway," she said. She gave Kick a wink, took a step back, snatched her white jacket off the bench, and jogged off.

Kick turned slowly and saw a quick flash from the back of a black SUV, the telltale reflection of a camera lens.

Paula was halfway across the park, a bobbing figure, getting more distant by the moment. The black SUV sped off with a squeal of rubber on concrete. Kick sank onto the bench, defeated. She should have taken advantage of the fact that Paula had removed her jacket. Kick knew four ways to kill someone with a jacket. Now she regretted not trying any of them out.

Monster nuzzled at her feet. Kick gazed across the park. Her mother was gone. She reached into her pocket and extracted the envelope. It already looked the worse for wear, wrinkled, its corners bent. She examined it with a blank kind of resignation, then slowly tore it open and withdrew the letter from inside. It had been months since Kick had gone to the Trident Medical Group to get tested. She hadn't told anyone, not even James. It was a simple blood test, funded by a prisoner rights organization. Full medical confidentiality. Kick had it all planned. The results would come back negative, she would be absolved, Mel would die, and that would be that. Kick had done the research. The odds of a kidney match between nonrelatives was 1 in 100,000.

And if she was a match, well, it didn't mean she had to do anything about it.

Kick unfolded the letter and read it. She stared at it for a long time afterward, not knowing how to feel. Then she worked the letter back into the envelope.

Across the park, the leaves on the trees were coming in and out of focus—one moment individual shapes, the next an indistinguishable blur.

14

SAN DIEGO SMELLED LIKE dust and salt, and it was exactly the same temperature indoors as it was outdoors. Beth was wearing her new blue swimsuit, an orange towel wrapped around her chest. The wet suit stuck to her skin. Her eyes burned from the chlorine. Everything was a little blurry. She blinked.

There was a boy in Mr. Klugman's kitchen.

She hadn't seen another kid up close in so long, she thought he might be imaginary.

Neither of them moved.

"Can I have a snack?" Beth asked.

Mr. Klugman appeared from the dining room and Beth could see her father leaning back in his chair, watching through the doorway. He always watched her when Mr. Klugman was around.

"Go back downstairs," Mr. Klugman said to the boy.

They had been in San Diego for two days. Mel and Mr. Klugman went to the store every day and came home with camera equipment and costumes.

"Let them play," Mel called from the dining room.

The boy was eyeing her like she might bite him.

Mr. Klugman shrugged.

Beth wanted someone to play with. "What's your name?" she asked the boy.

The boy looked at Mr. Klugman before he answered. "James," he said. "I'm James."

"Do you want to play in the pool?" Beth asked.

"I'm not allowed," the boy said.

"Oh," Beth said, with a rueful glance toward the pool in the backyard.

Her father got up from his chair and came through the doorway and stood behind her, and she pressed herself back against him.

"Why don't you show her your room, James?" her father asked the boy gently.

The boy gazed up at her father, right into his eyes. Beth could hear the blood rushing in her ears. Then the boy turned away and trudged across the kitchen toward the open door that led down the dark basement stairs. He looked back at her. "C'mon," he said.

Beth peeled herself away from Mel and followed him.

15

KICK DID NOT REMEMBER walking home from the park, so she was surprised when she found herself sitting on the front steps of her apartment building, Monster on his haunches next to her, head cocked attentively. The envelope from the Trident Medical Group was back in her hand. She touched her forehead and winced.

"I told you to get that checked out," Bishop said.

Kick whirled around, disoriented. Bishop was leaning against her building's front door. She squeezed her eyes shut, then opened them. There were two Bishops, actually—superimposed, one just slightly to the left of the other, both wearing black baseball caps, black jeans, and gray T-shirts. They merged and stopped shimmering. Kick stuffed the envelope back into her pants pocket, then got to her feet and pulled the keys from her other pocket so she could get inside and Google "concussions."

"We need to talk," Bishop said as she approached.

"Every time I talk to you, I regret it," Kick said. "You're not even a real person." She had to concentrate to walk straight, had to think about placing one foot in front of the other. Monster pressed against her calf, as if trying to give her ballast. But when they got to the door, Bishop didn't budge. A scar on his throat turned up slightly on each side. It looked like it was smiling at her.

"Move," Kick said.

Bishop stepped to the side. Monster leaned hard against her leg. If the dog moved suddenly, she'd fall. Kick looked at the key in her hand and went to insert it in the lock as she'd done a thousand times before. She missed. She tried again. Monster was panting. She jammed it toward the lock again, and this time the door seemed to sink away from her, and the keys fell from her hand.

Bishop caught her by the elbow as her knees buckled. She felt like she was floating, like the laws of gravity had changed. It took her several moments to get her bearings. Bishop didn't say anything. He just held her firmly, at a decorous distance, while Monster circled, nose in the air, whining softly.

"She's okay, buddy," Bishop said to the dog. "I got her."

Monster glanced at Bishop and then put his ears back and settled down in the space between their feet.

"I got you," Bishop told Kick. The grooves her nails had dug into his forearms were starting to scab.

"I'm fine," Kick said. "I just need a second." She

practiced her intentional breathing and tried not to stare at Bishop's scar. Her hair felt sticky with sweat. Her clothes stunk. He kept holding her. His fingers pinched her skin, but she didn't care.

"See? I'm real," he said.

Kick felt a feathering of nerves in her stomach. "I meant on the Internet," she said. "James researched you. He used a custom designed neural"—she searched her foggy brain for the right words—"something."

"A neural network filtering algorithm," Bishop said.

"Right. That," Kick said. She balled up her hand and then opened it between them. "Poof," she said, showing him her empty palm. "Nothing." She lost her balance, and Bishop tightened his grip.

For an instant Kick thought she'd caught him looking at her with an expression something like concern, but then it was gone, and she wasn't sure it had ever really been there. "How did you do it?" she asked him. "How did you erase yourself?"

"I told you," Bishop said. "I have a lot of friends."

"Can they help me?" Kick asked, regretting the words even as they left her mouth. She hadn't meant to blurt it out.

Bishop recoiled slightly, like he'd been burned, and he loosened his grip on her. "Erase your image from the Web?" he said.

She held her breath.

"No," he said, firmly. "No, Kick. They can't."

Kick's disappointment acted like smelling salts. It cut through the mental haze; everything was clarified. She shifted her weight to her own feet. "Let go of me," she said.

Bishop removed his hands, swooped down for the keys she had dropped, and placed them in her hand. "Double vision," he said as his fingers closed around hers, the keys in her palm. She steeled herself against his touch, growing armor over her skin. "Loss of balance." He was moving his hand up along the length of her arm, his fingers just above her skin, not quite touching her. "All expected side effects of a concussion." His hand hovered at the side of her face, then he brushed a stray piece of her hair behind her ear. "This is the worst of it."

Kick turned her head away from his hand and concentrated on putting the key in the lock. "Fucking a paramedic doesn't make you one," she said, pushing open the door.

"Ah, another classic symptom," Bishop said. He followed her through the door into the lobby. "Irritability."

Kick pulled Monster toward the elevator as Bishop tagged along, reaching down to pet her dog.

"I'm not going with you this time," Kick said. "Whatever game you're playing, I'm out. You're rich. You're bored. I get it. You want a hobby. You sold guns. Now you feel bad about it. So you want to track down missing kids. Whatever. I have a headache. And I want to lie down."

"You can't, Kick. I'm sorry."

His expression was impenetrable. The elevator dinged and the doors opened. Kick made a slight movement and he blocked the elevator door with his arm.

"Mia Turner had something you might be interested in," Bishop said.

Kick tugged Monster's leash and stepped back, away from Bishop. He didn't make a move to come after her. He kept his head down, his cap obscuring his eyes, like someone who was good at disappearing, like someone who had a reason not to be noticed; Kick recognized the tactics. Her eyes went up to the lobby security camera mounted in the ceiling corner. The camera. Bishop was positioning himself so that he couldn't be identified on the video feed.

The elevator doors had closed behind Bishop's arm. Someone who didn't want to attract attention wasn't going to risk making a scene. Kick stepped forward and reached around Bishop to press the elevator button. The car was still on the first floor, so the doors opened instantly. Bishop raised his eyebrows. She ducked under his arm and pulled Monster into the elevator with her.

"You can't walk away from this," Bishop said, letting his arm drop.

Monster looked back and forth between Kick and Bishop.

"Kick?" Bishop called as the elevator doors closed.

He tossed something through the narrowing gap between the closing doors. Kick caught it in her fist. She didn't want to open her hand, because she knew what it was, what she'd find in her palm. She could already see it in her head, the shape taking form in her imagination. She felt a stab of vertigo as the elevator went up, up, up.

Kick opened her eyes and unclenched her fingers, revealing the Scrabble tile, the letter *E*. The elevator stopped and the doors opened on her floor. She could see her apartment door across the hall. James's apartment was a mirror below it, a matching set. He was home right now and he'd know what to do. All Kick had to do was select the second floor, and ride the elevator down, and step off when the doors opened. Her hand hovered over the button. But her finger didn't select his floor; instead she pressed *L*, for "Lobby." Monster pulled at his leash, disoriented. The elevator began its descent. The doors opened.

Bishop was standing exactly where she'd left him. He stepped into the elevator and hit a floor without looking at the buttons.

The doors closed.

"It was found in Mia's pocket," he said.

He inserted a small key into a keyhole on the elevator control panel and Kick felt the elevator halt with a bump.

Bishop took off his cap and ran his fingers through his hair. "You should think about installing a camera in here," he said, looking around.

"You'd be amazed how much crime goes on in elevators."

Kick stared, mesmerized, at the nineteen-millimeter-by-nineteen-millimeter wooden tile in her hand. It was almost weightless yet seemed to burn a hole in her skin. "Where did she get it?" she asked.

"You first," Bishop said. "What does it mean?"

Kick glanced up from the tile. Bishop had his arms crossed, feet apart. The elevator remained frozen, a box in a wall. All the access Bishop seemed to have, and he didn't know this? "I thought you knew Frank," Kick said.

Bishop rubbed the back of his neck. "Yeah, well," he said with a shrug. "Frank kind of hates me." He raised his eyebrows and shared a conspiratorial smile. "He likes you, though. I've been through your case file. All fifty-eight file boxes. There are gaps in his notes. Like someone went back later and took out pages." Bishop's smile dropped away. "Here's what I do know, *Kit Lannigan*." He drew out every syllable of her old name. "I know that you walked out of that Idaho farmhouse with a Scrabble tile in your hand after you were rescued," he said. "I know it was the letter *K*. I know you had the tile in your pocket when you testified against Mel. I got that last bit from your mother," he added. "Or at least from her book—which, by the way, is staggering in its epic narcissism. I assumed you still had the tile, but—just between us—I poked around your apartment while you were at the park with your mother just now. Didn't turn it up."

Kick put her hands over her face, trying to block out the image of what else he might have found: the hundreds of victim notification letters, unopened, in her closet; the cards from Frank, neatly collected and hidden away in a drawer. "Ha!" she said. She closed her eyes and tried again. "Ha!" She peeked between her fingers at Bishop.

He lifted an eyebrow.

Kick rolled her eyes to the ceiling. "HA!"

"Is that helping?" Bishop asked.

The elevator felt like it was shrinking, like there wasn't enough air. "I feel sick," Kick said.

"Good," Bishop said. "That's a good sign, Kick. You *should* feel sick. That means you're not as fucked-up as you think you are."

Kick looked at him sideways, disgusted. "You would make a terrible therapist."

"Two kidnappings," Bishop said. "Two girls, two Scrabble tiles. That's a pretty meaningful coincidence, don't you think?"

A meaningful coincidence. The words snapped at Kick like rubber bands. "What did you say?" she asked.

"I said, that's a pretty meaningful-fucking-coincidence," Bishop said.

"That's an error of inductive inference," Kick said.

Bishop's eyes were attentive, his body drawn taut like a bow. "How so?"

"It's not *synchronicity*," Kick continued. "It's not even coincidence." She met Bishop's gaze. "Because they're all my tiles."

Bishop waited.

Kick held the Scrabble tile up between her thumb and forefinger. "This?" she said. "It's mine."

Bishop's brows drew together.

"I'd palm the tiles and hide them," Kick explained, folding her hand around the tile to demonstrate. "I'd tuck them behind rafters, between floorboards, under exposed insulation. I thought if someone ever found the secret rooms, they might find the tiles and know that I had been there." It had been a useless exercise. "Mel counted the tiles after every game. There are supposed to be a hundred, see: ninety-eight letters and two blanks." He'd never even acknowledged her act of rebellion, not once. "I always thought he'd get mad. But he never did. He'd just replace them. The next time he'd come to the box to play with me, all the letters would be there, like it had never happened."

She opened her hand again and looked down at the wooden square in her palm. The letter *E*. On its own, a one-point value. But for longer words, seven- or eight-tile long words, *E*'s became essential. Mel had taught her to hang on to *E*'s. Even if you turned in the other six letters on your rack, *E*'s always came in handy. "Only the original tiles, they were made from Vermont maple," Kick said. She showed Bishop the tile. "This is white oak. And the letter on this tile is carved and then inked instead of stamped." She shrugged. "It's a good copy. He stained them to match. But you can feel the marks from the bandsaw where it wasn't sanded down smoothly." She moved her fingers over the tile, noting the very slightest edge marking the path of a bandsaw blade. "He made this one. And I hid it. And Mia Turner found it because they put her in one of the rooms that I was kept in fifteen years ago."

Bishop's shoulders rose and fell. "Only she didn't find it," he said. "She said a boy gave it to her. The description she gave matches Adam Rice."

Kick could hear herself breathing; she could practically hear her own cells dividing. "So he's still alive?" she whispered.

"Maybe," he said. "I haven't talked to her myself, and she's five years old, so not exactly a reliable witness. But she says she was moved to at least three houses over the course of the day, always transported under a blanket in the backseat. She can't describe any of the houses she was kept in, just that she was kept somewhere inside and very dark. But if she's right, based on the time frame, the three locations must all be in the Seattle area."

Kick couldn't bring herself to ask the next question, but Bishop must have read it in her eyes.

"It doesn't look like she was physically or sexually abused," Bishop added.

Kick exhaled slowly.

"Do you remember being in Seattle?" Bishop asked.

Kick didn't know. There had been so many houses, and she had been kept inside so much of the time. In many ways, it was a blur. But if Adam had found her Scrabble tile, wherever he was, she had been there first. "I don't remember," she said. "But we moved a lot," she added. "Maybe we were there the first year, before they let me outside." The truth was, she couldn't locate the house any more than Mia Turner could.

The only person who could do that was Mel.

"Oh," Kick said, finally getting it. She felt foolish for not seeing what Bishop wanted from her sooner. He didn't care about her lock-picking skills or her steady shooting hand or her ability to squat deeply in a park for almost seven minutes. The thing that interested him was the same thing that interested everybody. Her enduring social capital. It would not matter what Kick did with her life, what she accomplished; her obituary would begin and end with Mel Riley.

The outline of the envelope in Kick's pocket pressed against her skin, like a hand on her thigh. Kick rolled her eyes to the ceiling and laughed at the bitter irony of her life.

"He has a world of information that could help us," Bishop said.

Us, Kick noticed, like they were a team now.

She cleared her throat. "He won't give up the safe houses," she said. "He's always refused to give up anything. You said so yourself."

Bishop nodded. He checked his phone. He rubbed the back of his neck. The air in the elevator had gotten thick. The steel walls gleamed. "You're right," he said. He pivoted away from her, turned the little key, and pressed the button for the fourth floor.

The sudden motion of the elevator was startling. Kick's eyes shot to the numbers above the door as they were illuminated one by one above the back of Bishop's head. *Second floor. Third floor.*

Monster looked at her and whined.

Fuck it. "Can you get me in to see him?" she asked.

"Yes," Bishop said, turning around.

"I haven't seen him since I was twelve, at the sentencing." The words tumbled out in a rush.

Fourth floor.

"I know," Bishop said.

Kick was holding the end of Monster's leash so tightly, she could feel it cutting into her palm. "He might not want to talk to me."

The elevator chimed and the doors opened.

"He wants to talk to you," Bishop said.

Monster tilted his nose toward the door and wagged his tail. He knew where they were, or at least knew they were somewhere. He headed off out of the elevator, pulling at Kick to follow.

"When?" Kick asked Bishop.

"I have a car."

Kick stopped mid-step. Something sour turned in her stomach. The world went shaky. Bishop couldn't mean today; he wouldn't make her do that, not on the ten-year anniversary.

"Drop the dog at your brother's," Bishop said, pushing the lobby button. "Put on something nice. I'll meet you downstairs. And, Kick?" he said, nodding at her hand. "I need the tile."

Kick didn't have time to think of a response. She tossed Bishop the tile. She hurled it, actually. He caught it through the doors, just before they closed.

16

NOT A LOT OF people on Kick's block drove black hybrid Porsche Panameras, so Bishop wasn't hard to spot. Kick got into the car wordlessly and buckled her seat belt with the kind of cautious attentiveness more often seen in electric-chair technicians. She kept her purse on her lap. She'd tucked the letter from the Trident Medical Group in the inside pocket at the last minute; she wasn't sure why. The purse was a cherry-red leather square the size of a vinyl record, with silver grommets punched into one side in the shape of a skull, which seemed especially apt. Kick didn't usually carry purses, but seeing as her backpack had been blown to smithereens, she'd had to improvise.

"What do you know about his health?" Bishop asked.

Kick reached into her open purse, past the letter, and pulled out a pair of handcuffs. "What I read on the Internet," she said. She snapped a bracelet on each of her wrists.

Bishop glanced at the cuffs without comment and then returned his gaze to the road.

"I know he's been on dialysis for three years,"

Kick said. She reached with her cuffed hands back into her purse and began feeling around for a paper clip. "I remember he would get sick sometimes. He had kidney infections. His lawyers tried to get the judge to consider his health at the sentencing." Her fingertips touched the paper clip and she fished it out and started unbending it.

"Well, he's in the prison infirmary," Bishop said. He wasn't looking at her. "Things seem to be deteriorating."

Kick pressed her fingers against the curve of the paper clip, forcing it apart until it gave. When she thought of her father now, she made herself think of Jerry, not Mel. It had been hard at first. Kick had few memories of before she was taken, and Jerry had left four months after her return. But she had one perfect memory of him from that earlier time, and she clung to it. It was her relaxing experience, her calm blue ocean. She used it to remind herself that she had, at least once, known normalcy.

The backyard. The tire swing. Her father's hands on her back, pushing her higher and higher, toward the clouds.

She flipped the straightened paper clip toward her cuffed wrists and used her right hand to guide it into the keyhole at the base of the left bracelet. With the tip of the wire inserted in the hole, she bent it about seventy degrees, one way and then the other, until the end of the wire formed a small notch. Then she removed the wire from the hole and, bending her wrists at angles that made them throb, wiggled the bent end of the wire back into the hole, hooking it so that the end of the wire pointed toward the locking arm, at a ninety-degree angle to the keyhole. Using her left hand, she turned the wire like a key, hooking and lifting the locking device. The right bracelet sprung open.

She freed her right hand and immediately transferred the wire to the keyhole on the left bracelet. She turned the notched wire. The locking device inside the cuff lifted. The bracelet opened. Kick glanced at the clock on the Porche's GPS screen. It had taken her just over two minutes.

Too long. She was distracted.

She snapped the handcuffs back on and tossed the mutilated paper clip back into her bag.

"You got a new car," she said as she felt around her purse for another clip with her cuffed hands.

"I have a lot of cars," Bishop said.

Kick located another paper clip, slid her purse from her knees to the floor between her feet, and began unfolding the wire in her lap. The dress came to her mid-thighs and her knees were pale and scabbed with scrapes. The wire straightened, Kick notched it in the right-side keyhole, extracted it, and then hooked the notch back into the hole at a ninety-degree angle, pointed toward the locking arm. Twist. Click. Spring. The air coming through the vents on the dash fluttered the hem of Kick's skirt. She turned her attention to the left cuff. Her mother had bought her the dress. It was not something Kick would have picked out: pale yellow patterned with tiny daisies. It looked like bathroom wallpaper to her. She'd never worn it. She didn't know why she'd chosen it today. Probably because it wasn't anything like her; it belonged to some completely different person. The left cuff opened. She glanced at the time. Just under two minutes.

"I shouldn't have said that to you, that thing about putting on something nice," Bishop said.

Kick snapped the handcuffs on and tossed the straightened paper clip into the purse. "You don't get to apologize and feel better," Kick said. She bent forward, reached into her purse on the floor, and dug for a fresh paper clip.

The truth was, she had torn apart her closet looking for the perfect thing to wear. Something Beth would like. Kick found a paper clip and bent it open.

Beth liked yellow. Because it was Mel's favorite color.

"Are you going to be doing that the whole drive?" Bishop asked.

It took an hour to get to Salem, Oregon, the state capital and home of the state penitentiary.

Kick jammed the end of the wire into the first hole. Her wrists were sore from overflexing them, and faint red welts had started to form. "It relaxes me," she said.

17

THE OREGON STATE PENITENTIARY was surrounded by guard towers and a twenty-five-foot wall topped with razor wire. Even after an hour to prepare herself, the prison appeared too soon, and Kick regretted the fact that there hadn't been a multivehicle accident to slow down the interstate. The gray Taurus that had been tailing them since they left Portland had dropped out of sight when they exited I-5. She knew that Bishop had seen it too. His eyes had returned, again and again, to the rearview mirror. But he hadn't said anything, and he hadn't tried to lose it.

She tossed the cuffs back in her bag as they were waved through the prison gates. The guards seemed to know Bishop by sight. He steered around the compound of institutional buildings and found a place to park like he'd been here before.

He didn't try to give her a pep talk; he didn't talk to her at all. When she got out of the car, she followed him. The closer she got to Mel, the more blank she felt. Like she was shedding herself, cell by cell, molting down to nothing.

She could do that. She could disassociate.

Reactive attachment disorder, one of her early shrinks had called it, when Paula complained that Kick wasn't showing the proper level of affection.

The spring after Kick's rescue, Paula had shipped her off to a clinic in Colorado for a week of in-patient rebirthing compression therapy. Every day, two practitioners would restrain Kick, wrap her tightly in sheets, and then simulate contractions by sitting on her until she managed to "emerge from the birth canal."

If Kick hadn't had an attachment disorder before that, she certainly had one after.

Years later she had found the clinic's report in some of her mother's things. They'd diagnosed her based on how she scored on a set of twelve items, including "seeking comfort when distressed," "responding to comfort when offered," and "willingness to go off with relative strangers."

"*Kick?*" Bishop said.

Kick looked up to find a prison guard in a blue uniform staring at her expectantly from the other side of a counter. A cacophony echoed from every surface: buzzers, walkie-talkie static, footsteps. Everything smelled like concrete.

"Ask her again," Bishop said to the guard.

"You carrying any weapons, sweetheart?" the guard asked Kick. She looked at Kick with an air of professional boredom. If she recognized Kick, she didn't show it.

Kick pulled open her red purse and showed her

the army fixed-blade survival knife, the recon camo tactical knife, a three-pack of throwing knives, the Leatherman, her lipstick pepper spray, a pouch of throwing stars, the handcuffs, and a pen with a steel tip that could be used as an emergency window breaker.

"Anything else?" the guard asked.

Kick unzipped one of the purse's inside pockets, reached behind the envelope from Trident Medical Group, retrieved her nunchakus, and dropped them on the counter with a *ka-thunk*.

Bishop gave the guard an apologetic smile. "She's safety conscious," he explained.

The guard handed her the key to a locker and told her to put her arsenal in it. Then she put two orange vests on the counter. Bishop reached for one and started to put it on.

"What are these?" Kick asked.

"Put it on," Bishop said. "If anything goes wrong, the guards will know not to shoot you."

Kick pulled the orange vest on over her dress.

Once they cleared the metal detector, the first full set of metal bars closed behind them, and they were issued prison ID badges that clipped to their vests.

Kick shed another layer of skin.

Bishop gestured for her to follow him, and Kick had the uneasy realization that they were not going to get an escort. "I know where I'm going," Bishop said, already walking. She followed him. It came easily, matching his steps as they moved down cinder-block corridors. She found it comforting, actually. A strange type of surrender. When they came to a barred door, Bishop would hold his ID badge up to the security camera mounted above it, and the door would unlock with a pop. Kick kept her face neutral and her head down, trying to disappear behind her hair. But there was no way to blend in. The guards they passed were in uniform; the prisoners were in orange jumpsuits; she was wearing an orange vest with the number three ironed on the back. Bishop stopped. They were outside a large gray door stenciled with the word INFIRMARY. On the other side of the door, she could hear someone crying.

This was really happening.

She was rooted to the spot. She couldn't move.

"You don't have to do this," Bishop said, in a voice so light it was barely more than a breath. "Just tell me no," he said. "I can't make you see him." He touched her arm. "Just say no and we walk out of here right now."

Kick pulled her arm away. "What happened to your brother?" she asked.

Bishop hesitated.

"The boys in the photographs at your house," Kick pressed. "One is you." She had wanted to knock him off balance, and for a moment it worked. "The other boy is your brother, am I right?"

"Yes."

"What happened to him?" she asked.

He regarded her warily. "What do you think happened to him, Kick?"

"I think he died," Kick said.

Bishop's face didn't show anything. "He did die."

"I think he was murdered," Kick added. "I thought maybe he was missing, but James and I searched, and we couldn't find him. Which means he's not missing. He's dead." Kick searched Bishop's eyes for some sign of pain. If it was there, he didn't let her see it. But she knew she was right. "That's why you do this," she said. "Why you don't care what it costs."

Bishop was motionless. "That is very observant of you."

She turned away from him, toward the door.

"I'm ready," Kick said.

18

THE LAMINATE FLOOR OF the infirmary was the color of a swimming pool. It gleamed, reflecting the fluorescent lights overhead, so that the floor seemed to ripple like water. Bishop didn't pause. He nodded at someone in a medical coat at the nurse's station and then led Kick across the room, through the sea of hospital beds, to an area partitioned with hanging-curtain dividers. A TV was on somewhere. A black man about Kick's mother's age was sobbing in a hospital bed nearby. Kick could feel his eyes following her.

When they got to the curtains, Bishop stopped. Kick reached out, lightly touching the thin cotton that separated her from Mel. It had a light-green checkerboard pattern, like children's pajamas. Her fingers were trembling. She looked down at her legs. She never wore dresses bare-legged. Her legs were too pale and scabby and bruised. Her blackened toenails were visible through her sandals. Act normal, Mel would say. Above all else, fake it till you make it.

He was right there. After all these years. She moved her hand into the fabric of the curtain. It was so light. Nothing, really. She moved forward, pushing the cloth to the side. The curtain rings jangled overhead. And then her hand touched air and the curtain fell behind her.

Her heart was racing. She couldn't look. She moved her hair in front of her right shoulder, the way that Mel had told her it was prettiest, and averted her eyes to the floor, emotions pressing at her throat. Bishop was right next to her; maybe he had always been next to her.

She heard a cough and looked up.

He had lost weight since she'd seen him in the courtroom. His blond hair had faded to the color of wet sand and had thinned to a fine, soft fuzz on top. His skin seemed delicate, almost transparent. He lifted his head weakly from the pillow. His lips were chapped. They cracked when he smiled.

"There's my girl," he said.

A flood wall gave way inside her. She felt everything all at once: the devotion, the fear. It was as easy as lowering a zipper. She had held so much in for so long. She had tried to do what people expected. She had been good. She had always done what he told her.

She sobbed and lifted her hands to her mouth in surprise at the sound. But it was like being caught from behind by a wave, like a force of nature overwhelming her. She rushed, shaking, to a plastic chair at his bedside.

His fingers struggled to touch her as his hands strained against the leather straps that bound his wrists to the bed. She moved her hands to his and wrapped her fists around his fingers. The moment their hands met, she lost it and dissolved into tears. His skin felt waxy and warm.

She was shaking all over. She laid her head down, her cheek on his knuckles.

Through the blur of her tears she could see Bishop standing stone-faced at the foot of the bed, watching.

"Thank you, John," she heard Mel say.

Bishop didn't bat an eye. "No problem," he said.

19

KICK KEPT BOTH HANDS wrapped tightly around Mel's fingers, her face pressed against his liver-spotted skin.

Bishop was ramrod straight with his hands clasped in front of him. She could feel his eyes on her, monitoring her, watching for clues, cataloging every reaction, every word.

She knew Mel's hand. Even swollen from edema, she knew his joints, his knuckles, the shapes of his nails, the map of his veins. Its familiarity was an anchor. Her tears drained onto his skin.

"I thought you'd be mad at me," Kick said.

"Never." Mel's voice cracked. His hand trembled under her touch. She knew he was struggling not to cry. "I want you to be happy," he said. "I always tried to protect you."

A rush of relief pressed at Kick's sternum and then escaped her mouth as a whimper.

"Let me look at you," Mel said.

Bishop was all soft edges now, an abstract shape through Kick's tears.

For a moment she couldn't move. It was like an electrical short circuit, a blown fuse. She wasn't sure which wasn't cooperating, her body or her brain. But she was frozen.

"Please, Beth," Mel said.

She lifted her head at the sound of his voice, as surely as if he had cupped her chin and raised it. She turned to face him, keeping one hand on his, afraid that if she let go, she'd be pulled away by some unseen, dangerous current.

He was trembling. The whites of his eyes were threaded with red. His scalp, visible through his thinning hair, was pocked with blemishes where patches of skin had flaked away. He lowered his head back onto the pillow and weakly squeezed her hand as his gaze traveled up and down her body.

She sat very still, on the edge of the chair, motionless, straight-backed, like she was posing for an old-fashioned photograph. Her hair hung in a curtain on either side of her face, strands of it stuck to her wet cheeks. Her eyes felt swollen. Her nose was running. Her yellow dress seemed inappropriate now, too bright, too cheerful.

His eyes continued to move over her with a sort of curious astonishment. And it dawned on Kick that while Mel had changed since she'd seen him last, she had been a child the last time he had seen her. And now she was sitting there, a grown-up.

She pulled at the hem of her skirt.

"You're still my girl, Beth," Mel said.

Bishop coughed, and Kick glanced at him. There was no judgment in his face; there was nothing at all. But as their gaze met, he moved his eyes pointedly up to the corner of the ceiling. Kick followed them to the dome security camera mounted there, aimed at Mel's bed. When she looked back at Bishop, he had returned to his sentry pose.

"You know what today is?" Mel asked.

His wide, hollow eyes brimmed with tears.

She knew he didn't mean the anniversary of her rescue. "It's the anniversary of Linda's death," Kick said.

Mel nodded, his weak grip spasming around her fingers. He gulped, his lips drew back over his teeth, and he began to weep. "She loved you," he said.

Had Linda loved her?

Linda had loved Mel. She had been good to Kick. She had said some of the things that mothers say and done some of the things that mothers do. She had taught Kick how to play the piano a little.

"It's my fault," Kick said quietly. She looked away, letting her hair form a wall between them so Mel couldn't see her face.

"No," Mel said firmly.

His tone stirred something in her. There was the Mel she remembered: that voice, always so full of authority and commands. Neither she nor Linda ever questioned him.

She threaded her fingers between his and leaned slightly forward. "Do you remember that house we lived in?" she asked. "In Seattle?"

Something changed. An almost imperceptible shift in the room. She could tell that Mel felt it. She could see it in his eyes. He was suddenly wary of her.

Kick snuck a peek at Bishop. His head tilted slightly. "Mel taught me how to pick locks," Kick explained. She smiled at the irony of it. All the drills, the target practice, paper clips and handcuffs. "He abducted me and then he taught me a hundred ways to get away." Mel's hand tightened around hers. "And you were right," Kick said, leveling her gaze at Mel. She slowly pried her hand from his. "It never occurred to me to use any of those skills to get away from you."

"I trusted you," Mel said, his fingers pawing the bed, reaching for her. "You're a good girl."

"Yesterday, I came across one of the locks we used to make."

Out of the corner of her eye, Kick noticed Bishop take a step closer to her.

Mel's face creased with pain. "Your mother and I couldn't work. We couldn't risk it. Those locks helped support us."

Your mother. It rolled off his tongue so easily. Kick's eyes started to fill, and she had to turn her head and clear her throat. Sometimes she had so many emotions at once, she couldn't put a name to any of them. Sometimes she had to put them in a box in a jumble and sort them out afterward. "A little girl was abducted in Seattle," Kick said, "and when they found her, she had one of my Scrabble tiles."

She could see the blood throbbing in Mel's

temples, the veins pulsing like they might burst through his fragile skin.

"She says she got it from a boy who was abducted three weeks ago," Kick continued. "The boy was kept in a house with a box, hidden behind a closet, behind one of our locks. I was there yesterday. I know your locks. But it wasn't a place I'd been kept in. When you are kept in the dark, with long periods of nothing to do, you explore. I know the shapes of all those rooms you locked me in. Which means the boy found the tile in another box, in another house." She looked at him intently. "Were we ever in Seattle, *Dad*?"

Mel's eyes were pleading, his mouth contorted.

Kick could feel his pain, like a physical presence, a band of pressure around her chest. She reached out and took his hand again, that hand she knew as well as her own. "I know you tried to be good to me," she said. "Be good to me now. The house I was in, there was an explosion. It was wired with a bomb. You want to protect me? I'm lucky to be alive." She moved her hair aside and lowered her chin so he could see the lump at her hairline. "I was knocked unconscious."

A flush of red washed across Mel's sweaty cheeks.

"Do you want to feel?" Kick whispered.

Beyond the curtain partition, the man started to wail again.

Mel nodded a fraction of an inch.

Kick scraped her chair across the bright blue floor and laid her head down on the bed, in front of where Mel's hand was tethered, and slowly eased back into Mel's grip. Bishop stood silently a few feet from the end of the bed. She was surprised he didn't stop her. His face didn't register any reaction. She locked eyes with him, made him watch, as Mel's fingers started to crawl along her scalp. Bishop didn't blink. Mel's fingers found her hairline, stroking the edge of her forehead. He paused at the knot of tissue.

Kick winced.

Bishop's body tensed.

"It still hurts," Kick said to Mel. She extracted herself from his hand, his fingers so entangled in her hair that even when she was free, a few long brown strands remained around his fingers.

Kick sat, dizzy, with her hands palm up in her lap. Someone was talking to the yelling man now, an insistent, calming voice. She couldn't hear the words, but the man stopped bellowing. In the absence of his complaints, smaller sounds appeared: the electronic pulse of medical equipment, the low hum of other conversation, the bright crackle of a television tuned to a show that no one was watching.

"You know I will never share the location of a single safe house," Mel said.

"Yeah," Kick said, unable to keep the anguish from her voice. She sighed and wiped the tears from her face as she stood up. "I know."

Mel squirmed against the wrist straps. "But the lock," he said.

She froze, waiting.

"I gave the specs to someone," he said. "Someone I knew online."

Kick and Bishop exchanged a quick look and Kick lowered herself back into the chair. "Why?" she asked Mel.

Mel hesitated. "He helped me out with a few things. I never knew his name. We used encrypted software to communicate."

"What did he do for you, *Daddy*?" Kick asked.

She could see him make the decision to give her this, this one thing. His body relaxed, as if he'd given up a struggle with himself. "He was a fixer. He took care of problems. Relocation issues. Fake IDs. Moving money around. The rumor was he was ex-military, or some kind of ex-spy. No one trusted him. But he could get things done. He lent me money once, when I needed it. And a few years before Linda died, he did some banking for us. Putting things in order, so that you and Linda would be taken care of if I ever had to go away. That was when I gave him the lock specs."

Kick glanced at Bishop and saw him stiffen slightly. She knew what was going through his mind. Mel's specs were probably all over the Internet by now. The information was useless.

"The boy who was abducted," Mel asked. "Light skin? Dark hair? Small for his age?"

Kick's breath caught in her throat. He was describing Adam Rice.

"Yes," Bishop answered for her.

Mel's yellowed eyes moved to Bishop, like he had been part of the conversation all along, rather than a lurking specter. "He liked to hang them by the wrists," Mel said. "He posted pictures sometimes, on the file-sharing sites. The boys' faces were always blurred. The man in the photographs was only visible from the shoulders down. He was big, at least back then. Looked Caucasian, but I can't be sure. I only glanced at the images. Once I realized what he was capable of, I cut off communication with him. He's a sadist. A man without a tribe. A stranger. He had no interest in the Family philosophy."

The Family. Mel had always used that term to describe them. Like they were a group of benign uncles.

"He used the Family to acquire used items," Mel said, and Kick understood.

"'Used items'?" Bishop asked.

"Boys," Kick said softly.

No one moved.

Bishop was going to make her spell it out. "The Family sold him boys," Kick said.

"Some children can't adapt as well as others," Mel said. "That doesn't leave a lot of options. Placing them in a new home seemed like a gentler alternative to a shallow grave."

A new home. Like a dog from the pound that didn't work out. This had always been the threat, growing up, that she could be turned over to someone else, someone not as nice as Mel and Linda, someone who would hurt her much worse. She knew it happened. She had seen it.

"But the boys this man acquired ended up in shallow graves anyway, didn't they?"

Mel nodded. "There were rumors."

The collage of Missing Child posters flashed in Kick's mind. All those dark-haired, slightly built boys. Almost elfin-looking. Adam Rice, with his dark eyes and hesitant smile—it had been his face that had set her off again, triggered something that had made her need to help him, to do something. She felt a connection with him. He seemed familiar somehow. She thought it was because he reminded her of herself.

The pieces were falling into place as if they had always been there, right there in front of her, waiting to be noticed, but too close for her to see them for what they were. So many parts of her childhood had been packed up and tucked way in the far-off dark corners of her memory, but she remembered the day she met James. He had been dark-haired, with a cautious grin. Poor James, whose circumstances she recognized even then were so much worse than her own. "He bought James."

"Good, Beth," Mel said, pleased.

"You remember Mr. Klugman's new car? The convertible? He used the cash he made on the boy to buy it. He went right to the dealer."

He had hurt James, and now he had Adam. Who knew how many other boys he had taken? She had to make Mel understand. "James found me," she said. "He saw me on the news and he wrote me. He's my *family*. We need to find this man."

"He's gone, Beth."

"What about Klugman?" Bishop asked.

"Gone," Mel repeated.

"He's right," Kick said. They had been experts at shedding their identities. "No one stayed anywhere longer than six months; every time we moved we changed our last name."

"Then we're done here," Bishop said.

Mel's eyes widened. "Just a few more minutes," he pleaded.

"You got what you wanted," Bishop said in a harsh whisper.

Kick was distracted, her mind on James. She got to her feet shakily.

"Remember that vacation we took to the desert?" Mel asked her with sudden urgency. "I taught you how to do a back float in the hotel pool. Do you still like to swim?"

Kick memorized him. This was the last time. She would never see him again. She knew that now.

"Everything else aside," Mel said, eyes burning into hers, "I'm still the guy who taught you how to swim. So if you want to remember me, you could remember that."

Kick heaved a tortured sigh. She hated him for making her grieve him. She kissed her palm and then leaned forward and placed her hand gently on Mel's forehead. His skin felt vaguely plastic, like he was already half corpse. He closed his eyes as she touched him. "'Bye," she said, her voice breaking.

Bishop had her by the elbow and was shepherding her away from the bed.

"Show me that pretty smile," Mel croaked.

Kick craned her head around. Mel had lifted his head from his pillow. His eyes were manic. Kick forced a smile.

Mel sunk back in the bed. "There she is," he said weakly. "There's my Beth."

Bishop drew the curtain partition open for Kick to pass through.

"Bishop," Mel called.

"Keep walking," Bishop said from behind her. "Walk straight to the door. Wait for me."

Kick moved through the curtain like she was slipping between worlds. On the other side, the TV was tuned to a game show. One of the jumpsuited volunteers pushed a mop across the swimming-pool linoleum. The old black man was still strapped to the bed. He was moving his lips, not making a sound. He and Kick locked eyes.

"This man you're asking about," Mel wheezed, on the other side of the partition. "He's not like me." He coughed, and Kick could hear him struggling to catch his breath. "He's dangerous."

She watched the old man's lips, curling around mysterious syllables, though Kick wasn't sure he was even making words. Maybe he was reciting a curse.

"You fucked up her entire life, Mel," Bishop said. He was straining to keep his voice hushed; Kick could barely hear him. "You think you're better than this guy because you didn't kill her?"

Her friend on the bed looked away. He closed his eyes. Not a curse, Kick realized, a prayer.

"I'm dying, Bishop," Mel said.

"Not soon enough," Bishop said back.

Kick heard Bishop's footsteps leave Mel's bedside and she pitched herself forward, hurrying across the infirmary to get ahead of him.

20

KICK HAD ALREADY DECIDED that she wasn't going to speak to Bishop until they were outside the prison, and very possibly never again. But as soon as he'd had them buzzed through the infirmary door, back into the cinder-block hallway, Bishop spun her around by the arm.

"What was that?" he demanded. He turned his head to look up and down the empty institutional corridor. " '*Daddy*'?" He threaded his hands through his hair. "Jesus Christ, Kick."

Kick could barely breathe. The hallway swam around her. Who was he to question her? She had done exactly what he'd asked her to. "I got you what you wanted," she said. "I didn't see you rushing to intervene."

"*We were on camera*," Bishop said.

She didn't know what that meant, why it was important. She couldn't think straight. "You shouldn't have taken me to see him," she said. "I have a concussion." Her skin was hot. Her eyes stung. She wanted out of this place, out of the vest, out of the building, away from all of it. She curled her lip at Bishop, her face burning. "You shouldn't have made me come here," she said.

Bishop exhaled and leaned against the wall. "I know," he said. His eyes looked pained. "I know."

No. He didn't get to be nice to her now. Kick backed away from him. "Don't talk to me," she said.

"You can't be alone in here," Bishop said, stepping after her.

Kick held up a hand. "I just need a minute," she said. She had to catch her breath. She had to process. If she didn't get control, the anger would trigger the anxiety, and then she'd go down the worry maze and . . . She couldn't concentrate. She looked at her hand, the one she had held Mel's in. She could still feel his fingers scraping against her scalp. Her eyes were hot with tears. She put her forehead against the cinder-block wall and pressed her skull into the concrete, into the contusion, until the pain started to push everything else out. "Ha!" she said.

She turned around, scanning the ceiling, squinting at the long rows of fluorescent lights. A security camera seemed to be aimed right at them. She held her arms out, opened her chest, and filled her lungs with air.

"Ha! Ha! Ha!" Kick said to the camera.

It had worked at the retreat. It had made her laugh. It had made everyone laugh.

She was out of breath again. She looked helplessly at Bishop.

He just stood there. "I need to know the level of your emotional entanglement with him," he said.

Kick flapped her arms around. What had he expected? "It's called acting," she said. "I grew up making movies, remember?" She was doing what she was supposed to do. "I was being who he wanted me to be. I was playing Beth."

"He's not your father," Bishop said.

Kick threw up her hands. She didn't know what the point was in trying to make anyone understand. She wiped some tears onto the shoulder of her orange visitor's vest and tried to compose herself. "How long does he have?" she asked.

Bishop sighed. "Weeks," he said.

Kick felt her features twist. She lowered her chin so that her hair would fall forward, covering her face. The key was not breathing. If she didn't breathe, she could keep it all in. She counted to ten in her head and slowly exhaled. *Change your thoughts and you change your world.*

"Talk to me about James," Bishop said.

Kick cleared her throat and nodded, then lifted her chin and swept her hair behind her ears. *James. Where to even start?* The corridor was still quiet. She didn't know how unusual that was—no guards, no prisoners—and she wondered if Bishop had that kind of power, to provide a few minutes of privacy in a maximum-security prison. Kick slumped against the wall. "He's not my brother," she said.

Bishop settled next to her against the wall. "I know he's not your brother," he said.

It was so quiet. How could a prison be so quiet?

"I know he started turning tricks at truck stops at age twelve and was convicted of stabbing a man to death off I-80 when he was fourteen," Bishop said. "I know they locked him up in a mental hospital. He was still there when he wrote to you four years ago. He must have meant something to you by then, though, because you used a chunk of your settlement money to get him out. Given that his psychiatric history indicated a textbook pattern of childhood abuse, I suspected that you might have known James when you were kids. But I didn't know for sure. Until now."

She was exhausted. She could feel every bruise on her body, every scrape and nick and sore joint. "He has scars on his wrists," Kick said. "I always thought he'd tried to kill himself." She had never suspected the scars were from being bound. If she had, she would have asked, she would have forced the conversation. "We don't really talk about that stuff," she added. It was obvious, but she said it anyway: "The bad stuff."

"Do you know how James escaped?" Bishop asked.

"I don't think he *did* escape," Kick said. "I think he just lost value. The guy Klugman sold him to sold him to someone else who sold him to someone else." From what she could piece together, James had been a part of at least three different "families" after San Diego. "He was used up. No one wanted him. So they let him go."

"And Klugman?" Bishop asked.

"Mel and I spent a few weeks at Mr. Klugman's house in San Diego," Kick said. "I never saw him before that, and I never saw him after. He was a creep. And like Mel said, he's long gone. These people are good at covering their tracks."

"There's no record of James before his first arrest. If he was abducted under a different name, it's possible he made it through the court system without anyone making the connection. But I've studied the missing-children database. I've memorized all those faces. I don't recognize James."

Kick's tears had dried and her face felt tight. "James was never reported missing," she said. "His mother sold him for drug money. There is no missing-kid photo to memorize. He was never on a milk carton because no one ever looked for him." She gazed up and down the empty corridor again. "Don't people have to use this hallway?" she asked.

"Are we done?" Bishop asked.

Kick ran her fingers through her hair. She felt a little better. "Let's go talk to James," she said.

They started to walk, and Bishop glanced back over his shoulder, his eyes directed upward, toward the security camera.

An instant later the hallway was bustling.

21

THE DRIVE HOME WAS taking months. Kick stole frequent glances at Bishop. She rubbed her palms against her thighs until they burned. She had washed her hands before they left the prison, but she could still smell Mel. It clung to her—the stench of raw meat—and underneath it something more familiar, more the smell she remembered. She crossed her arms and tucked her hands under her armpits. Then she snuck another peek at Bishop. He'd been sending and receiving texts for an hour now, his phone on the steering wheel, his eyes bouncing from the road to the screen. Kick uncrossed her arms and dug through her purse for her own phone. Still no reply from James. He was evidently pissed that she hadn't responded sooner to the fifteen texts he had sent her phone while it was in that prison locker. She sighed and leaned back in her seat and looked over at Bishop.

"You're breaking the law," she said.

Bishop kept typing.

"Texting while driving," Kick said. "There's a law against it."

Bishop's expression didn't register a reaction. "I'm an excellent driver. Why don't you practice some more with your handcuffs?"

"Just talk on the phone. Put it on hands-free."

He shot her a curt smile. "I don't want you to know what I'm saying," he said.

"So I have to die in a car crash so you can keep secrets?"

Bishop's eyes flicked down at his phone. "If necessary, yes."

Kick didn't like being ignored. She was the one who was mad at *him*. He'd taken her there; he'd made her see him. She was the one with the head injury. "You're not looking at me," she said.

Bishop continued to not look at her. "I'm driving," he said.

Her phone buzzed. Kick glanced at it to see if it was James. It wasn't. She gazed out the window at the agricultural fields on either side of the interstate. The crops were subsidized with billboards for mixed martial arts tournaments, cage fighting, and state fairs. The phone continued to buzz in her lap.

"Your phone's ringing," Bishop said between gritted teeth.

"It's my sister," Kick explained. Her head hurt again, a dull pain that gnawed at the back of her neck. "She calls every year on the anniversary. But she doesn't really want me to pick up."

Everyone said she and Marnie had been inseparable when they were little, but Kick couldn't imagine it. The Marnie she remembered had never liked her. She'd never forgiven Kick for splitting up their parents.

Kick wondered how long it would take for Mel's smell to fade from her hands. She had missed his smell at first. They didn't let her take anything from the house. They didn't even let her keep her nightgown. It was all evidence. All she had was the Scrabble tile. For a year, she slept with it in her fist. Every morning she'd have to find it in the bedsheets.

"It was an act," she said quietly.

She squeezed her arms together as tightly as she could. Her hands didn't burn anymore. They were numb.

"There's gum in the glove box," Bishop said. "Chew on a piece before you rub all your skin off." His eyes moved from the windshield to her hands and then flicked away again.

Kick lifted her hands from her lap and turned them over. Her palms were raw and red.

"It will help," Bishop said. "Peppermint kills everything."

22

JAMES STILL HADN'T RETURNED Kick's texts, which meant he was deep into programming or, more likely, playing Skyrim. Kick knew he wouldn't deal well with this, her just showing up with Bishop, all the questions about James's past. The elevator stopped on the second floor and Kick and Bishop stepped out.

"I think I should talk to him first," she said, four pieces of gum wadded in her cheek.

Bishop's hood was up so she couldn't see his face. He didn't break stride. "No," he said.

"He's fragile," Kick reminded him.

Bishop tipped his head slightly so it was angled away from the security camera and glanced back at her. "That's why I'm letting you be there while I talk to him," he said.

Kick worked the gum in her mouth. It was already losing flavor, getting blander with every chew. She'd left the pack in the car.

"Maybe we should call the police," she suggested.

Bishop stopped in front of James's door and knocked.

Kick crossed her arms. "It's not like he knows where the guy is now. It's not like they keep in touch."

"James?" Bishop called through the door.

They listened. Kick didn't hear the sound of James's steps.

"James?" she called impatiently. "Open the door."

She started digging through her purse, through the assortment of weaponry. "I have a key," she said. "He's probably at his computer with headphones on."

Bishop had pivoted slightly, his attention directed behind them. Kick could feel his body language had shifted, like a dog raising its hackles. "Here it is," she said, finding the key. They just needed to get inside. Bishop would see. James would be sitting at his computer. She started to turn the key in the lock.

"Don't," Bishop said, putting his hand on her wrist.

Kick swallowed her gum, startled. She could feel it stuck in her throat. She let go of the key and lowered her hand.

"It's probably nothing," Bishop said. He was still facing the door so she couldn't see his expression, only his hood and the tip of his nose.

"You made me swallow my gum," Kick said.

Bishop put his hood down and turned to her. There was no smirk anymore. He locked his eyes on hers.

"I need you to do something for me, okay?" His voice was even and calm. "I need you to stay right here while I go inside the apartment."

Kick knew James. He hardly ever answered the door. It's why she had a key. "He has his headphones on," Kick said.

"Please," Bishop said. "Do this."

A flutter of fear moved through Kick's stomach. She gave a small nod of assent.

Bishop exhaled slowly, turned the key, and pushed open the door. He lifted his phone to his ear as he went in and mumbled something into it. She thought she heard the word "backup."

Bishop had left the door slightly ajar and Kick kept her eyes on the sliver of hallway she could see through the gap. She could feel the pressure of the gum in her throat every time she took a breath. She waited.

"Well?" she called after a minute. "Is he playing Minecraft or what?"

No one answered.

"James?"

The gum throbbed as her throat constricted. "Bishop?"

She pushed the door open. James's recyclables were strewn on the floor. Kick felt around in her purse for the hunting knife. It made a satisfying sound as she unsheathed it. Her fingers wrapped around the rosewood handle. It was a fixed, full-tang stainless steel blade. She had never used it, but the guy who'd sold it to her had told her that it would split through rib cage and bone. She stepped over the threshold, the knife at her hip, her thumb at the hilt. She could hear faint sounds now, movement, coming from the living room. She stopped and switched the knife around so her thumb was at the handle base, holding the knife at shoulder level like she was about to kill someone in a shower. Then she started down the hall.

23

KICK HAD TO MAKE her way through a minefield of plastic water bottles and pop cans to get down the hall. She didn't know how Bishop had managed so soundlessly to avoid them.

The apartment smelled different. The stale pizza smell, James's unwashed sweet stink, they were there, but there was another smell, too, something on top of it, something fresh and metallic.

As she got close to the living room, she thought she could hear someone breathing.

Kick tightened her grip on the knife and stepped around the wall.

Somehow she knew to keep her gaze from the floor—maybe by instinct, maybe because some part of her saw what was there and warned the rest of her not to look. Her eyes fixed instead on James's workstation. She almost believed he'd be there, bent over his keyboard like always. But his blue chair was empty. Instead of displaying their usual coding and games, the monitors were in screen saver mode, rotating through a slide show of affirmations. Large white letters on a black screen read: *Anxiety is a normal emotion that I can control.*

She heard Bishop say, "Kick."

But Kick refused to look at him, refused to look down. She didn't want to see. She didn't want for it to be real. So Kick kept her eyes stubbornly glued to the monitors. The screen saver affirmations scrolled right to left. *There are good things about me. I deserve to be happy.* Kick could feel a film of sweat between her hand and the handle of the knife. *I feel calm.* The letters spun away and dissolved out of view.

She heard James's voice in her head. *I am safe outside. I enjoy meeting new people.*

"He's still alive," Bishop said.

Kick sobbed with relief and let her eyes fall. James lay splayed on his back, surrounded by blood-soaked printouts and notes. Pain twisted like a razor in Kick's chest. So much blood. She didn't know a person could bleed that much. James's entire midsection was red, his yellow shirt not yellow anymore, blood pooled around him. Bishop was kneeling at his side, blood seeping into his jeans, hands slick with red against James's belly.

The pain bounced and grew in Kick's chest. It was hard to breathe.

Change your thoughts and you change your world.

She hadn't paid James's water bill. It had been in her backpack, blown to smithereens. She hadn't even told him. She didn't know why it seemed important right then, but it did.

"Kick, I need you to listen to me," Bishop said.

One of his hands was inside James, his fingers pressed inside a bleeding wound.

"There are going to be a lot of people here soon," Bishop said. "You need to put the knife down. I need you to sit in that chair." He thrust his chin at James's desk chair. "And I need you not to contaminate the crime scene. Do not touch anything."

One of James's shoes was untied. His face was so pale.

Bishop was wrong. He couldn't be alive.

What would she and Monster do without their James?

The pain in Kick's chest tightened.

Monster.

She put her fingers in her mouth and tried to whistle, but her mouth was too dry and all she managed was a panicked croak.

"My dog," she said. She looked around, frantic. He was there. He was hiding. She took a step back and felt a piece of paper stick to the sole of her sandal. She kicked it off and saw that it had blood on it. She took another step, backing away.

"No," Bishop said sharply. "We have to wait for backup. I haven't cleared the apartment. It's not safe."

There was blood smeared on his forehead, like he'd touched his face with a blood-covered hand. "Stay here with me," he said. His gray eyes were intense, and she knew that he meant it, that it was important, that she should do what he said. "I can't leave James right now," he said.

It didn't matter. There was nothing he could say.

It was happening all over again. Monster was lost. It was Kick's fault. She had to find him. This time she would find him.

She stumbled out of the living room and into the hallway.

"Shit," she heard Bishop say under his breath.

She didn't even try to avoid the empty bottles now. She didn't care how loud she was. James's bedroom door was closed at the end of the hall. Kick felt a glimmer of hope. James had put Monster in the bedroom and closed the door. Monster was so blind and deaf, he wouldn't have barked; he wouldn't have made a sound. He was safe.

"Talk to me, Kick," Bishop called.

"I'm in the hall," Kick called back. "But it's okay. I think James shut Monster in the bedroom." Of course James had protected Monster. He loved Monster too. Kick had the knife at her side now and was batting water bottles out of her way with her feet. Poor dog, he'd probably been in there for hours. "I'm almost to the bedroom," Kick called excitedly. "I'm going to open the door."

"Don't touch it with your bare hand!" Bishop called back. "Find a clean rag or use—"

Kick didn't hear the rest. She had already turned the knob and thrown open the door, ready to welcome Monster into her arms.

The sound came out of her stomach, a gut-wrenching wail that made her light-headed, made her legs go weak. She dropped to her knees and the knife fell from her hand and clattered on the floor.

Bishop was hollering for her, yelling her name. She struggled through sobs for enough air to be able to respond.

"Is it the dog?" Bishop called.

Tears dripped down Kick's neck. She managed a great, shaking breath and called out, "Uh-huh."

Her shoulders heaved. She was sobbing so hard that no sound came out, so hard that it physically hurt.

He was lying by the foot of the bed. She crawled forward on her knees until she reached him. His frosted eyes were half open. "Pretty boy," she whispered, stroking the fur on his muzzle. Blood glistened around his mouth and ear. She glanced at his belly where he'd been opened up, his insides spilled out on the floor. Then she leaned forward and put her face against his, breathing him in. He was still warm. She had lost him once. And then they had been reunited. But he was lost forever now. He had died alone, with no one who loved him.

Kick lifted her head, choking back sobs, and slid her arms under her dead dog. Monster rolled against her chest as she picked him up, his head lolling over her arm. The weight of him was different, denser, like he was her dog but not. She struggled to her feet. She could feel the wetness of Monster's blood against the fabric of her dress, staining her. His tag jingled with each of her steps and she carried him down the hall into the living room.

Bishop was leaning over James and had started

CPR chest compressions. Kick stumbled toward them with Monster, but Bishop stopped her with a look.

"Put the dog down!" he commanded "That's evidence. Goddamnit. Kick, you're contaminating the scene."

Mucus clogged Kick's throat. She couldn't breathe. This wasn't evidence. This was Monster.

"Drop the fucking dog," Bishop snarled. "Now."

Kick buried her face in Monster's fur, sank to her knees, and let him roll gently out of her arms onto the floor. Now he looked dead, his body slumped unnaturally on the floor. Kick adjusted his legs so that he would look more like himself, like he was sleeping. Her hand grazed something on the floor. It was James's wire talisman. It had been flattened, stepped on. Kick reached for it. Bishop wasn't paying attention to her anymore; he was focused on James, his arms straight, his hands pumping against James's fragile breastbone. Kick stared, wide-eyed, at the disfigured wire man.

James.

Bishop's hands were covered in blood, his face taut with concentration as he compressed James's chest again and again and again. Kick scrambled on her hands and knees to the other side of James's body. She glanced around frantically for something she could do, some way to help. Bishop's sweatshirt sat in a heap on James's belly, soaking up blood. Kick pressed her trembling fingers against it and applied pressure. She copied Bishop's hands, palms stacked, the fingers of the top hand threaded between the fingers of the bottom one. The little wire man was wrapped around her finger like a ring. She could feel the pump of every chest compression under her own hand. It almost felt like James had a heartbeat.

24

JAMES'S ROOM WAS EMPTY. *It would not have been strange, except that James never went anywhere. Kick backed out of the room, into Mr. Klugman's basement, and ran up the stairs to the kitchen. She didn't see anyone. She ran to the back window and looked into the yard, but the pool was empty. She felt a tiny seed of panic tickle at her throat, like a spider crawling up the back of her tongue. She flew through the house, the dining room, the living room. Had everyone left? Had they left her alone?*

She was almost crying then, when she heard voices coming from the garage. She was so relieved that she almost opened the door without knocking. She caught herself, and knocked, and her father's voice called for her. When she opened the door, there they were, her father and Mr. Klugman. The garage door was open. The bright San Diego sun poured in. It was so warm, like not being outside at all.

"It's Miss America," Mr. Klugman said, and Beth beamed.

"I thought you'd left," she said.

"Mr. Klugman got a new car," her father said.
The car glistened red, like cherries.
"Where's James?" Beth asked.
"He's gone," her father said.
Beth knew better than to ask any more questions.

25

JAMES WAS GONE. THEY had taken him away on a stretcher.

Kick didn't know who these people were. But they were leaving her alone, stepping around her on the floor. She had pulled Monster halfway onto her lap and held him in her arms. His body was limp and heavy. Her dress was covered in dog hair and blood and something like blood, but stickier. The floor was red where James had been. Bloody footprints made tracks across the papers strewn around the room. Kick recognized the shapes of her own sandals.

James's wire man was ruined. She didn't know how to fix him. She twisted the ring she'd made of him around her finger. James would be furious.

Where was he? She remembered Bishop sitting back, letting the paramedics take over compressions, seeing them loading James on a stretcher. Someone took the sweatshirt out of her hand and put it into a plastic bag.

And then James was gone.

The paramedics were gone.

She smoothed down the fur over Monster's forehead.

Bishop was still there. He was talking to one of the men with guns.

FBI agents. That's who they were. They were all carrying Glocks. Like the ones who'd come for Beth. Only Kick was Beth. Kick was Beth that night at the farm. She could still hear Frank's voice in her head.

"I had a dog," she said, remembering.

Frank was motionless. "What was its name?" he asked.

There was shouting.

"You took her to see him?" a voice said incredulously. "What the fuck is wrong with you?"

It was Frank.

His voice—now, here, in this room. For real. Kick strained to locate it.

But it was Bishop's voice she heard. He was talking to someone who had just come in. "I don't work for you, Frank," Bishop was saying. "I didn't have to call you. I could have just walked away."

Kick threaded her fingers deeper into Monster's fur, unsure what was real.

She watched Frank point a finger in Bishop's face. "Not even you are that much of a prick," Frank said.

A poster on the wall had a picture of footsteps on a white sand beach. *Your Dream Vacation, Today!* it promised.

"It's him," Bishop told Frank. "James was one of his victims. This? It's him. There's security footage of the conversation at the prison. You know who to talk to about getting a copy."

Monster's head was so heavy. "She's a kid," Frank said, his worried eyes glancing in her direction.

"Not anymore," Bishop said.

Frank came toward her then, carefully making his way around yellow plastic evidence markers, pausing to find a spot to place his foot.

"Don't touch her," Bishop called to him. "Her clothing hasn't been processed. And she doesn't want to let go of the dog."

Monster looked peaceful. She had closed his eyes. As long as she didn't look below his shoulders, she could almost believe he was asleep. James was asleep. They could sleep together.

Frank was standing above Kick now, and she was gazing up at him. His rust-colored eyebrows were still thatched with blond.

"Are you really here?" she asked. She wanted to reach out, to touch him, to see if he was smoke. He was shorter than she remembered him. His eyes were squintier. Seeing him now, she realized that he wasn't even that old. She was the old one. She was as old as the universe.

Frank lowered himself into a squat. "I show up when you need me. That's our deal."

Kick moved her fingers over Monster's head, feeling his skull, his realness. "He killed my dog," she whispered.

Frank's mouth twitched. "I know." He turned

his face to his shoulder for a moment and when he looked back his eyes were red. "But it's time to go now."

"I don't want to leave him alone," Kick said. She could feel Beth's panic in her chest. Beth had never liked Frank. Beth had wanted to shoot him dead. "Don't take me away from him," she begged.

Frank rubbed his eyes with a thumb. "When I found you, you couldn't even say your own name, remember?" he asked. His shoulders rose and fell. "But you told me about your dog; you remembered Monster's name. And that's how I knew who you were. He helped get you home." His jacket hung open, and Kick could see his Glock 27 with Smith & Wesson .45 ammo, close enough to snatch. "And he has been a great dog, hasn't he?"

Kick looked down at Monster. This would be the last time she'd see him, his graying muzzle, his furry ears, his rough nose.

Oh, Monster, no.

Frank reached out and petted Monster's neck. He cleared his throat. "He's not warm anymore, is he?"

Kick swallowed back tears, coughed, and shook her head. He wasn't warm.

"It's time to go," Frank said again.

She could do this; she had to do this. Frank helped her slip out from under Monster's body. Frank got to his feet and held his hand out to her. "Come on."

She went with him. Maybe because that's what she had done all those years ago at the farm, when he'd led her out of Mel's basement, up the rabbit hole, out into the world. Maybe she was just tired. The blood on her yellow dress had started hardening and the fabric scratched her skin as she moved.

Frank pointed at the floor, at the blizzard of papers and blood. "Very carefully."

She tried to step where he pointed. Around James's Cthulhu mug, which lay broken on the floor. Dog hair fluttered from her dress as she moved. A dozen people inched around the perimeter of the living room, taking pictures, writing in small notebooks, coming and going. A Glock 22, a Glock 23, a Glock 27.

"Where's James?" she asked. Her voice no more than a whisper.

"I'm going to take you to him," Frank said. "We just need to have a look at you first." He led her over to where Bishop stood on a square of plastic sheeting and positioned her alongside him. The sound of the plastic crinkling under her sandals made her teeth hurt.

A camera flash went off.

A woman stepped in front of Kick. She was wearing blue latex gloves and a black FBI Windbreaker and she had a friendly, freckled face. She didn't have a gun. She gave Kick a reassuring smile. "I'm Mina," she said. "Short for Benjamina." She smirked. "My parents were expecting a boy."

She had kind eyes, and Kick concentrated on them. "I'm just going to do a once-over, make sure you haven't picked up any hair or fibers that might be useful in the investigation."

Kick felt her head nod.

Frank had his hands on his hips and was looking around the room, emitting a low whistle. "Was the place tossed?" he asked.

Notes layered the floor. Printouts papered the walls. James's dartboard was still on the floor where it had fallen. Kick felt a pang of guilt that she hadn't hung it back up.

"It's how she thinks," Bishop said. "She prints everything out and stares at it."

How did he know how she thought? He didn't know her at all.

"Well, it's going to take all night to process," Mina said. She made a swiveling motion with her finger and Kick, always obedient, turned around. The collage Kick had made the night before fanned out across the wall in front of her. All the missing boys, all her erratic notes, and behind them an array of exotic destinations: *See Italy! Cruise the Maldives! Visit Israel!*

Bishop turned around, too, so that they were now facing the wall side by side.

Between them, at eye level, was the photograph of Adam Rice above the Leaning Tower of Pisa. Around Adam, circling his image, ten pictures of other dark-haired Caucasian boys from the National Center for Missing & Exploited Children website. Kick's eyes moved from image to image, each one clicking into place.

"You figured out a lot," Bishop said, nodding at the wall.

"James saw the pattern," Kick said. Her voice sounded small and faraway. "He's good at patterns."

But she was not. She hadn't seen it, and it had been right in front of her. The coloring, the slight build. If she'd taken a photograph of James the day they'd met, she could have put it right up on the wall along with the missing boys. "The person who was here," she said. "It's him. The man Mel talked about."

"Did you see James's wrists?" Bishop asked.

Kick felt a flush of cold settle on her skin. She tightened her fingers together so that she could feel that the wire talisman was still there.

"Fresh ligature marks," Bishop said.

The activity behind them faded into white noise. It was just Kick and Bishop and the wall and James's blood. "Why?" she asked. After all this time, why would he come back for James?

"Take off your shirt," Frank said to Bishop, and Kick was startled back to the reality of the apartment, the police, the crime scene investigators, everyone picking over James's possessions.

"Excuse me," Bishop said to Kick. He turned around and pulled his T-shirt over his head and dropped it in a plastic bag. Kick was surprised to see the scattering of black stitches still in his back, the skin still inflamed; surprised to realize that it had only been a day since the paramedic had sewn up Bishop's wounds.

Frank held a box of Huggies baby wipes out to Bishop. "Clean yourself up," he told him.

Mina picked something off Kick's shoulder, and Kick turned her attention back to the faces of the missing boys. The wet slurp of wipes being pulled from the box punctuated the conversation behind her, and she could smell their distinctive talcum scent. Her eyes moved down the wall to the notes she'd written on torn copy paper. They were highlighted and circled in purple: *Former weapons dealer. But doesn't like guns. Excellent driver. Private jet. How did he get the scar on his neck? Island. Adulterer. Wife. Entitled asshole.*

Something plopped onto the plastic sheeting at her feet and she looked down to see one of the used wet tissues, pink with blood, discarded near Bishop's heel. Her gaze moved up his body. The muscles in his long arms tensed as he rubbed the blood off his hands.

"You're done," Mina said. Still dazed, Kick turned back to the room. Mina was putting away her tools. "We'll need the dress," she said to Frank.

Kick looked down at the front of the dress, the blood, Monster's fur, the last traces of her dog. "No," she said, pleading. "Frank, please."

Frank coughed and looked away.

"Everything on the dress is from the dog," Bishop said. "The blood on her hands belongs to the victim. And you'll want her shoes." Bishop drew another wipe out of the box and started scrubbing the blood out of the beds of his fingernails.

"Yeah, okay," Frank said.

Kick let them do what they wanted to her, position her for whatever photographs they needed. Someone unbuckled her shoes and spirited them away, leaving her barefoot on the plastic sheeting.

Finally it was over. Frank took her blood-caked hand and gently started dabbing at it with one of the wipes. It felt wet and cold. He touched the wipe against the wire-man ring.

"Stop," Kick told him.

Frank looked up at her quizzically. Kick took the wipe from him. "I can do it," she said, starting to clean her own palm. "I want my purse," she added. "It's in the hallway. It has my nunchuks in it, and my throwing stars." Frank gave her a slight nod. But what she really needed was information, and Frank couldn't help her with that. There was only one person who could. "I need a minute," she said. She shot a look at Bishop. "With him."

Frank's posture stiffened. "He will lie to you," Frank said. "I know him. And he will lie to you."

"*You* lied to me," Kick reminded him.

She saw Frank wince.

Bishop stood motionless, watching them.

Frank's eyes roamed to the ceiling, then landed on Bishop. His freckled ears were pink. "Tread carefully, my friend," he said to Bishop. "I don't care who you work for." He turned back to Kick. "I'm going to make a call. It will take about four minutes. We'll get your purse on the way out."

Frank stepped away, got his phone out, and slipped around the corner into the hallway. Kick heard the sound of a plastic bottle bouncing across the floor, and then Frank swearing. Mina was taking fingerprints off the surface of James's desk. The monitors had all been turned off, and another tech was packing all the computer equipment into evidence boxes.

"It didn't have anything to do with you," Bishop said quietly.

Kick gave him a sharp glance. "You don't know what you're talking about."

"He had an affair with your mother," Bishop said. "It didn't have anything to do with you."

Kick's pulse throbbed in her temples.

"Frank hasn't been promoted in almost a decade," Bishop continued. "So whatever happened between them, I'm guessing the Bureau knows about it."

"You don't know anything," Kick snapped, closing her hand into a fist. "You think you do, but you don't."

"Okay," Bishop said.

Kick took a fresh wipe from the box in his hand and began to scrub furiously at the blood on her palm. "You owe me," she said to Bishop. She looked him in the eye. "You're some kind of cop."

Bishop pulled out another wipe from the box. "I used to be some kind of cop. Now I work in private security."

"You said you were a weapons dealer," Kick said.

"I was," Bishop said, cleaning between his fingers. "Part of my responsibilities to my employer was to be the public face of his operation. Now I work on special projects."

"Who do you work for?" Kick asked.

"A man named Devlin." He pulled out another wipe and offered it to her.

"Devlin?" Kick said. "He just has one name?"

"David Decker Devlin," Bishop said. "But you won't find *him* on the Internet either."

Kick didn't know if she was supposed to believe him or not. She tossed the wipe she was using and took the fresh one from Bishop. "Why's he so interested in finding missing kids?"

Bishop's eyes were impenetrable. "His interest is in keeping me happy. I do a lot of work for him. This is just one piece of it."

"Bishop isn't even your real name, is it?" Kick said.

He smiled faintly. "You saw my driver's license."

Frank came back around the corner and strode toward them with something under his arm.

"I'll find whoever did this," Bishop said under his breath.

So will I, Kick thought.

Frank tossed Bishop something sealed in a

Visqueen pouch. "Mina wants you to take off your pants," he said. "You can put this on. I assume your employer will be wanting you to observe the processing of the crime scene?"

"He'll appreciate your cooperation, as always," Bishop said. He handed Kick the wipes and the Visqueen pouch, which had a label that read *Tyvek Coveralls*, and started unbuttoning his jeans.

Frank gave an exasperated sigh. "Jesus Christ," he said.

Bishop stood shirtless with his pants open and low on his hips. A trail of black hair led down his midsection to his black underwear. He shrugged at Frank. "What?"

"I'm taking the kid to the hospital to see the boy," Frank said.

The hospital.

The box of wipes and the Tyvek coveralls dropped from Kick's hands onto the floor.

James was alive.

"He's not out of the woods," Frank added quickly. "He's lost a lot of blood." Kick followed Frank, stunned, as he led her off the plastic sheeting. "They transfused him in the ER and he just went into surgery." He shot a begrudging glance back in Bishop's direction. "But apparently our friend is not a half-bad medic."

"You should put a guard on his room," Bishop called after them. He had stepped out of his pants and was stuffing them into a plastic bag.

"Protect the only person who can identify a child

killer," Frank replied. "I would never have thought of that."

Kick looked at her hand, at James's wire talisman, then back at the place on the floor where she'd found it, where Monster lay sprawled.

"You want the boxers too?" Bishop called to Frank.

Monster didn't look like he was asleep anymore. He looked too flat somehow, like some substantial part of him had deflated. Next to him, on the floor, was a yellow plastic evidence marker with the number *24* printed on it in black. That's what he was now: evidence. Another crime scene biohazard.

"What's going to happen to my dog?" Kick asked Frank.

Frank sucked in a long breath and looked like he had a sudden headache.

He had never been good at giving her bad news.

Kick looked over at Bishop, who had one leg in some kind of white zip-up paper suit. "What's going to happen to my dog?" Kick called to him.

Bishop paused, pants around his knees, and his eyes went to Frank.

"There are protocols," Frank said, touching his ear. He couldn't even look at her. "For disposing of crime scene . . . biological evidence."

"You mean," Kick said numbly, "that he's going to get incinerated with a bunch of biowaste." Thrown away and burned up. Discarded. It made it worse somehow. Made her failure to protect him more complete.

"I'll take care of it," Bishop said.

"What?" Kick asked, unsure she had heard right.

Bishop had the suit on and was zipping it up, not even looking at her. "I'll take care of your dog," he said. He adjusted the cuffs on the white paper arms. "I'll bury him. When we're done."

And despite all his lies, Kick believed him.

26

THE HOSPITAL WAITING ROOM was cold and the yellow dress felt threadbare and insubstantial. A pair of hospital footies did little to warm her bare feet. Kick picked a piece of Monster's hair off the daisy-printed fabric and set it gently in a little stack she was making on the couch upholstery next to her. Everything seemed louder, brighter: she was acutely aware of the hospital's ventilation system blowing air against her skin, the incessant hum of the fluorescent can lights overhead. The static of the hospital intercom announcements seemed ear-splitting. Colors looked different; even the drab earth tones of the furniture seemed electric. But the color in the room that stood out most was the red on Kick's dress. It was the reddest red Kick had ever seen. She peeled a piece of Monster's hair from the blood-encrusted fabric and set it with the others.

She heard Frank's footsteps in the hallway, and then the door opened and Frank backed into the room with two cups of coffee. She had her head lowered so that her hair formed a screen around her face, and he must not have been able to see her eyes, to see that she'd looked up at him. For an instant she saw his real face, spent and haggard, stained with weary sadness. But when he set one of the coffee cups down in front of her a moment later, his features had rearranged into gentle concern.

How strange that he would be here, now, for this.

The shrinks always asked about Frank. Kick had made the mistake of telling the Jungian about the Christmas cards. She hadn't said a word about Frank to a therapist since.

Kick looked at the coffee that Frank had set in front of her. She didn't touch coffee, but Frank would have no way of knowing that. The only version of her that he knew was twelve years old.

"He's still in surgery," Frank said. He took his time taking off his jacket and draping it on a nearby chair. His soft belly hung over his belt. The armpits of his white shirt were darkened with sweat. He rolled up his sleeves and stretched, then gingerly sat down next to her. Kick felt the couch slide back an inch. He didn't say anything. She didn't mind. It had been nine years. And Frank had never been good at small talk. The only person she'd ever seen him make sparkling conversation with had been her mother. They had been at the hospital for three hours now, and Kick hadn't said a word the whole time, so he was probably used to the silence. He stared contemplatively at the lid of his coffee, and his face went hangdog again. He exhaled a deep sigh. As Kick studied him through her hair, she realized that he wasn't sad at all; the lines had just etched in his face this way.

Frank caught her looking at him and his eyes brightened. He reached for his jacket and pulled a candy bar out of the pocket. He held it out to her. "Here, eat this," he said. He lowered his eyebrows. "You still like Snickers?"

He had done this during the trial: brought her candy to keep her spirits up.

"You bought me a candy bar," Kick said skeptically. It was such a strange gesture, she didn't know what to make of it.

Frank shrugged. "You're too grown-up for candy bars now?"

Actually, she was starving. She snatched the Snickers bar from Frank's hand, tore the wrapper open, and took a bite of the chocolate. For an instant she actually felt better.

Frank took the plastic lid off his coffee cup and blew on it, looking pleased with himself.

Kick ate half of the candy bar, swallowing sometimes after only a couple of chews. She could feel flakes of chocolate at the corners of her mouth.

"You get my cards?" Frank asked.

Kick stopped chewing in mid-bite.

Frank must have realized that this wasn't the time, that she wasn't ready, because he withdrew slightly on the couch. "It's okay," he said, scratching his neck. "Never mind."

She started to chew again, but the chocolate had

made her saliva thick and her mouth felt sticky. She set the rest of the candy bar on the table. "Do you know his real name?" she asked.

Frank blew some more on his coffee. "Nope," he said.

They sat in silence for a while, Frank blowing on his coffee, scratching his beard, then taking a tiny sip from the cup, then blowing on it some more; Kick picking the hairs of her dead dog off her dress and adding them to the stack on her cushion. "And the FBI just lets private citizens elbow in on investigations now?" she asked.

Frank breathed a heavy sigh and slugged back a full sip from his cup even though it was still steaming and looked like it hurt. Then he settled the cup on his knee and held it there.

"The guy he works for," Frank said, "this guy, he topples regimes." His eyebrows lifted an inch. "He wins wars, Kick. If our government has a special interest in the outcome of a revolution—and we always do—Bishop's boss gets a call. He gets the weapons in. He gets the blood on his hands. No congressional hearings. The U.S. gets to look above the fray. Our international interests are protected." He chuckled and shook his head. "A guy like that? You give him anything he wants."

Kick noticed that Frank had never used Devlin's name, so she didn't either. "I thought Bishop's boss was retired," she said.

"Guys like that don't get to retire."

"And what about me?" Kick's voice wavered. "I

just go home and pretend none of this has happened?"

"I don't want you to go home, kiddo," Frank said. "Not until we know the situation."

Kick saw him sneak a glance at his watch.

"But I've got to get back to work," he announced, standing up. He got his jacket from the chair. He wasn't looking at Kick; it seemed to her that he was making a special effort not to.

She knew then what he'd done. It made perfect sense. Even as a kid, she'd figured him for a sentimentalist.

"You called her, didn't you," Kick said.

He looked sheepish, found out. She didn't know how he'd been able to carry on an affair for a year. He cracked under the slightest pressure. "I called her."

Kick took a shaky breath and her eyes fell on the pile of dog hair she'd made. It really wasn't much when it was all put together.

Frank scratched the back of his neck. "She's your mother," he said.

Paula had made a career out of it.

"I'm sorry I can't stay," Frank said, pulling on his jacket. "They'll let me know about James."

Kick saw through him. She always had. "You're just trying to make an escape before she gets here," she said.

Frank hesitated. "I know you think I'm a coward," he said.

Kick wished she could take it back. They were

bound, she and Frank. They understood something about one another. "You saved me," she said.

Frank gave her a bitter smile. "Then I broke up your family," he said. He lowered his head and turned for the door. "I'm a real white knight."

Kick gathered the dog hair into her palm. "Well, there's that," she said under her breath.

She heard the door open and looked up to see Frank standing face-to-face with her mother. Kick had thought she had met some emotional quota for the day, some point where the universe says, *Enough*. Frank jumped back, looking almost comically panicked. Paula Lannigan breezed past him with a phone to her face, wearing a shimmering gold satin blouse and chartreuse trousers. Her blond hair had been crafted into an up-do. She was in full makeup. Kick wondered bleakly if her mother had stopped for a media interview on the way to the hospital.

Paula lowered her phone. "Hello, Frank," she said over her shoulder.

"Hello, Paula," Frank mumbled. He made a jittery motion with his hands indicating the coffee table. "There's coffee there for you. Two Splendas."

Paula gave him a distracted nod, then she hurried to Kick, sat down beside her, and reached an arm around her shoulder.

Kick had a vague awareness of Frank saying good-bye and leaving. Her mother gave her shoulder a squeeze. Kick couldn't look at her. The dress looked like bathroom wallpaper, but it had been expensive. Her mother's gifts were always expensive.

Instead Kick fixed her gaze on her lap. There was a dog hair on the hem of the yellow dress and she picked it up and moved it to the pile. Her mother's arm remained around Kick's shoulders, a steady, patient pressure.

Her mother smelled like Eternity by Calvin Klein. She had smelled like that for as long as Kick could remember.

Kick knew what her mother would say: that Kick should have put Monster down months ago; that she'd been selfish. And Kick knew she was right, because if she had done that, then she would have been there, and her dog would not have died alone.

Her mother patted her awkwardly on the shoulder. "You gave him a good life," she said.

It was the first time Kick ever remembered her mother saying exactly the right thing.

Kick hiccuped back a sob. Then the floodgates opened. Her mother pulled her close and Kick clung to her and cried.

27

"I SPENT THE NIGHT at my mother's," Kick told James. She was dressed in her mother's clothes, her brain fogged by her mother's pharmaccuticals: Ambien to help her sleep last night, Klonopin for anxiety in the morning. The pills made Kick drowsy and thirsty, but she took them without protest. She wanted to dull her senses.

"If you could open your eyes," she continued, "you'd laugh." Her mother's dark denim designer jeans were an inch too long, and the heather-gray jersey top with the cowl neckline and the asymmetrical peplum had looked edgy in her mother's closet but on Kick just made her look like she was wearing a shirt backward. The only pair of her mother's shoes that came close to fitting were hot-pink plastic flip-flops with silver-sequined straps. "You'd die laughing."

James's head was tipped back on a pillow and his mouth was open around a clear tube that had been forced down his throat and secured with clear surgical tape around his lips. The other end of the tube led to a ventilator. The hiss of every forced breath had a mechanical quality, each breath lasting exactly the same duration, spaced exactly the same length apart. His slender shoulders were bare. He had too many surgical dressings to wear a gown; the bandages had to be changed, ports flushed. Tubes drained from his abdomen; a catheter fed fluid into a bag below his bed. His thin arms were threaded with IVs and wrapped with more surgical tape. Bandages covered the fresh ligature marks on his wrists.

He wasn't asleep or even unconscious; he was sedated, which was worse. He didn't stir or flinch or flutter his eyelashes. His chest and chin rose in rhythm with the machine. Otherwise he lay there like a corpse.

Kick watched him for a while, then she dug her handcuffs out of the purse under her chair and she cuffed her wrist to the side bar of James's hospital bed. It was an activity, a way to stay focused, like playing solitaire. Kick could do it in her sleep. But something went wrong. She flattened the paper clip, she notched the end, but it wouldn't catch in the keyhole. She wiggled it, but it was no use. Frustrated, Kick started over, this time notching the other side of the paper clip and trying that. The metal cuff rattled against the bed railing as she worked the paper clip fruitlessly in the lock. Kick started to sweat. James's chest expanded and deflated. Kick's own breathing was twice as fast. She glanced at the door and tried to figure out how she was going to explain this to the next nurse who walked in. "This isn't funny," she told James.

The paper clip slipped from Kick's hand and bounced under the bed.

Kick rested her forehead against the edge of the mattress and tried to collect herself.

The door opened. She peeked up, expecting to see a nurse. Instead, Bishop strolled in. He tipped his head to the side and looked at her curiously. Kick tried to seem casual. She lifted the hand she had cuffed to the bed and waved. "Hi," she said.

"Hi," Bishop said. He crossed to the computer terminal opposite the bed and typed something on the keyboard. Kick watched as James's medical reports appeared on the screen and Bishop proceeded to page through them.

"Things seem to be in a holding pattern here," he said, scanning the screen. He turned his attention to James. There was no reaction on his face, but he looked at James for what seemed like a full minute. Then he bent over, scooped the paper clip up from the floor, and handed it to Kick without comment.

Kick started working the keyhole again.

"I spent the night at my mother's," she said.

"That explains the clothes," Bishop said. "And why you smell like Eternity."

Kick looked down at her shirt with a stab of self-consciousness. "She gave me pills," she said. "My head's a little muddy." Eternity? How did he know her mother's perfume? He hadn't had trouble obtaining a fresh change of clothes, she noticed. Black jeans, gray T-shirt, black blazer—he probably kept a bloodstain-free ensemble in every city, just in case. She gestured helplessly at the cuffs. "Can you give me a hand?"

Bishop glanced at the cuffs. "I don't know how to pick a lock."

"Seriously?"

"No idea," Bishop said.

"Why are you even here?" Kick said, peering into the keyhole, trying to see what she was doing. "He can't answer any questions."

"I can access his medical chart from my phone," Bishop said. "I wanted to check on you."

She could feel him looking at her; it made the back of her neck warm. "Did you find anything useful at the apartment?"

"It's possible the lab might still turn something up," he said.

She knew that meant they had turned up nothing. She'd known it the moment Bishop walked through the door, because he could be there for only one reason. Kick wiggled the paper clip.

"You want me to talk to Mel again," she said.

The ventilator hissed. James's chest rose and fell.

"No," Bishop said.

Kick looked up, the paper clip poised in her hand. "James can't help," she said. "Mel knows everybody in that world. If he can't give us more information, he can tell us how to find someone who can. I can handle it. I want to talk to him. I want . . ." She stopped herself before she said it.

"Mel slipped into a coma this morning," Bishop said quietly.

Kick's hand shook and the paper clip made a frantic tapping noise against the cuffs. "Oh," she said. She set the paper clip on James's white hospital blanket.

Compared to the smooth pace of the ventilator, Kick's own breaths seemed suddenly shaky and shallow.

She fixed her attention on the paper clip. She made it her whole world. She didn't try to laugh, or scream, or tell herself affirmations. She didn't want to feel.

"I need to ask you some questions," Bishop said.

She didn't answer.

"What year was it when you were in San Diego?" he asked.

Kick was aware of her hand hanging limp in the cuff; of James's wire talisman, still snug around her finger; of the paper clip on the white blanket. "I don't know."

"How old were you?" Bishop asked.

The ventilator hummed. "James was nine," she said. "So I was seven." She picked up the paper clip and pushed the end back into the keyhole.

"How long were you there?"

"A few weeks," Kick said. "It was summer."

"It's always summer in San Diego," Bishop said.

"No," Kick said firmly. "It was July. I remember the fireworks on the Fourth. I could hear them."

James's breaths were like a ticking clock. Each mechanical lungful of air counted against him. Every day that James was on the ventilator increased the chances he wouldn't wake up.

"Could you find the house?" Bishop asked.

Kick looked up, puzzled. "In San Diego?" she said. "Klugman is gone. He's probably changed his name ten times by now. Even if you could find him, he sold James to this guy fourteen years ago. He's not going to be able to help you find him."

"Can you find the house?" Bishop repeated evenly.

Kick jammed the paper clip around in the hole. James didn't even look like himself. He looked like a shell, like a skin he'd shed and left behind.

She could sit there in her mother's clothes, listening to a machine count down the minutes to her brother's death, or she could find out who did this. Kick felt the paper clip catch, and she turned the wire ninety degrees. The lock clicked and the bracelet opened.

She sat back in her chair with a sigh. The pills were wearing off and her brain was feeling sharper. "That jet isn't yours, is it," she said.

"No," Bishop said. "But I get to use it. It's one of my corporate perks."

She had conditions. "I want a gun," she said.

Bishop smiled. "Is that a yes?"

"It's a maybe." It would be something to do; it would get her out of that room. The idea of a life without Monster or James made Kick more terrified than she could ever admit to anyone. "I could maybe find the house."

Bishop reached underneath his jacket, to the small of his back, and pulled out a 9mm semiautomatic and handed it to Kick.

Kick turned the pistol over in her hands, her heart quickening. The polymer construction, the black finish, the hammer-forged, Tenifer-coated barrel, beveled at the front for easy holstering. She knew this gun. It was her Glock. "You said . . ."

"I lied," Bishop said.

28

"DO WE NOT GET fancy cars anymore?" Kick asked, gazing glumly around the bland interior of the Chevy Impala that Bishop had rented at the San Diego airport.

"Fancy cars stand out," Bishop said.

"This car is electric blue," Kick said.

"It's topaz, and it was the only full-size model they had available," Bishop said. "Besides, it has a big trunk."

Kick let the topic drop. She didn't want to know why Bishop considered a big trunk a plus. They certainly didn't need it for their luggage. Bishop had a carry-on-size suitcase and a duffel bag, and Kick had her red purse and a shopping bag from the Target they'd stopped at so she could get supplies on the way to the airport. They could have fit all they had with them in the trunk of a Miata.

She had changed out of her mother's shirt and into a black T-shirt with studded sleeves that she'd picked up at Target. The gray shirt was probably more suitable to San Diego's climate, but Kick felt better in the black shirt. She wanted all her clothing to have studs. It felt like armor.

"Anything?" Bishop asked.

They had been driving around for over two hours. Every so often Kick would glimpse the Pacific Ocean down a side street. The car's outside temperature reading said it was eighty-three degrees—not that they'd know it, since Bishop had the AC cranked up so high.

"No," Kick said. Bishop had signed into the hospital network from her phone, allowing Kick to see James's digital chart in real time as it was updated. Kick glanced down to check it.

"Eyes up," Bishop said.

"The light hurts my head," Kick said. It wasn't true, but he was starting to annoy her. "Concussion, remember?"

"You're fine," Bishop said. "If you were going to have an intracranial hemorrhage, it would have happened by now."

Nice.

Kick sighed and stared out the window. There was nothing to see. None of it looked familiar, and yet every block was the same as the one before it. Gated condos, adobe-style houses, manicured lawns.

"Is that place on the island even your house?" she asked.

"Technically it belongs to my employer," Bishop said. "He lets me live there when I'm working in the area." They stopped at a light. "I'm not there a lot."

Kick was tired of looking out the window. She

turned her attention back inside the car. "What about the old ball and chain?" she asked, with a nod at the naked left hand Bishop had on the steering wheel. "She mind you not wearing a wedding ring?"

"Eyes up," Bishop said.

Kick crossed her arms and looked back out the window. "It was light colored and one-story," she recited by rote. "It had a pool. And it was near the ocean."

Two boys played basketball in the driveway of a house with a red clay roof and two palm trees in the front yard.

"There was a school," Kick said. She had forgotten that until now. "An elementary school. I could hear the kids at recess. I wasn't allowed outside. But I could hear them." She twisted to look up and down the street they were on. "Have you noticed that half these houses are for sale?"

"Public or private?" Bishop asked.

"Huh?" Kick said.

"The school," Bishop said impatiently. "Was it public or private?"

She caught a glimpse of the ocean again, a chunk of blue at the end of a street. She had a feeling this was the closest she was going to get to it. "Do they sound different?" Kick asked.

"You said it was July," Bishop said. "It was probably a public school. They go year-round here."

All the cars they passed, the houses, they were too fancy.

"Te:l me about the pool," Bishop said.

"I don't know," Kick said helplessly. "There was one." She didn't know what he wanted from her. Her memories were fragmented, like a series of clips in the wrong order. "It was in the backyard," she said. "The backyard had a wooden fence. It had some vine growing on it. It had dark-pink flowers."

"Bougainvillea," Bishop said. "Who maintained the pool?"

She didn't know. "I was a kid," she said. "We were there for two weeks."

"What was over the fence?" Bishop asked.

"I wasn't allowed near the fence."

"Did you see airplanes flying overhead? Were there trains? Ship horns?"

Kick looked at her wire-man ring and felt a pang of guilt for not being with James. "I don't remember."

"How do you know you were near the ocean?"

She wanted him to leave her alone. "I could hear it. I could hear the roar of the waves."

Bishop pulled to the curb and lowered Kick's window from the driver's-side controls. "Listen," he said.

Kick listened. It made Bishop shut up for a minute, at least. She focused all of her attention out the open window. She practiced being present in the moment. She didn't know what the hell she was supposed to be hearing. She could see a slice of the ocean between condo buildings. She could smell the salt water. But she couldn't hear the waves. So she didn't know what good this was doing. She couldn't hear the ocean at all. Then it dawned on her: if she couldn't hear the ocean now, then she wouldn't have been able to hear the ocean then. "It wasn't the ocean," she said.

"It was a freeway," Bishop said.

This was good. This was a breakthrough. So why didn't Bishop look more excited?

"Doesn't that help?" Kick asked.

Bishop leaned back against the headrest. "There are more houses near freeways in San Diego than near the ocean."

Kick inventoried her mind for anything, any detail no matter how random, that might possibly help. She came up with nothing. Just one small fact that was probably stupid to even bring up, but she did anyway. "The basement leaked," she muttered.

Bishop turned slowly toward her. "The house had a basement?"

"The houses always had a basement," Kick said. She'd told him that, in Seattle. It was a given. She looked out the window. A five-year-old kid on a Razor scooter sped past on the sidewalk, followed by his father.

"This is San Diego," Bishop said.

"So?" Judging by the For Sale signs up and down the street, no one wanted to live there.

Bishop rubbed his temples like he was the one with the concussion. "Do you know why people build basements?"

"Storage?" Kick guessed.

"To stabilize their homes," Bishop said. "Soil, when it's saturated, expands, causing anything built on top of it to shift. That's why building codes require foundations to go below the frost line." He gestured with his chin out the windshield. "There's no frost here. The frost line is, like, a foot underground. You don't need a basement. They're not required by code. No developer is going to sink a shitload of money building a basement unless the code says they have to."

Kick was starting to feel a little defensive. "The house had a basement," she insisted. "A cellar, or whatever. Mr. Klugman had partially finished it." She could see it as clear as anything, as clear as any part of the house. She could remember the stale air and how dust came off when she ran her finger along the concrete wall.

She would always remember that basement.

The kid on the skateboard fell. Kick didn't see it happen. He was down the block, a small, distant figure. But the window was still open and she heard him start to wail. His father rushed to him and held him in his arms. Kick felt a stab of bitterness. She didn't know why she had assumed the man was the boy's father. He could be anyone at all.

"We made the first movie down there," she said. "Mr. Klugman filmed it. That's why we were staying there. Mel used the money he made to buy his own equipment."

She glanced at Bishop, to see how he'd react.

He was already getting out his phone, dialing a number. He held up a finger for her to be quiet. She saw his eyes on the For Sale sign across the street. The sign had a photograph of the Realtor, Stacy Smith, *San Diego's Prime Bungalow Specialist.* She had a dark mane of hair, a bright smile, and a 1-800 number.

"Hi, Stacy," Bishop said smoothly into his phone. "This is Phil Marlowe." He winked at Kick. "Barbara recommended I give you a call. My wife and I are looking to buy a house sometime next year, but we're in town unexpectedly for the afternoon and wanted to take the opportunity to get to know the area so we can move quickly when the time comes. Well, my wife's from back east and she's set on having a basement. I know. I explained that, but she's insisting. We want an area with some privacy, a little space between houses. A fenced-in yard. Maybe a pool. Also, we've got a third grader, so we're looking for a property with an elementary school within walking distance. And I'll be working up in Irvine, so I'm going to need access to the freeway. Can you give me a few ideas? Thanks. She's checking. Yeah, I'm here. Excellent. Okay. Read that to me again. Okay. Got it. Well, we'll take a look. Thanks so much. We'll be in touch."

He turned to Kick. "She said she hasn't sold a house with a basement in this town in nineteen years as a real estate agent. But there are two older neighborhoods we should take a look at. She says most of the houses have at least partial basements. They don't come up on the market much. Most of them are rental properties. She was worried about our son walking to school in this one, because there aren't any sidewalks."

29

THE NEIGHBORHOOD THAT THE Realtor had sent them to was ten miles from the ocean and tucked next to a tangle of interstates. The houses were mostly one-story and ranged from Spanish-style adobe to bomb-shelter-style cinder block. Many of the homes were run-down but they were on big lots and had fenced-in yards.

Bishop followed the directions to the elementary school and started circling the neighborhood from there.

Kick had the window down again, hoping that the din of the playground would spark some other memory, but it was Sunday and the school was closed.

The street gently curved around a bend. She could hear the irregular pulse of interstate traffic in the distance, and birds. Her eyes studied the houses they passed. She didn't really expect to recognize the house from the front. She didn't know what she was expecting—maybe a psychic recognition, like she'd see an aura or something.

But she knew the place the instant she saw it.

It was entirely indistinct, a one-story rectangle

266 • CHELSEA CAIN

with gray siding and white trim. Someone had added a covered patio in front, and two neatly painted aqua chairs sat side by side. The yard was sand. She remembered that now. Rocks were arranged here and there, along with a few scrawny palm trees, as if the house had been set down in the middle of the Mojave Desert. She had looked at it from the front window, a sandbox she could never play in. In the middle of this arid landscape an American flag fluttered on a pole planted in the sand. The flagpole was twice as tall as the house.

"There," she said.

Bishop didn't question her. He pulled the car over and they got out. Above the house, white clouds floated by in the blue afternoon sky. A fifteen-foot wall of bushes separated the property from a neighboring house to the west, and an empty lot, overgrown with foliage, sat to its east.

Behind the house, Kick could see the school in the distance.

They walked toward the front door. The path had been repaved and two names had been drawn into the concrete: *Stella and Eliza*. A third name followed a few steps later: *Grandpa Bob*.

"I can pick the lock," Kick said, already eyeing the door's medium-priced dead bolt, a Schlage five-pin by the look of it.

"Was the flag here?" Bishop asked.

"I don't remember it," Kick said.

Bishop buttoned his blazer and grinned at her. "Flagpole in the yard. Grandkids' names in the front walk. Navy emblem on the mailbox. What does that tell you?"

Kick didn't see what he was getting at. "The people who live here are old and patriotic?"

"Exactly," Bishop said. "So why don't we try knocking first?" He brushed some lint from his shoulder, stepped up to the door, and knocked.

They hadn't even worked out their cover story. They were totally unprepared. But Kick didn't have time to protest. The door opened and a grandfatherly man appeared with a neighborly yet cautious smile. His baseball cap announced that he was a U.S. Navy veteran.

"Hello, sir," Bishop said smoothly. "We're investigating an abducted child, and it's possible a man who may have information about the case used to live here about fourteen years ago. Do you mind if we come in?"

Kick gave Bishop a sideways look. She hadn't expected him to tell the truth.

The man in the doorway regarded them with sharp eyes. He was in his mid-seventies, Kick guessed, and still broad shouldered and strong. His T-shirt and cutoffs were layered with the paint of a hundred projects.

He adjusted his cap. "I expect you'd better come in," he said, opening the door.

Kick tried to hide her amazement. The guy was just going to let them in out of some sort of civic duty. He hadn't even asked for identification. *Old and patriotic.*

"After you," Bishop said, giving her a push.

She stepped inside.

"Name's Collingsworth," the man said to Bishop. "I'll help in any way I can."

Kick moved past him toward the living room. Her stomach tightened with anticipation. Since they'd pulled up to the house, her memories had gotten clearer, more detailed. She could see the brass gas fireplace in the living room wall and the built-in bookshelves where Klugman had kept the paperbacks that she wasn't supposed to read. She remembered the brown shag carpet and how it smelled like cats, even though Klugman didn't have a cat.

But when she turned the corner, everything was wrong.

It wasn't how it was supposed to be. There was no gas fireplace, no brown carpet, no bookcases. The room wasn't even the right shape.

This was not the house she remembered.

She turned back to Bishop. "This is wrong," she said.

"We've done a lot of work to the place," Collingsworth said almost apologetically.

Family photographs adorned the wall behind him. A picture of two little girls hung in a frame decorated with the words *World's Best Grandpa*.

"When did you buy it?" Bishop asked him.

"Ten years ago this November," Collingsworth said. "Bought it from the bank. A property management company owned it before then, but they went belly-up."

That fit the time frame.

Kick continued into the kitchen, scrutinizing every molding. The counters were configured differently, and new shiny white appliances had been installed. She remembered an ancient refrigerator with a heavy door she needed help to open. She remembered wallpaper with pale pink and yellow flowers.

She went to the kitchen window and looked out, but it was a different backyard. All she saw was an expanse of grass. "There's no pool," she called to Bishop.

"First thing I did was fill that in," Collingsworth said from behind her. "It was leaking. Would have cost five thousand dollars to repair. And Estelle worried about the grandkids. That was my wife, may she rest in peace."

"What about the basement?" Bishop asked.

Kick spun around.

Collingsworth gave a nod toward a closed door at the far corner of the kitchen.

Kick's heart was in her throat as they descended the basement stairs. Each step came back to her: the sound the wood made as it creaked under her feet, how the center of each step had a worn spot in the gray paint. The wood underneath the paint was polished from a thousand footfalls. It gleamed.

"You know, it's really unusual to find a basement in San Diego," Collingsworth was saying to Bishop. "One of the reasons we bought the place. Estelle was from back east . . ."

Kick cleared the stairs and stepped into the basement. She knew better than to let herself hope, but the stairs had seemed so familiar, she allowed herself a brief fantasy that this might be the place.

But confronted with the new drywall, lighting, and carpet, she hesitated. Basement stairs were basement stairs. They all creaked. They all had worn paint. Now that she was in the basement, it was nothing like she remembered it. She had no reference point to get her bearings. She looked despairingly at Bishop.

"Give it a minute," Bishop said.

Collingsworth's white eyebrows drew together. "Say, you don't think someone is buried down here?" he asked.

Bishop didn't answer. Something had caught his eye. He turned to Collingsworth. "You do a lot of this work yourself, Mr. Collingsworth?" he asked.

Collingsworth glanced away sheepishly. "Yeah."

"So no permits, then," Bishop said slowly.

"I, uh . . ."

"It's okay," Bishop said. He gave Collingsworth a reassuring smile. "We don't work for the city."

Kick was looking around the basement, trying to figure out what Bishop was seeing.

Then she spotted it. The other walls were drywall, but this one was paneled with knotty pine, like a rustic accent wall in some 1970s rec room. Kick moved toward it.

"That's not a load-bearing wall," Bishop said to Collingsworth. "Was that here when you bought the place?"

Kick knew the answer was no before Collingsworth even grumbled a response. The wall was out of place. The geometry didn't fit.

"You know what's on the other side of it?" Bishop asked.

"Dirt?" Collingsworth guessed. "It's a half basement. Not uncommon around here. If you're lucky enough to have a basement, you take what you can get."

Kick scanned the room again, trying to overlay her memories on top of the well-lit, well-scrubbed, finished space she was standing in. The concrete floor, the cobwebs, the old sheet Klugman had hung to act as a backdrop for filming. She had crossed that concrete floor to visit James. She had come down the stairs and walked straight across the basement. The pine wall was in the right place.

"You have the house inspected before you bought it?" Bishop asked.

"Bought it for a song," Collingsworth said. "Didn't need a loan."

Kick put her cheek to the wall and pressed her skin against the knotty pine until it felt like the wood grain was being imprinted on her flesh. Then she knocked—*shave and a haircut*—and listened for a mechanical click.

"Exactly what do you two think is on the other side of that wall?" Collingsworth asked.

"The cell the man who used to live here kept a child in," Kick said.

Collingsworth reddened and stepped back. Bishop sighed and shook his head.

She didn't care.

She moved her face along the pine boards and then stopped and knocked again. She didn't know if the room was still there, if the locking mechanism would even work after all these years, if she'd even hear the click through the knotty pine. But for the first time since they'd walked into that house, she was certain that this was the place. Her skin prickled. Her mouth felt hot. She moved her cheek and knocked again. She had to concentrate, to listen as hard as she could.

Someone tapped her on the shoulder and she turned. Collingsworth stood behind her with a sledgehammer. Behind him, a utility room door was open.

"Step aside," he said. He lifted the sledgehammer. "I was a Seabee in the navy. I've got grandkids. If there's some kind of cell back there, let's find it."

Kick ducked out of the way and Collingsworth swung the sledgehammer at the center of the pine wall. Wood splintered and the hammer stuck in the wall for a minute before Collingsworth pulled it free. Muscles rippled underneath the loose skin of his arms. This time drywall dust filled the air and whole boards clattered to the carpet.

Kick could taste the drywall dust grit in her

mouth. She took a few steps back, covered her mouth with her hand, and closed her eyes.

She heard Collingsworth whack the wall again, and there was another great thwack as more wood gave way, and Kick felt the dust in the air thicken.

Collingsworth started coughing. Kick peeked an eye open. Collingsworth was covered with a fine white powder like he'd been rolled in flour. Splinters and chunks of drywall lay on the floor at his feet. He heaved the sledgehammer into the air again, but his lungs gave out before he could get it above his shoulder. He spit on the floor, set his mouth determinedly, tried again, and started wheezing. Kick was certain that he was going to have a heart attack. She wondered bleakly if they could be blamed for it.

Bishop was already taking off his blazer. He laid it across the back of a recliner and approached Collingsworth with a polite smile. "May I?" he asked, indicating the sledgehammer. "I have always wanted to use one of these things."

Kick was breathing through her fingers. Dust was settling on Bishop's gray shirt like snow.

Collingsworth turned the sledgehammer over to him and stepped out of the cloud. Bishop swung it above his shoulder, held it like a batter staring down a pitch, grinned happily, and slammed it through the wall.

A few minutes later Bishop, sweating and beaming like a kid, had smashed a four-foot-square hole into the wall. "That was fun," he said. He lifted his

T-shirt up and wiped some of the pulverized dry-wall off his face.

Kick tried to peer through the opening, but it was too dark and the dust was too thick.

"Is there a room?" she asked.

"Oh, there's a room," Bishop said, and he picked up the hammer, held it forward with a straight arm, and extended it beyond the wall into the darkness, all the way to his armpit. Kick's eyes stung from the grit in the air. More chunks of dry-wall and splinters of wood littered the carpet.

"You need a flashlight?" Collingsworth asked Bishop.

They both had white dust in their hair and on their eyelashes.

"That's exactly what I need," Bishop said.

Collingsworth tromped off to the utility room, leaving a trail of white footprints, and came back with an assortment of industrial flashlights and lanterns. "Earthquake country," he said, by way of explanation, and he handed an LED camp lantern to Bishop.

Bishop turned the lantern on and stretched it into the darkness.

"Oh my God," Kick whispered, feeling the hair on the back of her neck stand up. Bishop leaned in, moving the light around, but Kick stood ramrod straight, trying to absorb what she saw.

A rotting mattress lay on the concrete floor sur-rounded by stacks of yellowing paperbacks and moldy posters curling from the walls; a seatless toilet sat in the corner, and pop cans were scattered across the floor, coated with dust. Beyond the effects of age, the room had been preserved exactly as it had been when James was kept in it.

"Is it what you remember?" Bishop asked her.

"It's exactly how I remember it," Kick said slowly. She felt dazed, like she was entering a dream. "I don't think anyone's been in this room since James."

"Hold this," Bishop said, handing Kick the lantern. He pivoted away, already dialing someone on his phone.

Collingsworth stepped forward, gazed solemnly into the room, and took off his cap.

"It's me," Bishop said into the phone. "I need you to run a check on a name and address for me. Rental records. Tax records. Anything you can find." He paused. "Klugman. . . . I don't know how it's spelled. You find out for me. . . . I don't know the first name. He was at this address fourteen years ago." He rattled off the address.

The posters were so moldy that Kick couldn't make out what they were; she couldn't remember.

"I'm going to take a look around," Bishop said. He was wearing latex gloves now and took the lantern back from her, then stepped through the broken wall.

"I'll come with you," Kick said quickly.

"It's a crime scene," Bishop said, looking back at her through the hole, his face lit by the lantern. "Think back: we've been over this."

"His mother sold him," Kick said. "He wasn't abducted." Bishop had already turned away from her and was moving toward a far corner, his body blocking her view of what the lantern was revealing. "Without a complaining victim, the statute of limitations on child sex abuse is ten years," Kick continued. "You'd need James to wake up and file a police report, and that will never happen. Even if he does wake up, he would never agree to go through a trial—that would mean dealing with people. So, assuming you manage to someday find Klugman, which is highly unlikely, you're better off prosecuting him for human trafficking. Or you could have the bastard put away for life for child pornography. Then you don't need the room at all." She didn't want to testify, but she'd do it for James. "You just need me."

The lantern appeared again, and Bishop with it. "Congratulations on the law degree," he said.

"I have a special interest in this area," Kick said.

He extended a hand to help her step over the lower part of the wall. Kick ignored the gesture and clambered through the passage unaided. The floor on the other side was concrete. The air felt immediately colder. Everything smelled sour and dank. She lit a path with her flashlight and made her way past the mattress to the posters on the wall. Even up close, in direct light, she couldn't make out the images. The bloom of mold had blotted out everything.

"You know what they are?" Bishop asked, stepping beside her.

The light of his lantern, combined with her flashlight, brightened the wall just enough that a sliver of stone crenellation was visible in the poster's image. It was a castle—Kick could see its shape now—one of those old castles tourists visit in places like Bavaria.

"They're travel posters," Kick said. How many hours had James spent, locked in this room, dreaming of faraway lands? "Places he wanted to go."

"What's this?" Bishop asked. He moved his light to where the corner of the poster had curled off the wall, and Kick saw a piece of paper tucked there. Bishop reached for it with his latex-gloved hand and slid out a postcard.

It had been protected somewhat from the entropy of the room, but when he held it in the light, they saw that the image on the front was largely consumed by mold. He flipped it over. The back was blank except for a logo: *The Desert Rose Motel*. Kick felt a jolt of recognition. She looked around for something she could use to clean the card.

"Take off your shirt," she said.

"Excuse me?" Bishop said.

"Your shirt's already dirty," Kick said. There was no way she was taking her shirt off. "Mine isn't."

Bishop hesitated and then put the lantern on

the floor and pulled his shirt over his head. "Now what?" he said.

"Clean off the front of the card," Kick said, picking up the lantern.

Bishop placed the postcard against the wall and used his shirt to scrub at the mold. Kick turned her head as tiny spores rose into the air and floated in the light.

"That's the best I can do," Bishop said.

Kick inched closer to the card. The mold had smeared and formed a fine, streaky gray paste. But Kick could see a ghost of an image underneath. A fifties-style courtyard motel with a pool, surrounded by desert. A neon sign in front read *The Desert Rose Motel, Vacancy*.

She knew it. She'd been there.

"This place," she said. "We went there on a vacation. They let me play in the pool. Be outside. Linda met us there, but Mel and I were there for days, alone." The Desert Rose pool—that's where Mel had taught her how to do the back float. He'd mentioned it at the infirmary. "Yesterday," she said. "I think he mentioned this vacation. He told me to remember it. I thought it was after San Diego. But it must have been before. I think this is where Mel met Klugman."

Bishop worked a finger under the moldy poster where they'd found the postcard and a moment later another square of paper came free from underneath and dropped into Bishop's waiting hand. He wiped it with his shirt and then planted it on the wall in front of her. "Is this Klugman?" he asked.

The photograph was surprisingly well preserved. James as she had first known him, a gawky nine-year-old, with a bad haircut and too-small clothes. In this picture he was grinning. A man had his arm around him. The man was turning his head away from the camera, his anonymity protected except for the side of his jaw, his ear, and his sideburn. They were standing side by side in the shallow end of a swimming pool. James, his bare chest sunken and skinny, looked puny next to Klugman's hairy barrel shape. But he was outside, in the backyard pool. He had not always been kept in the dark.

Kick looked away. "It's him," she said. She didn't need to see his face; she recognized his shape, his torso and limbs, his square head.

Bishop pocketed the postcard and the picture and they looked around some more, carefully peeling the posters off the walls, but they didn't find any more hidden clues. Kick leafed through James's sci-fi paperbacks. Bishop went through the pockets of a small pile of rotting clothes. They flipped the mattress over.

That's where the little figure was, so small that when Kick first saw it in her flashlight beam, she thought it was an old screw. It was only when she picked it up that she saw it was a little man made of wire, a twin to the talisman she wore on her finger. James had probably found the wire scraps in his room or pilfered them from the basement.

"What is it?" Bishop asked.

"A toy," Kick said. She couldn't take it with her. It would be like stealing something from a grave. She set the little man back down in the dust.

When they climbed back through the wall, Collingsworth was waiting for them, his cap still in his hands. "I didn't know it was there," he said shakily. "All this time, I didn't know." He was still covered with debris. Drywall stuck to his eyelashes.

Bishop glanced at Kick. "The boy who lived in there," he said to Collingsworth. "He got away."

It wasn't exactly a lie, it just wasn't the whole truth. Bishop sold it, though. Collingsworth looked relieved.

Bishop used his shirt to clean the sweat off his chest and the drywall dust off his arms and head, and then he tossed it over his shoulder through the hole they'd smashed in the wall. "Thanks for your time, Mr. Collingsworth," he said, shrugging his blazer on over his bare torso.

Collingsworth looked confused. His eyes went to the dungeon on the other side of his rec room.

"What do you want me to do with all that?" he asked.

Bishop produced a checkbook from the blazer pocket and scribbled something out on it. "Gut it," he said. He tore the check out and handed it to Collingsworth, who looked agog at the amount. "Put in a playroom for your grandkids."

Collingsworth gave Kick a questioning look.

"Spare no expense," she said.

"Besides, look on the bright side," Bishop added, clapping Collingsworth on the back. "You just doubled the square footage of your basement."

30

IT TURNED OUT THAT the Desert Rose's neon sign was the most glamorous thing about it. The sun had not quite set when Kick and Bishop pulled up and parked. The foothills were distant humps on the horizon, and the setting sun had turned the sky deep periwinkle. The motel was fifteen miles from the nearest town and surrounded on all sides by the empty desert. When they parked the car and got out, Kick could have sworn she heard a coyote howling. It was eighty-nine degrees in the shade.

She followed Bishop into the lobby. A counter stretched across one side, and a mud-colored Naugahyde sectional formed a seating area at the lobby's center. A set of glass doors on one wall led to the pool; glass doors on the opposite wall led to a restaurant, which was, according to the handwritten sign on the door, Open Most Mornings. The lobby floor was ceramic tile. Kick remembered slipping on it once when she had wet feet from the pool. Other than that, nothing else about the lobby struck her as particularly familiar.

The only motel staff appeared to be the clerk minding the check-in counter. She was engrossed in a celebrity magazine, a position that effectively displayed the cleavage her V-neck T-shirt exposed. Her thick, dark hair was blown out into soft shoulder-length waves and her caramel-colored skin was flawless. She looked up from the magazine with glazed eyes, but when they landed on Bishop, they instantly brightened. She batted her false eyelashes. "Can I help you?" she asked.

Bishop grinned. Kick could practically hear the blood rushing to his crotch. He slid her a sideways glance as if to say, *I got this.*

Kick hung back a few feet as he swaggered up and slid the photograph of James and Klugman on the counter in front of the clerk. The clerk leaned forward, arching her back a little, so that her T-shirt drew tighter in the right places. Bishop's eyes moved over her breasts with an appreciative smile.

Kick wondered if she should wait in the car.

"Have you seen this man before?" Bishop asked. His voice sounded different, like he was auditioning to host a late-night radio show.

The clerk looked up from the photograph. "He's not as cute as you are," she said.

"No, he's not," Bishop agreed.

The clerk blushed, and Bishop shifted his weight forward so that his forearms and elbows were on the counter.

"I'm going for a walk," Kick announced.

"Wait," Bishop said. He put his palm on the counter and slid the magazine toward Kick. "Take something to read," he said. He tapped the magazine with his finger, drawing Kick's attention to it.

She did a double take.

Her own image was splashed across the cover; she was crouched in horse pose at the park next to her mother and Monster. A bright yellow headline announced the cover story: *Ten Years of Freedom! Kidnap Mom, Paula Lannigan, Exclusive!*

Kick flipped the magazine over and drew it toward her.

"That's mine," the clerk protested.

Bishop stepped between them, and Kick saw his fingers brush the clerk's bare arm.

"What's your name?" he asked her.

"Carla," she said, her eyes back on him.

"I'm John," he said.

Kick backed away with the magazine, toward the sliding glass door.

She noticed how Bishop leaned his head toward the clerk's, repositioning the photograph on the counter so that the clerk was entirely in his orbit. "Do you recognize him, Carla?" he asked.

"I can only see his ear," the clerk said.

"Does his ear look familiar?" he asked, and Kick wondered if the clerk could hear the flicker of impatience in his voice.

Apparently she couldn't. "Do you work out?" the clerk asked. "I work out. I'm only doing this job for the summer. I'm an actress. In LA. What do you do?"

Kick neared the door.

"I'm a casting agent," Bishop said without missing a beat.

The clerk giggled uncertainly. One of Kick's palms was on the glass, the other on the plastic door handle. The door was sticky, and Kick jiggled it, trying to get it to glide along its track.

"Are a lot of the staff here seasonal?" Bishop asked.

Kick glanced back at him. He was entirely focused on the clerk, his fingertips on her forearm. Screw it. Kick muscled the door open, stepped through it, and slammed it behind her. Ten percent of the moisture in her body immediately evaporated in the desert air. Her lips instantly felt chapped. The warm, dry heat made her skin buzz, like the faint electrical current created when you put a tongue to a battery.

And a weird thing happened: Kick relaxed. Maybe it was the pool. It was lit from below and glowed in the twilight like an aquamarine jewel. Even Kick, who hadn't liked pools since she was a kid, found herself drawn to it.

The courtyard itself was nothing special. The two-story concrete-block motel surrounded it on three sides and the kidney-shaped pool was at its center. The pool was empty, the courtyard abandoned. Most of the motel room windows were shuttered and dark. A child's pink foam pool noodle floated discarded in the shallow end.

Kick sank down into a white plastic lounge chair, tossed the magazine aside, and took off her mother's flip-flops. The concrete under her feet was warm. She used her phone to scan the latest updates in James's medical file and then sat watching the changing surface of the water, how the slightest breeze created ripples that changed how the blue light moved.

It was this blue light that drew Kick's attention back to the magazine. It winked across the cover, reflecting off a pale face in a corner box. Kick reached for the magazine and squinted at it. She had been too distracted by her own image to notice it before—featured in the top right corner was a photograph of Adam Rice. *The New Face of Missing Children?* the copy asked.

Kick opened the magazine, paging past the images her mother had sold, and the quotes that her mother had given, and the ads for her mother's book, until she found the half-page story about Adam. It was all a rehashing of what Kick knew. Even the photographs were recycled from other articles. The main image was the one that Kick had clipped and put up on her bedroom wall: Adam's mother at the press conference, clutching her son's stuffed elephant. The article had one new quote, from the utility worker who had seen Adam playing in the yard before his abduction. "I noticed him because of the monkey," the utility worker was quoted as saying. "It looked loved, like a stuffed animal my kid's got."

A white butterfly alit on the surface of the pool and immediately started to drown.

Kick rolled the magazine up and stuck it in her purse, then unzipped the interior pocket and extracted the envelope from the Trident Medical Group. She unfolded it and stared at it dumbly; it was so official-looking, with its medical seal and the American flag stamp. Kick's name and her mother's address were visible through the plastic window. It hadn't been a mix-up. She had given them her mother's address on purpose because James always went through Kick's mail, and she knew that if he had intercepted the letter, he would never have given it to her.

Kick slowly extracted the typed letter from inside. The pool reflected off the white paper, rippling it with aqua light.

Seeing the report in black-and-white made it real somehow.

She didn't like to swim. She didn't even like baths. She didn't like being in the water. It was one of her triggers.

She didn't know why.

This place . . . she barely remembered it. But she remembered the pool. Even as a kid she had appreciated its color, that perfect Caribbean blue.

She heard the sound of plastic scraping against concrete, looked up to see Bishop dragging a deck chair parallel to hers, and quickly folded the letter from Trident back into her purse. He sat down, tossed the plastic Target bag with her overnight things on the ground at her feet, and then dangled a room key over her lap.

She took the key. Not a key card, she noticed. A real key. It was attached to a shiny red plastic key chain that had the number *18* stamped on it.

"They have a lot of seasonal employees," Bishop said. The key chain on his room key was stamped with a *6*. "But Carla says that a few of the restaurant staff have been here almost twenty years. We'll show them the photograph in the morning."

"Carla?" Kick said, looking at him sideways.

"I think she likes me," Bishop said.

Kick scanned the surface of the pool. She couldn't see the butterfly anymore. "Are we spending the night here so you can have sex with a motel clerk?" she asked. "Not that I care," she added quickly. "I'm just wondering, so when I'm eaten alive by bedbugs I'll know at least it's in service to a larger goal."

"We're staying because it's late," Bishop said, "and all the longtime staff will be here in the morning." He stood up, scratched the back of his neck, and looked away. "And so I can have sex with the motel clerk."

"Good night," Kick said, settling back into her deck chair.

"Good night," Bishop said.

She felt him start to step away, a shift in the light where his shadow had been.

"Bishop?" she called. She was staring straight ahead, at the pool. She couldn't see Bishop, but she knew he was still there. "You know how Mel said that Klugman spent the money he got for James on a new car?" she asked. "I remember that day. I remember looking for James. I found Mel and Klugman in the garage with the car. They told me that James was gone. And you know what I did?" It was the first time she'd ever said it out loud. "I went swimming." The knot in her throat felt like a hand around her neck. James wasn't allowed in the pool, so when they played, they had to play inside. With James not there, she could do what she wanted. She had played in Klugman's pool all afternoon, happy that he was gone.

"You were a kid; you didn't understand what it meant."

Kick sat forward, distracted. The edge of the motel pool was ringed with ceramic tiles. She had remembered it wrong. The two pools, Klugman's and the Desert Rose's, had merged in her memory. "I was wrong about the photograph," she said. "I thought it was taken in Klugman's backyard." She lifted her finger, the one with the wire talisman, and pointed at the shallow end of the Desert Rose Motel pool, where the lip was checkerboarded with black and white tiles. "It was here," Kick said.

31

"THE KEY TO DOING *a back float is to relax,*" *her father said. Beth leaned back into his hand and let his palm support her at the surface of the water. The sky was the same color as the pool, and her body burned with excitement at Mel's attention. "Just stay clam and relaxed," her father said. "And do what I tell you."*

They weren't alone in the pool; there were other grown-ups: the big man in the black swimsuit with the pale legs and the arrow tattoos, and his wife, who didn't like to be splashed, sat on the edge with their legs in the water. The pool cleaner, who always said hello to her, was using a pool skimmer to scoop up the dead palm fronds.

Her father's voice always made her calm, and she knew that if she just did what he said, he would keep her safe. "Very slowly, tip your head back until your ears are underwater," he said, guiding her forehead back with his hand. "Good. Now lift your chin." It was scary. The water seemed so close to her eyes. "More. Point it up toward the sky." She lifted it a bit more. She could feel her whole body becoming more buoyant. The water was at her mid-cheek. "Keep your head centered," he said, "arms a few inches from your sides. Keep your palms up. Now arch your upper back just a few inches." He moved his hand along her spine. "Lift your chest just a bit out of the water." He moved a hand and held it just above her belly. "Now lift your stomach until it touches my hand," he said. She pushed her belly out until it met his palm. "You're such a good girl, Beth. Now bend your knees and open your legs slightly." She did what she was told, and he withdrew his hands and stepped away, and for a moment she was terrified, all by herself, in water above her head. Then the thrill of her achievement hit her and she squealed with delight. She was floating. "Listen to your body," her father called from the edge of the pool. "You're doing it."

32

KICK POUNDED ON THE door to Bishop's motel room. After a minute the door opened a few inches and Bishop peered out across the chain.

"I want to talk," Kick said. She had come straight from her room and was barefoot, wearing what she'd bought at Target for sleepwear: a black tank top and boxer-like pajama shorts.

Bishop closed the door in her face. Kick waited. Bugs batted against the caged light fixture overhead. Every room was fitted with a chain lock above a standard doorknob lock, both easily defeated. All Kick would have needed was a paper clip and a rubber band. She hadn't even locked her room, because why bother?

Kick heard the chain drop.

"It's two a.m.," Bishop said. He was standing in the doorway, wearing black jeans he'd clearly just pulled on, and no shirt or shoes. The scratch marks she'd left on his arms looked like they had been drawn on with a shaky red ballpoint. A plastic jug of juice dangled from his hand.

Kick peered past him, into his room. It looked identical to hers. Green carpet. The same psychedelic tropical-leaf pattern on the bedspread. The bed looked like it hadn't been slept in. "Are you alone?" Kick asked.

Bishop looked over his shoulder into the clearly empty motel room. "Uh, yes?" he said.

Kick was relieved. Purely on Bishop's behalf. Because he had probably dodged an STD, and self-restraint was not exactly his style. "I thought the motel clerk might be here," she said, walking past Bishop into his room. His air-conditioning worked better than hers, and she crossed her arms, her skin pebbled from the artificial chill. It smelled like mildew and stale cigarette smoke. A print of a coyote howling at the moon in the desert was bolted to the wall over the bed. His suitcase was still packed, next to the wall. "Or has she already come and gone," Kick said.

Bishop closed the door, took a slug from the juice, and wiped his mouth with his hand. "You know, contrary to popular belief, I can go a night without getting laid," he said.

Kick snorted.

Bishop turned his desk chair around and sat in it, and Kick caught a glimpse of the stitches that still peppered his back. His laptop was plugged in behind him on the wood laminate surface that passed for a desk. He had been sitting at his computer when Kick had knocked, she guessed. The laptop was closed, but it was on.

Besides the desk chair, the other seating options were the bed and a stained orange-upholstered reading chair.

Someone was listening to a Spanish-language radio station on the other side of the wall.

Kick didn't know where to sit. The carpet felt sticky under her feet. She stepped over to Bishop and took the jug from him and tipped it into her mouth. It was orange juice, sweet and pulpy. She looked at the label. Fresh-squeezed. There was no way he got this at the pool vending machines, which meant that, at some point earlier that night, he'd made the twenty-minute trip into town without her.

She passed the jug back to him and he took a swig.

"Was there something in particular you wanted to talk about," he asked, studying her, "or did you just want to infect me with your insomnia?"

He didn't seem to register that she was practically naked.

"How many women have you had sex with?" Kick asked. The question sounded as awkward out loud as it had in Kick's head.

"More than you," Bishop said. His gray eyes were fixed on her. "I mean, I don't know that. I'm assuming." He grinned to himself as he took another slug of juice. "I don't know what you're into."

Kick let herself stare at him. The scar on his neck was beautiful, as thick as yarn.

She had thought that she would tell him about the Trident Medical Group, about the test results, that he might talk her out of what she was thinking. But that's not why she was here. The back of her neck was on fire.

A mariachi band started up on the Spanish-language station.

Bishop rested the jug on his thigh and looked at her expectantly.

Kick hesitated, then took the juice from his hand, tipped it down her throat, and drained it.

"Help yourself," Bishop said wryly.

Light-headed, Kick tossed the empty jug behind her on the carpet, wiped her mouth, and climbed on Bishop's lap, straddling him.

She was startled by how surprised he seemed. The muscles in his chest tensed and he lifted his hands reflexively from the chair. Kick guessed the paramedic and the flight attendant had been more subtle. At that moment Bishop could have stopped her cold with one devastating rejoinder, but he didn't. He lowered his hands back to the armrests and was motionless. It flustered her. She didn't know what he wanted. She thought he wanted sex, all the time. She couldn't bring herself to make eye contact with him, worried that he'd look horrified or something. Instead she divided his sum into parts: the angle of his jaw, the smiling scar across his neck, the black hairs on his chest, the sinewy muscles of his scratched arms. Her whole body buzzed with warmth now. She interlaced her fingers at the nape of his neck and pulled his mouth to hers. Their tongues met. He tasted like orange juice. She moved her tongue around his mouth, exploring him. He kissed her back but he was cautious, and he still hadn't actively touched her.

When Kick had played out how this would go, she wasn't sure what she wanted him to do; part of her had wanted him to give her a fatherly speech, pat her on the head, and send her back to bed.

But something had changed, and she felt overcome by an almost desperate physical longing that was making all her other plans seem hazy. Her fingers, behind his neck, brushed against the nylon thread that sutured a wound.

She rocked forward in his lap. She could feel his abdomen clench, heard him inhale, and then his hands brushed up along her thighs to her lower spine. A pulse of pleasure radiated down her legs as he pulled her toward him, his tongue pushing deeper into her mouth and his hands moving under her shirt. He pulled his mouth away from hers as he lifted her shirt off over her head, and she realized how out of breath she was. She expected him to ask then the usual questions: if she was "sure," or "ready," or "okay."

She knew what she'd say. But it never came up. He picked her up and carried her to the bed, and after that they didn't do any more talking.

33

KICK FELT FOR HER underpants in the dark with her foot, managed to find them, inched them over to the bed, and pulled them on. The air conditioner was blowing full blast, making her sweat-dampened skin cold. Bishop was asleep on the bed, a motionless silhouette, breathing like a tranquilized goat. Kick found her shorts balled up in the bedsheet and wiggled them on. The digital clock on the bedside table said it was 5:15 a.m. She shifted her weight carefully off the mattress onto the floor. Her tank top was somewhere on the carpet by the desk. She crept across the room, found her shirt on the floor, pulled it on, and unlocked the door.

Kick was good in the dark. Stealthy. That's what she was thinking, anyway, when she was suddenly aware of the sensation that she was being watched.

"Where are you going?" Bishop asked quietly.

Kick froze, her hand on the doorknob. He sounded perfectly awake. Which probably meant that he'd been awake this whole time.

She felt foolish, fumbling around in the dark for her clothes, sneaking out like a teenager. "My room," she said over her shoulder. She wanted out of there. She opened the door and was a half step over the threshold when Bishop turned on the bedside lamp and said, "Wait."

If only she had been faster. Kick stopped and stepped back into the room. The strap of her tank top slipped off her shoulder and she pushed it back. Bishop was sitting up on his elbows in bed, not making any effort to cover himself.

He took in a breath to talk.

Kick cut him off. She hated this part. "Don't apologize," she said miserably. "Everyone apologizes after." If he'd just let her leave, everything would be fine, but he was about to turn all Boy Scout on her. "Just once," Kick said, throwing up her hands in disgust, "I would like to be able to have meaningless sex just like everyone else."

"I was going to say that I want to hit the road by ten tomorrow," Bishop said.

Kick fiddled with a piece of her hair, flustered. "Oh," she said. She cleared her throat. "Okay. I'll be ready." She snuck a glance at him through her veil of hair as she stepped outside. He was already lying back down, reaching for the light.

"Get some sleep," he called as she closed the door.

Kick hurried, smiling to herself, across the concrete courtyard toward her room. It was still dusky, but the eastern horizon blazed with red and there were fewer stars in the sky. This was a revelation: sex without psychodrama. Is this how people did it? They just had sex and didn't have to talk about it with therapists?

Kick stepped over a flexible vacuum hose that had been unspooled across the deck and slung over the edge of the pool. She paused and took an inventory of her surroundings. Two rooms, both on the second floor, had lights on. The white plastic lounge chairs had been stacked for the night over by the soda machines. Kick was drawn toward the aquamarine light of the pool and stood on the edge, combing the snarls out of her hair with her fingers.

She was surprised by how refreshing it looked, and she remembered now that feeling of weightlessness that came with being in water. She was hit with a sudden urge to jump in. She almost giggled at the idea. It was crazy. She didn't like swimming. She didn't have a suit. The last time she'd been in a pool, she had a massive anxiety attack.

But the urge was so unexpected and strong, she wondered if she should take advantage of it. She could wear what she had on.

The pool was tranquil. The pink noodle was gone. The end of the pool vac hose bobbed listlessly underwater in the deep end. She dipped her bald big toe in the water; it was cool and sent shivers up her leg. The ripples of blue water reflected off her pasty bruised shin, so that it looked like it was almost liquid too. Her body was disappearing. Becoming water.

"Pool's closed," a man's voice said.

Kick jumped and jerked her foot out of the pool with a little splash. She had thought she was alone.

She forced herself to slowly turn around. The courtyard was empty. It was so quiet that she could hear the vending machines humming. But now that she was paying attention, she noticed things that she hadn't seen before. A pool skimmer abandoned on the deck. The door to the corrugated metal supply shed that was ajar. Something about the pool skimmer made her skin crawl.

A stocky, middle-aged man stepped out of the shed. Kick thought she was seeing things. She gaped at him, unable to speak. It couldn't be him— her mother was right; she was crazy, she was a fucking nutcase. But that silhouette, she knew his shape.

It was Klugman.

Kick knew without even being able to see his face. The man she was looking at right now—the man cleaning the Desert Rose Motel pool—was Klugman. She knew the slope of his shoulders and the way his arms bowed at the elbows, his tree-trunk thighs. That is what she remembered most: Klugman's silhouette behind the bright light of the video camera.

But it couldn't be Klugman.

One hundred billion nerve cells were screaming at Kick to run. Her heart was beating so fast that she couldn't even feel it anymore.

But fear was a skill. And Kick had practiced it.

The growing dawn light blushed Klugman's white pool cleaner's uniform with pink. His hair was thick and untrimmed. He lifted his chin and smiled at her, and his teeth glimmered. "Nice morning, isn't it?" he said. He strolled forward and his face came into focus, those smooth cheeks and almost colorless lips.

He was so short. Maybe five-foot-seven. Kick had remembered him as a giant. Everyone had been bigger back then. But now Klugman and Kick were the same size. Now she could look him in the eye.

"Pool opens at seven," he said.

He didn't recognize her.

She *was* crazy. It wasn't him. This man didn't even know her. And yet . . . his shape, she knew it. She knew it was him.

"I know who you are," Kick said.

Klugman cocked his ear at her. "What?"

"I stayed with you in San Diego. I know what you did to James. I know what you did to me. I remember. I remember all of it."

A light went on in his eyes and a slow grin spread across his face. Kick felt acid rise in her throat.

"Miss America," he said, wiping his upper lip. "I remember you now."

What was he supposed to say? She didn't know. But she expected him to say something, to apologize, or justify himself, or deny everything—something. She didn't know how long they stood there. It felt like five lifetimes. Finally, Klugman gave the back of his head a scratch. "Listen," he said, "it was good seeing you, but the pool won't clean itself."

She watched uncertainly as he set off across the

courtyard. *That was it?* "Don't you have anything to say to me?" she called.

Klugman looked over his shoulder. His face was a shadow. "Like what?" he asked.

Kick's fear dissolved into rage, which was a lot more satisfying. Fear came with two options: fight or flight. Rage offered more shades of possibility. She could have gone to her room for her Glock, come back, and shot him in a nonessential organ. She could have impaled him with throwing knives, or pepper-sprayed him, or gone and hollered for Bishop, or even called the cops. Kick wanted to use her bare hands.

She wrapped her thumb around her index and middle fingers, between the first two knuckles, and made a tight fist.

Klugman had hauled a lidded white plastic bucket out of the shed and was walking it slowly back to the poolside, grunting with every step.

She could knock him out cold. If she aimed for his throat, he'd see it coming and automatically bring his chin down in line with her fist. She could punch him in the gut so he couldn't breathe. She could aim for his liver on one side, then his ribs on the other. She could kick him in the groin. But she didn't just want him to hurt. She wanted him to bleed.

Klugman set the bucket down and rubbed his lower back. "You want to give me a hand?" he asked her.

She raised her fist alongside her face, tilted her

wrist down slightly to align her first two knuckles with her forearm, and checked that her arms were level with her shoulders. Then she put her chin down and threw a punch.

Her knuckles made contact above his jawbone and moved inward. She felt the meat of his face and the hard bone underneath as her fist drove his head sideways. She rolled her hips into the punch and followed through. Blood spewed in an arc from Klugman's nose onto the concrete and he lifted his hands to his face. Kick pulled her fist back, ready to go again, balanced on the balls of her feet. She thought he'd yell and she'd have to punch him again, but he sank to his knees, whimpering.

Kick stood over him, her whole body vibrating. Every cell in her body cheered. "Remember me now?" she said.

34

KICK RAPPED LIGHTLY ON Bishop's door. "Bishop!" she whispered hoarsely.

The door opened instantly and Kick gave Klugman a hard push, then followed him into the room. Klugman stumbled forward, clutching a blood-soaked towel to his face. Kick felt immensely proud of herself, like a cat dropping a plump dead bird on a doorstep.

Bishop had closed the door after them and was now leaning up against it, completely naked, a picture of insouciance. "So this isn't another booty call?" he asked.

"It's him," Kick said. She waved an arm at Klugman, who was huddled against the wall outside Bishop's bathroom.

Bishop gave Klugman a glance as he walked over to the bedside table. "I'm glad you didn't attack a stranger," he said to Kick, picking up the TV remote.

"He cleans the pool here," Kick said. And she understood then why the sight of the pool skimmer had made her skin crawl.

"She broke my goddamn nose," Klugman said, his voice muffled by the towel.

Bishop pointed the TV remote at Klugman. "You," he said. "No talking."

Klugman lowered his head.

Bishop directed the remote back at the thirty-year-old TV that faced the bed. He flipped through a few channels and then settled on an infomercial. A woman on the screen was talking about how she'd lost a hundred pounds working out just ten minutes a day on the Total Gym home fitness machine.

"I don't want to watch TV," Kick said.

Bishop slid a duffel bag out from under his bed. "You sure?" he said. "It's a great product." He set the duffel bag on top of the mattress and unzipped it. Kick couldn't see what was inside, but she had a feeling it wasn't a Total Gym. It wasn't clothing, either, because Bishop didn't get dressed.

"Did you break his nose?" Bishop asked casually.

Judging by the swelling, and the copious amount of blood flowing from Klugman's nostrils, and the pitch of his whining, Kick had no doubt she'd broken his nose. "I think so," she said.

"Bad idea," Bishop said. He was bent over the bag, sorting through it, things just sort of swinging as he moved. It made it difficult for Kick to concentrate.

"I was subduing him," Kick said.

"I know," Bishop said. He straightened up and

306 • CHELSEA CAIN

faced her, full frontal. "But it makes the next part harder."

"The next part?" Kick looked away, exasperated. "You know you're naked, right?"

"I sleep naked," Bishop said. "That way I'm ready to go when the ladies drop by in the middle of the night 'to talk.'"

"Well, I would like you to put on some pants," Kick said.

"I will," Bishop said. He smiled to himself as he extracted a pair of handcuffs and a roll of duct tape from the bag. Klugman was already backing against the wall. "In a minute."

35

KICK KNEW SOMETHING ABOUT being scared. James was scared, every night in that basement, when the rats would come out through the toilet pipes. Kick had lived in terror, in the dark, for months before she was allowed into the rest of the house. Her childhood had been defined by fear: fear of Mel, fear of being taken away from him. So she was not particularly concerned when Bishop wrestled Klugman to the ground, handcuffed him to the metal frame at the bottom corner of the bed, taped his mouth, and left him bug-eyed and moaning as Bishop went about casually putting on his pants.

Kick understood then why the TV had to be so loud.

The stained orange reading chair smelled like dirty socks. Kick sat in it with her bare legs pulled tightly under her, her eyes on Klugman, who was huddled on the floor against the bed, blood bubbling from his nose as he struggled for breath.

On the TV, Chuck Norris was making the Total Gym workout look easy.

"He's suffocating," Kick said.

"Remember when I said that breaking his nose

was a bad idea?" Bishop said, buttoning his pants. "That's what I meant."

He got a roll of plastic sheeting out of the duffel bag and rolled it out on the carpet in front of Klugman. Then he grabbed Klugman by the back of the collar and wrenched him forward, on top of the plastic. "We need to talk about James," Bishop said.

Klugman twisted his head toward Kick, his eyes rolling in their sockets. She could smell his sweat and blood, the chemical odor of the plastic.

"Don't look at her," Bishop said, taking Klugman firmly by the chin. "Look at me. Do you remember James?"

Klugman was right to be scared. Bishop was scary. He was scarred and scratched and stitched together. The angles of his face made him look hard. It was like that night he had come for her in her apartment, like he could make himself into a different person when he wanted to.

"Well?" Bishop said.

Klugman hesitated and then made a little noise under the duct tape.

"No?" Bishop said. He frowned and released Klugman's chin. "The little boy you kept behind the wall in your basement with all the travel posters and the broken toilet?" He pulled the photograph from his jeans and held it in front of Klugman's face. "Bring back any memories?"

Kick was filled with loathing. Klugman hadn't recognized her at first. But James? He had sold James like he was some used piece of furniture.

She wanted Bishop to make him pay.

"Give me the name of the man who bought him," Bishop said.

Blood frothed from Klugman's deformed nose. It gurgled and popped as he tried to breathe. The tendons on his neck were like rails and his face was growing steadily more purple.

On the TV, Chuck Norris was talking to someone who'd lost thirty pounds working out just ten minutes a day on the Total Gym.

"Do you have something you want to say?" Bishop asked, ripping off the tape.

Klugman sucked in a huge gulp of air. "I can't breathe," he gasped.

Bishop dangled the piece of tape in front of Klugman's face. "How can you expect me to help you with your problems if you don't help me with mine?" Bishop asked.

"I never met him," Klugman said, still panting. Blood ran from his nose like snot, his white shirt already stained with it. "We made arrangements online."

"How did you make the transfer?" Bishop asked.

Klugman didn't answer.

"He took James somewhere," Kick said. "He left the house with James and came back with a new car."

Bishop reached for the duffel bag. The muscles in his torso cast shadows as he moved. The tiny black stitches poked out of his back like quills on a porcupine. "Do you think of yourself as lucky?" he asked Klugman.

Klugman's eyes were huge.

"Look at this," Bishop said, showing Klugman his neck. "You see this scar? My brother was abducted and murdered by a man like you when we were kids."

He took a pair of latex gloves out of the bag and put them on, stretching them and snapping them into place like a surgeon.

"He could have taken both of us," he said. "But he cut my throat and left me for dead."

The room was cold, but the AC didn't switch off. Kick's arms were covered in goose bumps, but she didn't move, didn't dare breathe.

"I don't know why he took my brother and not me," Bishop said. He extracted a straight razor from the bag and set it on the plastic sheeting.

Klugman looked terrified, his eyes pleading at Kick. She didn't offer anything in response; she kept her face expressionless.

"Do you think that makes me lucky?" Bishop asked. He took Klugman by the chin again, forcing Klugman to look at him. Tears streamed down Klugman's face. "Yeah," Bishop said slowly. "I go back and forth on that one too." He dropped his hand and sat back on his heels. "It made me angry for a long time," he said. "I'll admit, it led to some unhealthy life choices." His hand moved back to the bag, and Kick saw Klugman start to blubber before she even saw the orange Black & Decker drill. "But then I had the opportunity to spend time with that man again. And I—" Bishop glanced at Kick and then leaned in close to Klugman. "Let's just say that I was able to work through some of my anger," he said.

Klugman squirmed and wrenched his wrists against the cuffs.

"And you know," Bishop said, sitting back with a wistful smile, "ever since, I've felt a lot better."

Klugman was shaking now. "You're crazy," he rasped.

Bishop picked up the straight razor. He *did* look crazy. "But I'm fun."

The moment Bishop started to move that razor toward him, Klugman went to pieces. "He left the cash at a bus stop," Klugman stammered, sniveling. "And I left him the boy."

"What do you mean you left him the boy?" Bishop asked.

"I told him his mother wanted him back," Klugman said, cringing against the side of the bed. "I told him to wait right there on the bench for her."

The image of James sitting on that bench, buoyant with anticipation, made Kick's throat burn. "You son of a bitch," she said.

"That's all I know," Klugman whimpered.

"I need you to go back to your room, Kick," Bishop said.

The razor was still in his hand.

Kick hesitated. She studied Bishop for some clue, some indication of what she was supposed to do. But he gave her nothing. She took a deep breath. "I want to watch," she said.

Bishop looked at her, but his face was a mask.

"This isn't pretend," he said carefully. "I'm going to start hurting him. So if you're uncomfortable with that, you should go now."

Klugman was crying, shoulders heaving, sputtering blood. If he was holding back anything, they would know. If they were going to sell it, Kick knew she had to play along. "I'm not uncomfortable with that," she said.

Bishop moved so quickly, Kick wasn't sure what happened next. He held Klugman's head to the ground, on the plastic, and then Kick saw the razor in the air, and Klugman howled. Bishop cupped his hand over Klugman's mouth until the howls turned to quiet weeping.

Then he let him go and sat back on his heels, slightly out of breath, a fine spray of blood on his bare chest.

Vomit burned in Kick's throat. Klugman was in a fetal position, blood where his ear used to be.

"Holy fuck," she said through her hands.

Bishop dropped a small chunk of flesh on the plastic sheeting. "I told you it wasn't pretend," he said as he wiped the blood off the blade onto the thigh of Klugman's white pants.

An overwhelming smell of urine filled the room. Kick suppressed a gag.

"I know his online handle," Klugman croaked through his sobs.

"I'm listening," Bishop said.

"It's Iron Jacket," Klugman said. "I don't know anything else, I swear."

Bishop exhaled. "Okay," he said. He closed the straight razor and dropped it back in the duffel bag. "That name mean anything to you?" he asked.

The first infomercial had ended, and now dozens of people were doing Zumba on the TV screen while an instructor shouted encouragement over Latin dance music.

"The name, Kick, does it mean anything?" Bishop said.

Kick took a shaky breath and lowered her hands from her mouth. "No," she said.

Bishop peeled off a bloody latex glove. "Why don't you go to your room and get dressed," he said to her. He gazed around the room. "It will take me a few minutes to pack and clean up."

Kick nodded and got up and walked wordlessly to the door. The plastic orange juice jug was still on the carpet.

"Iron Jacket tried to buy you," Klugman called after her. "He offered Mel ten grand, but Mel said he wouldn't part with you for less than fifteen."

"That's a lie," Kick said. She faced forward, not looking back. "Mel was nothing like you."

36

KICK HAD PACKED HER plastic Target bag and
was perched on her psychedelic tropical-print
bedspread, waiting, when Bishop knocked. She
opened the door to her room and found him
fully dressed, the suitcase in one hand, the duffel
bag slung over his shoulder. He was in a jaunty
mood.

"You ready?" he asked. "We're all checked out."
He offered her a stale-looking pastry on a small,
limp paper plate. "Danish," he said. "From the
lobby."

Kick looked down at the Danish. Then up at
Bishop. "Did you kill him?" she asked.

She could see her reflection in Bishop's sunglasses, but she couldn't see his eyes. He leaned
forward, his expression unchanged. "No," he said
quietly. "I called the police. They'll be by to pick
him up by checkout. I left the TV on so he can
learn to Zumba. Can we go now?" He adjusted the
shoulder strap of the duffel bag. "Or am I going
after Iron Jacket by myself?"

Kick picked up her purse and the Target bag
and followed him out the door with the Dan-

ish. The sky was bright peach and the motel had
started to come alive. A couple of kids played in
the pool while their dad drank coffee and looked
at his phone on a deck chair. A housekeeper in
a pink dress pushed a cart full of folded white
towels along the veranda. Kick glanced across
the courtyard at Bishop's room, where a Do Not
Disturb sign hung on the doorknob. Her hair
was wet and fell in heavy curtains on either side
of her face. It smelled like hotel shampoo, a scent
she recognized but couldn't place. They were
crossing the concrete deck near the pool's edge
when Kick stopped. She studied the pool around
her feet.

"Bishop," she called hoarsely.

He turned and sighed and walked back to her
with his bags.

"This is the spot," she whispered. She had
punched him hard. He had bled. She'd seen him
bleed. Kick's voice caught in her throat. "The
blood's gone."

"I cleaned it up," Bishop said.

Kick glanced around the courtyard. The pool
vac, the skimmer, all of it was gone.

Now she felt bad for taking a shower when he'd
been so hard at work. "I have incredibly long hair,"
she tried to explain. It took a lot of upkeep. People
didn't understand.

"I didn't notice that," Bishop said, starting to
walk again.

Kick could see the roof of the Impala over the

concrete-block wall that separated the courtyard from the parking lot.

"We have to talk," Kick said.

Bishop stopped. "Can we do it in the car?" he asked over his shoulder.

"No."

Bishop exhaled. "Okay." He dropped his bags and walked back to her. He scratched the back of his neck. "Which talk do we need to have?" He raised his eyebrows. "The sex talk?"

"Oh," Kick said, alarmed. "No. I'm fine about the sex."

Bishop visibly relaxed. "That's a relief," he said. "Okay, what, then?"

"You cut off his ear," Kick hissed. She sucked in a breath and put her hand over her mouth. She looked around. The kids were splashing and squealing. The father was half asleep.

"Part of his ear," Bishop corrected her, lowering his voice. "He'll be fine. If he has anything to worry about, it's his nose"—he pushed his sunglasses up—"which I had nothing to do with."

Kick hesitated. "So that was all an act?" she asked. "You weren't really going to torture him?"

"Of course not," Bishop said.

Kick laughed with relief. Bishop had been trying to scare Klugman. And it had worked, and now they had a lead. They were that much closer to the man who had hurt Monster and James. This was all very, very excellent. She tore off a piece of Danish and ate it, and her eyes fell back on the door to Bishop's room.

Bishop started for the car.

The back of Kick's neck itched.

"Of course not, it wasn't an act?" she asked, running to catch up with him. "Or of course not, you weren't really going to torture him?"

37

KICK STARED STRAIGHT AHEAD out the windshield and tried not to think about the fact that she was speeding through the desert in a dirty Impala with a trunkful of torture implements and a man who packed plastic sheeting and duct tape in his carry-on.

Bishop was eating sunflower seeds he'd bought at a gas station a few miles back. Adam Rice's face had been on a Missing Child poster on the gas station's front door; Kick spotted it when she went in to ask for the bathroom key. But if Bishop had noticed it, he didn't say anything. Every so often he spit five or six sunflower seed shells into a Styrofoam to-go coffee cup. The sound rattled Kick's nerves.

"Does the name help?" she asked.

Bishop had been texting or on the phone since they'd left the motel. He glanced over at her. "Iron Jacket," he said. "Catchy, right?" The road in front of them was reflected in his aviator sunglasses, empty desert on both sides.

"That's a no, isn't it?"

"It gets us closer."

Kick rested her head against the seat back. The

Impala's windshield was spattered with dead bugs. They passed a billboard for some tribal casino.

"There's a lot of data to sift through," Bishop said. "The big users are actively monitored. He's not one of them, at least not with that handle. It may take a little time." He dribbled some more sunflower seed shells into the coffee cup.

Kick fiddled with her seat belt. Then adjusted the sun visor. Then readjusted the sun visor.

She dialed up James's digital medical chart. His blood pressure was down and they'd started him on broad-spectrum antibiotics.

Kick let her eyes drift out the side window. In front of them, the foothills were shades of violet. Except for the occasional billboards, the landscape, as far as Kick could see, was barren. The window was hot from the sun.

Another billboard for the same casino appeared on the horizon. An Indian chief in full headdress was extending a peace pipe in apparent celebration of the fact that Dionne Warwick would be appearing. But the illustrator had given the chief a pipe tomahawk. It could be used as a pipe or as a hatchet in close combat. One end was the pipe of peace, the other was the ax of war.

"Can I see the photo?" she asked Bishop.

He dipped into his pocket and handed her the photo of James as a kid with Klugman. Kick held it delicately in her palm. The corners of the photo were soft, and it was warm from Bishop's body heat. It smelled like mildew.

"Mel said that Iron Jacket posted pictures," Kick said. "And Klugman said he communicated with him online. If Iron Jacket is a pedophile and he's on the Internet, then he's on the porn sites. You have to upload new images before they give you access. So he's communicating with people. There's an online trail."

"If he's trading images, he's careful," Bishop said. "He probably uses peer-to-peer file sharing."

"Someone knows who he is," Kick said. "It's a community. And he's putting the community in danger. He makes them look bad."

"He makes pedophiles look bad?"

"He's a sadist," Kick said. "A killer. Yeah, I'd say he makes pedophiles look bad. But they're all too afraid to report him because if they know him, he knows them."

"How does that help us?"

"Put me in a chat room," Kick said. She didn't know why she hadn't thought of it before. "I grew up with these people. I know how to talk to them. Someone knows who this guy is. We'll do a video. So they can see me. We can upload it to a few of the popular sites. I'm a legend, Bishop. Someone will want to impress me."

Bishop's attention wavered between Kick and the highway. He didn't exactly leap at the idea.

"You took me to see Mel," Kick pressed.

"Yeah," Bishop said. "One dying pedophile strapped to a bed. And for the record," he added, "I was against that. You're talking about going in front of a million pedophiles, many of whom have probably jacked off to your image."

"I know," Kick said. She fiddled with the wire ring. She had done all kinds of things that scared her. She had jumped out of an airplane with a parachute on her back; she had testified in court; she had gone off with Bishop despite the fact that she knew she couldn't trust him. She could do this one thing, for James.

Bishop was looking at the road. Heat rippled the pavement ahead of them. "Okay," he said. "I'll set it up. I know some people in Portland who are good with computers."

"Good," Kick said, a little surprised that Bishop hadn't tried harder to talk her out of it.

The landscape went by in shades of brown.

They passed the exit for the casino, a tall, shimmering gold tower of glass attached to what looked like a mall. The parking lot was filled with cars. Where did all those people come from?

"You're not really married, right?" Kick asked.

"*Now* you ask," Bishop said with a smile.

"Those sunflower seeds are disgusting," Kick said.

Bishop emptied some more into his mouth. "It was the healthiest thing they had," he said.

38

BISHOP EMERGED FROM THE airplane bedroom looking relaxed and well rested. Kick, on the other hand, had dozed in her chair and had a pit in her stomach and a dull ache behind her eyes. Her hair still smelled like cheap motel shampoo. She smelled it on the airplane and could still smell it now in Bishop's Panamera. By the time they parked in a no-parking zone in front of the Crowne Plaza office building on the corner of SW Bill Naito and Clay, she had braided her hair into a long, tight rope.

"This is where the FBI offices are," Kick said.

"Yep," Bishop said. He slapped a parking pass on the dash and got out of the car.

Kick grabbed her purse and followed him. "These are the 'people you know in Portland'?" she asked. "The FBI?"

"I know them; they're in Portland," Bishop said.

Kick sighed and gazed up at the Crowne Plaza. It took up the whole city block, eleven stories of 1970s dark glass and concrete. The FBI was on the fourth floor. She had visited many times in the months after her rescue, staring into the middle distance while men in pleated suit pants questioned her.

She jogged up the wide front stairs after Bishop and followed him through the revolving door.

The lobby of the Plaza was like any other office building lobby: there was a café and a building directory and a security desk and people in business attire drinking coffee and sitting on benches. Kick and Bishop walked across the lobby to a bank of elevators, stepped in one, and pressed the button for the fourth floor. The elevator started going up. It had brushed steel walls and tasteful lighting, but in the end they were still trapped in a metal box.

"Does Frank know about this?" Kick asked.

"Sure," Bishop said.

Of course Frank knew. Kick didn't know why, but the thought made her feel a little queasy.

The elevator chimed and came to a stop at the fourth floor. When the doors opened, Frank was waiting for them. But instead of them getting out on the fourth floor, Frank stepped into the elevator with them.

"Hey, Frank," Bishop said. "We were just talking about you." He pressed the button for the basement level and the elevator started to descend.

Frank glowered at both of them. "I don't like this," he said.

"Her idea," Bishop said, jerking a thumb at Kick.

"She's a victim," Frank hissed.

Kick waited for one of them to acknowledge the fact that she was standing right there. Neither of them did.

"You obviously have never been kicked in the nuts by her," Bishop said. "Trust me, she can take care of herself."

Frank sighed, held his hand up, and dangled a visitor badge on a black lanyard in front of Kick.

"And hello to you," Kick said, putting the lanyard on.

The three lapsed into silence.

"You slept with him, didn't you?" Frank said. He held up his hand to stop her before she could answer. "Wait. I don't want to know."

The elevator doors opened.

"You're not my father, Frank," Kick said, stepping into the basement.

"If I were, I would kick his ass," she heard Frank grumble under his breath.

The two men exited the elevator and Kick followed their lead down a concrete corridor, past the building mail room toward a fire door.

"You armed?" Frank asked Kick.

Kick adjusted the strap of her purse. "Kind of," she said.

She saw Bishop smirk.

Frank waved the ID badge clipped to his belt in front of a card reader mounted next to the fire door and the door opened. There was a desk on the other side, and a security guard, and an American flag, and a metal detector. The corridor continued beyond it.

"You sure you want to do this?" Frank asked Kick. "You've thought about what it will mean?"

Kick met his gaze. "I was there," she said, keeping her voice measured. She made a fist and felt the talisman sting her palm. "I saw what he did to James. If this will help catch him, it's worth it."

The muscles in his cheeks slackened; his eyebrows dropped. "Okay," Frank said. "This is where I get off."

"You're not staying?" Kick asked. She hadn't wanted him there, but now that he was here, she didn't want him to leave.

"I can't," Frank said simply. He looked away from her and rubbed the back of his neck.

"He doesn't want to watch," Bishop explained.

Kick nodded and took a shaky breath. That was fair. She didn't want to watch either. Frank held the door open for her. She couldn't hesitate, couldn't let them see any doubt. She squeezed the talisman tighter and stepped over the threshold. Bishop followed, and the door closed behind them.

39

THE SECURITY GUARD WHO greeted them on the other side of the door was wearing blue mascara and carrying what looked like a Glock 21 in her holster. She took Kick's purse and gave her a claim check with a number on it, then made her go through the metal detector four times. Bishop didn't have to go through the metal detector, but Kick did notice that the security guard took her time frisking him.

When the blonde decided that Bishop had been frisked enough, they were able to continue down the hall. The concrete walls were painted bone white. Fluorescent lights buzzed overhead. Corkboards lined the hall on either side at eye level, layered with bulletins and internal memos and Wanted posters and Missing Person fliers interspersed with random posters for local events. A high school production of *Joseph and the Amazing Technicolor Dreamcoat* was coming up, as well as someone's yard sale.

Kick stopped cold. Next to the yard sale notice was a new Missing Child flier for Adam Rice. In the picture he was hugging a worn stuffed monkey to his chest and his mouth was open, laughing.

"Take it," Bishop said. He was a dozen steps ahead of her.

Kick took the flier. In another six months they'd issue another one, and then one every year after that, showing computer-generated age progressions. Adam's avatar would continue to age, even if Adam didn't.

"This is it," Bishop called from an unmarked door up ahead.

Kick tucked the flier into her pocket and hurried to catch up.

"Welcome to the cybercrime center," Bishop said.

He pressed a buzzer mounted on the wall and gave a merry wave at the camera above the door. The door unlocked and Bishop reached for the knob. "They all call it the bunker," he said. "You'll see why."

They stepped through the door, into a darkened, windowless room lit only by the glow of dozens of computer monitors. Each station had three or four flat screens of various sizes. At the front of the room, on the wall, a larger screen spun with an FBI logo screensaver. A half dozen people sat hunched over keyboards, their faces luminous in the reflected light of their monitors. Kick couldn't help but think how much James would love it.

One of the technicians pushed his task chair back from his station and stood up to greet them.

"That's Joe," Bishop told her. He smiled as Joe approached. "Joe, this is Kick Lannigan."

Joe gave Kick's hand a firm shake. He had the soft, pale physique of someone who spent most of his time motionless in a chair in a dark room. "Pleased to meet you, Ms. Lannigan," he said. "You're the reason we're all here."

"Excuse me?" Kick asked.

"Your case," Joe said. "If we'd had this up and running back when you were abducted, we might have found you a lot sooner. You're the reason we got funding."

Kick looked behind him at all the gleaming screens, every one a different image, a different website or chat room or string of addresses. "You monitor everything?"

"As much as we can," Joe said. "We also work to flush out predators. It's an uphill battle. There are hundreds of thousands of websites. We've logged ten million public IP addresses offering child porn or peer-to-peer file sharing in the U.S. alone."

The meaning of what he was saying was sinking in. "So you've seen me," Kick said.

Joe hesitated. "We have to look at the images to identify victims and perpetrators, locations," he said. He wiped his lip. "No one here enjoys it."

Kick smiled weakly. "Am I still popular?"

"The Beth Movies are still the most downloaded child pornography on the Internet," Joe said. A flash of regret crossed his face. "You probably didn't want to know that," he said.

Kick tried to shrug it off. It's not like it was news. Kick had a closet full of victim notification letters, a living memorial to her continuing presence on the Internet.

She looked over at Bishop. "I told you I was famous."

Bishop was staring intently at his phone. He glanced up distractedly. "Where do you want to do it?" he asked Joe.

"Right," Joe said, with an apologetic glance at Kick. "Follow me."

He escorted them to the back corner of the room and through a door into a small conference room with a computer station against the wall. Kick pulled the rubber band off her braid and started to untwist her hair. "Have a seat here," he said to Kick, motioning to the conference table. She glanced nervously at Bishop and then took a seat at the table. Joe sat down at the computer station and powered up its four monitors. Then he hit a switch, and a light came on directly over Kick's head. The sudden spotlight made her squirm. She dragged her fingers through her hair to comb out the tangles, snagging the talisman ring in the process. Joe placed a web camera in front of Kick on the table. The sight of it made Kick's stomach hurt.

"I'm looking at a live video feed right now," Joe said. One of the monitors showed an image of a satellite map. He tapped the webcam. "You're going to look into that camera right there," he said. "Keep it short and sweet. Start by telling them who you are. We can do as many takes as you want, so no pressure."

"Wait," Bishop said. He had his hands pressed together, prayer-style, his index fingers against his lips. "You want a minute?" he asked her.

Kick dug her fingers into her thighs under the table. "Don't watch me," she said to Bishop. "Watch the monitor. I don't like being watched." She shook her hair out and quickly rebraided it to the side, in front of her left shoulder: if this was going to work, her hair had to be on the left. Then she inhaled and lifted her head, and she gazed directly into the camera. All she had to do was believe in two facts. Adam Rice was still alive. He was out there, and Iron Jacket was responsible.

She drew a picture of Adam's face in her mind's eye. "I know you know who I am," she said to the camera. "And I know you can help."

It was like she could feel the men on the other side, through the lens, their eyes roving her body; it made her skin crawl. But she couldn't think about that. She forced herself to continue. "I'm looking for a murderer, a man we think was in Portland, Oregon, just yesterday. He's been active for at least fourteen years, and he may go by some form of the name Iron Jacket." The picture of Adam shifted in her mind, and now she could only see James, the boy he'd been when they'd first met. Pain darkened Kick's face before she could stop it. She could feel herself losing control. Her throat closed. "He has a special interest in dark-haired Caucasian boys," she said. She had to clear her throat to get the words out. Her mental picture of James shifted again, and now she saw him unconscious on the ventilator. "Maybe you fool people in your lives. Maybe some of you have families." She pulled at her braid, twisting it around her fingers, eyes still fixed on the camera. Under the table, her free hand was balled into a fist. "But I know who you are." Kick stared hard at the lens. "I see you," she said. "And you owe me."

"Okay," Joe said softly. "I think we got it."

Kick lifted her eyes to Bishop. She felt lightheaded, out of breath. The back of her neck was wet with sweat. "Do you want another take?" she asked. "I can do another take."

"No," Bishop said. "It's perfect."

Joe was typing away on a keyboard, opening websites on his monitors. "Okay," he said. "I'm uploading it on several popular sites, and including a contact email." Kick watched the monitors. Red dots peppered the world map, blinking across almost every continent.

"What's all that?" Kick asked, leaning on her elbows.

"Those are all the servers currently hosting Beth Movies," Joe said over his shoulder. "We wanted to be sure to post this where you're most popular."

"Sure," Kick said.

"We're getting some responses," Joe said, focused on his center monitor.

Kick glanced brightly at Bishop. But he looked cautious. He walked over to Joe's chair, positioning himself between Kick and the screen. She stood and edged around the table. She could see part of the monitor, messages popping up one after the other.

"Anything?" she asked.

"Don't read it," Bishop said.

"If you're trying to keep me safe from the fantasies of pedophiles, you're too late," Kick said, elbowing him aside.

Bishop made room for her.

Kick put her hair behind her shoulder and leaned in so she could see the screen.

Messages were coming in so furiously that Kick barely had time to skim them. Message after message about what men wanted to do to her, what they fantasized she'd do to them, how wonderful they'd make her feel.

"It's already getting reposted to other sites," Joe said, glancing at another monitor.

"It's okay," Kick said tonelessly. Sometimes she felt so hollow it scared her. "It's not me. I don't mind."

That was Beth they were talking about, not her. And Beth was a ghost.

Kick was real; she was the one with the power now. She was the one laying the trap. The thought made her stand up a little straighter.

"I'm done here," she announced. The flier of Adam Rice that she'd taken from the bulletin board was still folded in her pocket. She was going to find him, one way or another. She made herself a promise.

There wasn't much time.

40

"IT'S TIME, BETH," HER *father said. She could hear the frustration in his voice, but she kept swimming.*

The sky was dark and full of stars. Beth's fingers were pruned. She kicked her legs and propelled herself on her back over the surface of the pool. "I don't want to."

"She's tired," her father said to the man with pale legs. "She's not usually like this."

"Let me try," the man said. He lowered himself over the edge of the pool and swam toward her. Beth kicked harder, pushing through the water, but he had long arms and caught up with her in a few strokes.

"I see you," he said. He was a head in the water now, his feet planted on the floor of the deep end. The arrows tattooed on his chest, sharp points and feathered fletching, distorted under the water, so that they seemed broken. "Are you having a nice vacation?" he asked.

She nodded, paddling in place, the water lapping at her ears.

"Your father worked hard to bring you here. He counts on you to be a good girl." The man's voice sounded muffled through the pool, distant, but there was still something in his tone that made Beth's stomach hurt. "Don't you think you owe him that?"

She could feel him getting close to her, and she strained her eyes sideways. His wet, dark hair was flattened back, like paint. The water came to his bottom lip, so that his face seemed divided into two different shapes. One of the tattooed arrows stretched up his neck, the tip pointing at his jawbone. "I know who you are," he breathed. "I know your real name."

Beth swallowed a gulp of pool water and choked, and her legs sank as she paddled frantically with her arms to stay afloat. She was still sputtering on the chlorine when she felt a viselike grip on her arm, propelling her to the black and white tiles at the edge of the pool.

41

BISHOP HEADED EAST, OVER the Hawthorne Bridge. Below them, the Willamette River looked so tranquil, but even in the summer it could kill you—if the currents didn't get you, the hypothermia would.

"Are you all right?" Bishop asked.

"Yes," Kick lied. She glanced down at the flier with Adam's photo on it in her hand.

"They don't know where you live," Bishop said.

She could tell he was trying to make her feel better; the problem was, he didn't know what was wrong.

"It's all words," he continued. "They wouldn't know what to do with you if they had you." He caught himself. "That was the wrong thing to say, wasn't it?"

Kick could feel the barrel of the Glock through the leather of the purse on her lap. "I knew what I was doing, John."

Bishop looked at her sideways. "*John*?" he said. "I'm *John* now?"

Kick shrugged. "I was just trying it out." It had sounded all wrong coming out of her mouth. It probably wasn't even his real name. "I don't like it," she added.

"I don't like it either," Bishop said.

Kick put the flier back in her purse and pulled out the Glock.

"You want me to drop you off at the hospital?" Bishop asked, with a glance at the gun.

Kick ejected the magazine, inventoried the ammo, and inserted it back in the well. It needed cleaning. "Can I get into my apartment?"

"James's place is still sealed, but there's no reason you can't access yours. You'll be alone, though: all the neighbors are out until tomorrow."

"I want to go home," Kick said. "I can drive myself to the hospital." She swallowed hard. "Will you be by later?" It sounded like a proposition. Maybe it was. She didn't know yet.

Bishop hesitated. "I'm going to head back and help Joe."

Right. He had to scour her deviant fan mail for clues. That wasn't humiliating at all.

"You need to dry-fire that before you clean it," Bishop said, nodding at the Glock.

"I know," Kick said. She peered over the sky-line at where Mount Hood was supposed to be and wasn't, but it was like it had never been there in the first place. She wanted to ask Bishop where he was going to spend the night, but it wasn't any of her business, really. She didn't know what she was to him.

"It's the right thing to do," Bishop said.

For a moment she thought he had seen through her plan.

But when she looked over at him, he seemed completely unconcerned, gazing out the windshield, one hand on the wheel. "You'll feel better sleeping in your own bed," he said.

She couldn't figure him out.

"I'm going to see you again, right?" she asked.

"We will see each other again," Bishop said.

He said it with such absolute authority that Kick almost thought he meant it.

"Good," she said.

42

"I KNOW WHO HE is," Kick whispered to James.

James's eyelids twitched. Kick lay next to him on the bed, on the side with fewer tubes, wedged between his body and the rail of his hospital bed.

His skin felt clammy and cold. "Breathe," she reminded him. The muscles of his neck strained. His forehead was shiny with sweat. His vitals skyrocketed, matched by the quickening electronic pulse of the monitor alerts, lights blinking. The doctors were weaning him off the ventilator, forcing him to take every other breath on his own. He had to decide, with each breath, if he wanted to live or die. It made Kick sick to see him struggle. She closed her eyes and put her forehead against his cheek. She could barely smell him anymore. The machine took a mechanical breath, and she felt James relax. The electronic pulses slowed.

"I've seen him," Kick whispered.

All those years, Mel was teaching her escape tricks, teaching her to be afraid. It wasn't the FBI he was worried about. He had borrowed money from a dangerous man, a fixer for the Family, a man with a military background and a child bondage fetish. A man like that, he wouldn't just invest blindly in a project: he would want to know what he was getting into; he would want to inspect the merchandise. She had met him, when she was a kid, at the Desert Rose Motel. He had made her get out of the pool that night. *You owe him,* the man had said. But a child's description and a vague memory of a tattoo were not going to help Bishop find him.

"He'll come tonight," she said.

She knew Iron Jacket was watching her. The gray Taurus had been behind them on the way down to the state pen, but it hadn't been there on the trip home, because it had turned around and doubled back as soon as Iron Jacket realized where she was headed. Her visit with Mel had been the trigger.

James was struggling to breathe again. Kick caressed his cheek. If they made it through this, she would tell him everything. All he had to do was breathe.

Poor, sweet James. "I think all of this might be my fault," she said. They had assumed that James had been attacked because of his history with Iron Jacket. But why now, after all these years? No, it had been about Mel. James and Monster had been hurt to send Mel a message. It had been a threat. *Give me what I want or I will kill your daughter. I will kill Beth.* James and Kick lived in identical apartments. If he could get to James, he could get to her. She remembered how her skin crawled when

Iron Jacket came up out of the pool next to her. *I see you.*

She took James's hand, the wire talisman pressed between them. She wondered if he could feel it too. If he even knew she was there.

The round clock on the wall said it was almost six p.m. She had to go. Kick felt a strange kind of calm settle over her.

Mel had known this day might come. He had taught her about the Comanche, about their raiding parties, how they murdered adults and took children captive. Most of the children were slaughtered, but some, the cooperative ones, the pliant ones, would be given Indian names and welcomed into the tribe. One of the greatest and most arrogant Comanche chiefs wore a vest of Spanish armor, and many believed him to have supernatural powers because the vest repelled bullets so easily. They called him Iron Jacket.

Tonight she would be ready for him. And she would make him tell her where Adam was, and she would make him pay for James, and she would get vengeance for her dog.

43

KICK TOOK HER TIME making preparations. She fieldstripped the Glock at her kitchen table, cleaned it, reassembled it, and loaded it. She kept it out as she padded around the apartment. Her apartment felt alien to her. Monster's food bowl sat half full on the kitchen floor. His toys lay strewn around her bedroom. Everywhere she looked, she saw a ghost image of James's apartment imprinted over her own. His blood on her floor. Monster, dead, in her bedroom. Kick looked for a place on her bookshelf to hide the knife, and her gaze fell on a framed photograph of her and Marnie. Her childhood pictures were limited to Befores and Afters. There were no photographs of her from the five years she'd spent with Mel and Linda, only photographs of Beth. Kick smiled faintly at the framed photo: two little kids grinning madly at the camera. They looked happy. Kick had no memories of her sister from Before, but she liked the idea that they had once gotten along. It was a good place to hide the survival knife. This one was military-grade. Case-hardened steel, and a leather grip darkened with the patina of her sweat and hand oil. She liked it so much, she'd bought two.

The throwing stars were flat and easy to stow. Kick tucked them between the pages of books that she positioned at strategic areas around the living room. She opened the end table drawer and slipped a star on top of the rubber-banded stack of Christmas cards from Frank, and the bulldog wearing a Santa hat on the top card looked back at her supportively. She said the name of each location out loud so she'd remember it. "In the book on the coffee table." "In the drawer of the end table." "Under the couch cushion." The Taser went into the utensil drawer with the forks. She folded the new Adam Rice flier on the kitchen counter and tucked a throwing star under it for good measure.

She carried the pepper spray and the rest of the knives to her bedroom, careful to keep her eyes up so that she wouldn't see Monster's blanket, and balls, and rope toys. The throwing knife with the nine-inch carbon steel blade went into her bedside table. That was the one with its center of gravity at its midpoint; it was heavy and hit hard. She scattered the four-inch blades around the room, repeating each location aloud: "In the change bowl on the dresser." "In the sock drawer." "Under the pillow." She could feel Adam watching her from the Missing Child posters on the wall. She opened her closet. The four white card-board file boxes of victim notification letters were carefully labeled with black Sharpie. One word, scrawled across each box: *Assholes*.

She tucked the pepper spray on the top box.

Satisfied that her apartment was well armed, Kick stretched, loosening up her legs with squats and lunges. Then she did fifty push-ups just to get her blood pumping.

Once she had worked up a sweat and her mus-cles felt warm and responsive, she made herself jar spaghetti sauce and meatballs and ate it alone at the kitchen table with the Glock on her lap.

She was rinsing her bowl out in the sink when she finally heard him coming. She hadn't even bothered to activate the alarm. She wanted to make it easy for him. She turned the faucet off and lis-tened. The sound of her apartment door opening was barely audible, like someone whispering in the next room. If she had not been paying atten-tion, she would not have heard it. But she'd been expecting him to come through that door. It was how he'd entered James's apartment; otherwise, why go through the trouble of disabling the hall-way security camera?

Kick put the bowl down in the sink, tossed a dish towel over the Glock, and waited. It felt strange not to have Monster there, head cocked, gazing up at her. It made her feel alone. She listened as the faint beat of footsteps moved down her apartment hallway toward the living room. She placed her feet parallel, shoulder width apart, and closed her hands into fists at her navel.

His shape came from the shadows. She saw a figure darken the far end of the hallway where it opened onto the living room. There was a flash of movement and then stillness. Kick remained motionless, watching. Slowly, excruciatingly, the shadow bent and stretched and Iron Jacket stepped into the light. He was dressed head to toe in black: a black watch cap, black gloves, a black backpack. He was as big as she remembered him. A hulk of a man, both tall and substantial. But his round, elastic face looked soft, like it belonged on someone else's body. He came at her, toward the kitchen. The tip of the arrow tattoo was just visible above the neck of his shirt. The muscles in his arms and chest seemed to pulse as he breathed. His hair, from what she could see under his cap, was cut military short.

Kick inched her hand to the edge of the dish towel and let him come to her. Like she had that night in the pool at the Desert Rose Motel. As he stepped into the kitchen, she shifted her body forty-five degrees from his centerline. Her fingertips found the butt of the Glock. "Where's Adam Rice?" she asked.

"You have something for me?" he asked. The knife seemed to come out of nowhere; he must have had it pressed against his thigh. Suddenly it was just there, in his hand, a ten-inch steel blade.

Kick kept her eyes moving between his face and the knife, alert for any shift in his movement that might signal an attack. "What do you want?" she asked as she slid her hand under the dish towel.

"The password to the offshore account," he said. His voice was low and pleasant and sent chills down her arms.

She had hoped, somehow, that in the end it would be about more. "Money," she said.

"I was supposed to get a piece of everything. Mel and I had a deal."

He had been in a neutral agile position, but now he lowered slightly into a crouch.

"Maybe we can help each other," Kick said. "Tell me where Adam is. I'll tell you the password."

The blade was angled up. She saw his thumb move on top of the knife's spine. It made for a harder thrust, so that it could penetrate more muscle, cut deeper. "What do you have under the towel, Beth?" he asked.

She closed her hand around the grip of the Glock and raised it straight out in front of her, one hand closing around the other, elbows locked, as the dish towel fell away. Her thumb hugged the grip, her index finger stretched along the muzzle, the other three fingers were secured around the grip high up, the way she'd been taught. The fingers of her left hand wrapped around the fingers of her right, her left thumb making an X over her right thumb. Feet planted under her shoulders now, she leaned forward slightly so that her hips would take the brunt of the recoil. Then she adjusted the sights to eye level and lined up the three white dots, centering the middle one on Iron Jacket's sternum, and placed her finger gently over the trigger. Her grip was relaxed, her breathing even. She had practiced this a thousand times. She knew how to squeeze the trigger, to wait until the end of an exhalation, and then tighten her finger slowly until it fired. "Where's Adam Rice?" she asked again.

Iron Jacket smiled at her. She tried to stay focused on the gun sights, on his sternum, but she could see his slow grin at the top edge of her vision. He shrugged his backpack off his shoulder and let it drop to the kitchen floor. It made a loud sound, like it was full of tools.

Kick leveled the Glock's sights at the center of his face. "Stop," she said, but he continued toward her.

"Kill me," he said, "you never find the boy."

She hesitated, shifting her aim, trying to find a safe place to shoot him. The head and torso had too much bone mass, vital organs, nerve bundles; between the shock wave and the shrapnel, she couldn't risk it. But if she went for an arm or leg, she might nick his femoral or brachial arteries. He'd bleed out in minutes.

She angled the muzzle downward and aimed the sights at his foot. The bullet would shatter the bones, hobble him, make him hurt. But before she could fire Iron Jacket lunged toward her and she had to raise the gun to keep him back. He held the knife in his right hand, his left extended toward her. She'd studied knife combat. The left hand was his lead hand, the one that would set up the attack. He was in a mobile stance, his weight on the balls of his feet, knees slightly bent.

She saw his eyes flick over her arms. That's how you disarmed an opponent: you went for the joints above the wrists and elbows, or for the veins on the insides of the arms. You cut the tendons, you let the person bleed, you took the weapon. It was easy then to take your opponent by the head and thrust your blade into the hollow cavity below the jaw.

Iron Jacket was inside the grappling zone. She only had a second to react.

He brought his lead hand in toward her shoulder and she fired reflexively, jerking the trigger rather than squeezing it.

Iron Jacket grunted when the bullet hit. An exhalation of surprise, followed by a sigh. Kick staggered back, out of the grappling zone, breathing hard. The smell of gunpowder filled the room. Iron Jacket was still standing, the knife in his fist, upright, alert, seemingly unharmed. She searched his body for the entry point, hoping for a through-and-through, something painful but not deadly.

Then Iron Jacket slowly stepped sideways and pivoted, revealing a figure behind him. Kick's stomach dropped. Bishop stood there, one hand pressed against his shoulder, blood between his fingers.

Kick glanced down at the Glock she had just fired. Then back up at Bishop.

"That's . . . why . . . I don't . . . like guns," Bishop said.

Iron Jacket stepped beside Bishop and drove an elbow hard into his skull, flattening him.

44

KICK WATCHED, TERRIFIED, AS Iron Jacket unpacked his backpack on her kitchen table. He'd pushed the table to the wall and she couldn't see exactly what he was unpacking from her position on the floor, but every item he set down made a sickening clunk. She tried to wriggle her hand out of the handcuff that Iron Jacket had used to cuff her wrist to Bishop's, but it was useless. Their hands were secured on either side of the steel handle of her refrigerator. Sitting on the floor with her back against the fridge, her wrist shackled above her head, she couldn't get a good angle to even see the lock.

She nudged Bishop with her foot, trying to rouse him, but he was deadweight, his arm hanging like meat from the cuff, his body slumped to the side, head hung over his chest. His blood smeared the fridge door between them. The bullet had gone through his shoulder and out his back, leaving a silver-dollar-size hole in his T-shirt and exposing flesh the color of raspberry jam underneath.

He'd come to help her. He *had* figured out what she was up to. He must have noticed the hair, that she'd put it to the left. Beth had done that only once, only in the first movie, before Mel had told her it was prettier on the right.

She bent her knee, drew her leg up, and thrust the ball of her foot into Bishop's thigh.

He drew a sharp breath and opened his eyes, then winced in pain as he pushed himself up into a sitting position with his feet.

He was awake. Kick practically sobbed with relief. She glanced at Iron Jacket. He was examining the edge of a new knife he'd just unpacked.

Bishop blinked woozily down at his shoulder. "You shot me," he said.

"Sorry," Kick said. They didn't have time for this. Iron Jacket looked over at them from the table. "You need to get us out of here," Kick hissed at Bishop.

"Where's the gun?" Bishop asked.

"On the table," Kick said. What was she supposed to have done? "He made me give it to him. He threatened to cut your throat."

Bishop glanced bleakly up at their cuffed hands. "He's going to cut my throat anyway," he said.

"No he's not," Kick said. "Because you're going to get us out of here."

Bishop gave the handcuffs an obligatory tug. "Can you open these?"

"I only know how to do it with a paper clip," Kick said. She didn't have a paper clip. Couldn't he see that? Bishop was looking past her. She saw his eyes darken, and she turned to see Iron Jacket swinging a length of heavy chain and gazing up at the exposed beam that ran the length of her kitchen ceiling. He positioned one of her kitchen chairs under it, slung one end of the chain over the pipe, and hooked the chain to some sort of winch. "What's he doing?" she whispered.

Bishop took a slow breath. "He thinks you have some kind of password?"

Kick nodded.

"Do you, by any chance?"

"No," Kick said. Iron Jacket attached the nylon cord from the winch to his belt loop and snatched something off the table before he crossed toward them. Kick pressed herself against the fridge and wedged herself against Bishop. A black strap dangled from Iron Jacket's hand. The winch made a *click-click-click* sound as the cord unspooled. Kick squeezed her eyes shut.

"He's not coming for you," Bishop said.

She opened her eyes. Bishop gave her a wan smile. She didn't understand. *Click-click-click.*

Iron Jacket squatted in front of Bishop and squinted at the wound in his shoulder. "I don't like people sticking their noses in my business," Iron Jacket said.

Bishop didn't look away. "Whatever happens, I can handle it," he told her. Iron Jacket slapped him hard across the face, and Bishop's head slammed against the fridge door. Kick screamed and curled her knees against her chest. Iron Jacket took Bishop's free hand and wrapped the black strap several times around Bishop's wrist.

"It's okay," Bishop said to Kick. His cheek and jaw were red. His eyes swam. Blood collected at the corner of his mouth. "I can handle it."

Iron Jacket lifted Bishop's wrists together overhead, wrenching Bishop's shoulder. Bishop made a grunting sound, and Kick could see him steeling himself against the pain as Iron Jacket bound his wrists together with the strap.

This wasn't how it was supposed to work.

Bishop was going to rescue her. That's why he was here.

Iron Jacket unsnapped the cord from his pants and hooked it to Bishop's wrists, then unlocked Bishop from the handcuffs they shared and secured Kick directly to the fridge.

"I'm sorry," Bishop mumbled to her.

The winch started to retract, and Bishop's arms lifted as the nylon cord stretched taut. *Click-click-click* went the winch. Kick watched in horror as the cord lifted Bishop's wrists.

"I don't have the password," Kick called after Iron Jacket, panicked. "I swear. I don't know anything about it." But Iron Jacket barely glanced at her as he walked back to the winch and then stood there, waiting.

Bishop was pulled forward, onto his knees. He swayed there briefly. "I'm going to try to stay conscious long enough to buy you time," he said to Kick.

She didn't know what he meant. Buy her time to do what?

He wrapped his hands around the cord, got one foot in front of him, and managed to get shakily to his feet, then stumbled forward, away from her, following the cord drawing him to Iron Jacket. He came to a stop underneath the winch, next to Iron Jacket, and gazed upward as the retracting cable lifted his wrists above his head. *Click-click-click-click.* Bishop took a sharp breath, arched his back, and was lifted off the floor.

He hung like that for a long moment, dangling there, his back to her, every vein in his arms visible, fingers splayed.

And then Iron Jacket spun him around toward her. Bishop's face was red and contorted, the muscles of his neck taut, threads of saliva hanging from his chin, and she could hear him wheezing, struggling to breathe, his arms pressed against the sides of his head, his toes just inches from the floor.

"Wrist suspension puts pressure on the muscle sheath around the chest, compressing the lungs," Iron Jacket said. He threaded his gloved hands in front of him and leveled his gaze at her. His face was smooth, unworried, a man without a concern in the world. "He'll suffocate if we leave him there too long." He lifted his chin toward Bishop's bound wrists. "Then there's the strap," he said. "It presses against nerves and cuts off circulation to the hands." He frowned sympathetically, and Kick noticed that Bishop's hands appeared to be darkening even as she watched, going from dark pink to crimson. "See there, how his finger's twitching," Iron Jacket said.

Kick would have told him whatever he wanted to know. He should know that. He should know that she would cooperate if she could. "I swear," she pleaded with him. "I don't know any passwords. I don't care about some old bank account. You can have it."

"You think you're so clever," Iron Jacket said. "You had Mel wrapped around your little finger. But you don't fool me. You think he came up with the idea of putting all the proceeds away for you on his own?"

All the proceeds?

"You're still a big earner," he added. "I see the statements every month. That was Mel's way of shoving it in my face."

Bishop had his head back and was looking up at his wrists, his fingers pulling uselessly at the cord. His shirt was darkened with sweat and blood, so that she couldn't tell where one left off.

"What kind of password is it?" Kick asked, stalling. "A word? A number? Does it have to have a symbol? I can figure it out. Give me a minute."

Iron Jacket unthreaded his hands and looked right at her as he shifted his stance. She knew what was coming an instant before Iron Jacket placed his palm over his fist and drove an elbow hard into Bishop's gut, before she heard Bishop's sharp, guttural exhalation of pain. Iron Jacket stepped away, and Bishop swung back and forth from the winch.

Kick's mind grasped for anything. "The Desert

Rose? Or November tenth—that was the birthday Mel made up for me. Or Kwikset—that's the first lock I learned to pick."

It worked. Iron Jacket left Bishop, went to the table, where he had unpacked his backpack, picked up a BlackBerry, and typed with his thumbs on the keypad.

Kick willed one of the passwords to work. Bishop swung from the winch, pale and limp. His body seemed longer, more concave, like he was slowly deflating.

Iron Jacket threw the BlackBerry down on the table in disgust. "I never liked you," he said to Kick. "I always thought you were a spoiled little bitch." He dug through his backpack, and Kick half expected he was looking for a weapon to kill her with right there, but instead he pulled out a plastic bottle of water and drained it. He put the empty bottle back in the pack and grinned to himself. "That's better," he said, wiping his mouth. He turned on his heel, stepped back to Bishop, and took him by the waist of his pants. His eyes gleamed as they roamed Bishop's weakened body. "How do you feel?" he asked Bishop.

Bishop lifted his head and Kick could see him muster his strength. "Never . . . better," he said.

Iron Jacket gave him a little push, so Bishop swayed away and back; then Iron Jacket leveled his shoulders and brought his fists in front of his own face. He danced around Bishop, like a boxer circling a punching bag, face merry, throwing

fake little jabs as Bishop hung there, too weakened to flinch as the fake punches crossed in front
of him.

"Mel's birthday?" Kick tried in desperation.
"Linda's maiden name?"

"Think harder," Iron Jacket said. He pushed off
his back foot, took a small step forward, and threw
a real punch, jabbing his fist into Bishop's rib cage.
Bishop's lips contracted and he groaned horribly.
The tendons in his neck drew taut like ropes. Iron
Jacket returned his punching arm to starting position, his left fist at his ear. Bishop's head flopped
forward.

Iron Jacket put his weight on his back foot again.

"You had a wife," Kick said quickly. "Back at the
Desert Rose." She was desperate to distract him, to
keep him talking.

"So?"

"She's dead, isn't she?" It was a shot in the dark,
a wild guess. Kick barely remembered her from the
motel, just a vague presence, but she'd be the right
age, and matched the general physical description,
of the dead body they had found in the house in
Seattle. Iron Jacket pitched forward, slightly off
balance, and had to adjust his stance, and she knew
that she was right. "She rented the house using the
name Josie Reed," Kick said.

Iron Jacket wiped the saliva off his mouth again
with the back of his glove. "Twenty-five years we
had an arrangement. She didn't have a problem
with it until I brought home a girl." He leaned

back, pushed off, and punched Bishop in the solar plexus. Kick heard herself cry out. Bishop's body buckled, his face twisted, his fingers splayed, then he hung limply. Iron Jacket swung him gently back and forth.

Bishop coughed, so she knew he was still alive. When he lifted his head, his eyes were bleary and there was blood and saliva on his chin. "Ever thought of using power tools?" he asked. Even half dead, he managed a smirk. "I find . . . it adds . . . a little finesse."

Iron Jacket's eyes glowered, and Kick could see him draw back his elbow.

"*Watership Down*?" she called out. "That was my favorite book. Mel read it to me."

Iron Jacket hesitated, and then opened his fist, pivoted smoothly away from Bishop, and picked up his BlackBerry again.

The wheeze of Bishop's breathing was barely audible now. Every few moments his mouth would open and his rib cage would jerk, and he'd suck in a small gulp of air. It wouldn't be much longer. The blood slowed in Kick's veins and a cold chill settled on her skin. And then Iron Jacket would kill her.

Iron Jacket put the BlackBerry down, and when he returned to Bishop this time, there was something impatient about his posture, his shoulder twitched, and his mouth was tight.

"She doesn't . . . know . . . the fucking password," Bishop muttered between agonizing gasps.

Iron Jacket snarled at him, leaned back, and jammed his fist into the side of Bishop's face.

Kick's hands fisted reflexively. Why the idea came to her this time, and not after any of the other punches had been thrown, she didn't know; maybe because this particular hit was so brutal, her whole body winced. This time she clenched her fists the way she'd been taught, thumb outside, wrapped around her fingers. And that's when she felt the ring.

James's talisman, his wire man, still wrapped around her finger.

Wire would work just like a paper clip.

Kick's heart skittered as she tried to pick the end of the wire loose.

Iron Jacket was focused on Bishop, his back to Kick.

Blood ran down Bishop's face and neck where Iron Jacket's fist had connected. He looked dazed. His head lolled. "There you go," he murmured to Iron Jacket, though Kick felt a stab of certainty that the words were intended for her.

Her fingers were clumsy from being elevated in the cuffs, but Kick managed to unwind a finger's length of wire. She tried to keep it hidden in her hands, but it was too hard to manipulate. If Iron Jacket looked at her, he was sure to see what she was doing. But she had to risk it. Bishop was barely conscious. Kick felt for where the notch should go and then bent it.

"I'm going to bleed you out through your

abdominal aorta," Iron Jacket announced, and Kick almost dropped the wire.

She looked back and forth between Bishop and Iron Jacket.

Bishop's glazed eyes appeared sightless, fixed straight ahead. "Sounds messy," he mumbled.

Kick's hands trembled. She couldn't manipulate the wire. Her fingers were cold and clumsy, like they belonged to someone else. She watched as Iron Jacket slid a rectangular leather case from his backpack and folded it open on the table. Kick tried to block out the fact that she recognized that case, that she knew it was for hunting knives. She just needed another minute or two. "Please," she begged. "Iron Jacket, please."

His head jerked up at her. "My name's Dennis," Iron Jacket said with an amused smile.

Dennis. He was looking right at her now. She kept the wire tucked in her palm, afraid to move.

"How are you going to do it?" Bishop asked, drawing Iron Jacket's attention away from her again.

Kick bent the second notch on the wire.

"Eight-inch carbon steel blade," Iron Jacket said. He lowered his head back to the table. "It's sharp. Sometimes I have to dig a little to find the aorta."

Bishop coughed, and more blood gurgled down his chin. His teeth were wet with it. "What's that take you . . . three, four minutes?" he asked.

She could tell it was requiring everything he had to stay conscious. He could barely lift his head anymore. His mouth was having trouble forming words.

Kick felt around for the first keyhole and managed to insert the end of the wire.

"Closer to three," Iron Jacket said distractedly.

Bishop's eyes fell on Kick. "That should be enough time."

She felt the give of the wire as it hooked the inside of the lock, and she twisted her hands around to rotate it. The bracelet opened and Kick felt tears of relief slide down her cheeks. She kept her hand in the unlocked cuff and worked on the second keyhole.

"What are you using?" Bishop asked.

"A modified spear-point blade, plus a combination saw and deer-gutting hook blade."

Hook blades were used to "unzip" the deer without puncturing its innards, like what had been done to Monster. But Kick couldn't think about that—not now.

"You like the polymer handle," Bishop asked, "or wood?"

"Polymer."

"I like a . . . wooden grip," Bishop said, his words slurring. "Feels . . . warmer."

She almost had it. Bishop was quiet, his chin against his chest. But she couldn't think about that now, couldn't notice how still his body was, or the fact that he wasn't making any sounds at all. He'd been quiet before. He was gathering his strength.

The second lock clicked open.

Kick quietly slid her wrists out of the cuffs and started to back away on the kitchen floor as Iron Jacket turned to Bishop with a knife in his hand.

Kick fought frantically to mentally catalog all the weapons she'd hidden in the kitchen, their locations and functionality.

She would have one chance.

She had to make the right choice.

Iron Jacket slid Bishop's T-shirt up and felt along his rib cage and over his sunken abdomen, as if locating the correct incision spot by touch.

Kick got to her feet. "Dennis," she called.

Iron Jacket turned, startled.

Kick snatched the throwing star out from under the Adam Rice Missing Child flier, held it horizontally, aimed, and then, keeping her elbow close, extended her arm straight forward and released the star with a flick of her wrist. For a second she wasn't sure she'd hit her target. Everything slowed. The blade sank into the wall. Iron Jacket whirled toward it. Bishop seemed to pause, suspended in the air. Then the nylon cord snapped in two where she had sliced it, and Bishop slammed into the floor.

Everything was still.

"Bishop?" Kick called. He lay on the floor, not moving.

Iron Jacket pointed at her with the end of his knife. "I see you," he said in a singsong voice, like that night at the pool. "You fucking little bitch." He drew toward her, keeping the knife between them,

and adjusted his grip, extending his thumb alongside the blade so that the knife was poised to slash.

Kick backed away from him. When he lunged he
wouldn't go for her torso—too much muscle and
bone; he wouldn't want to risk getting the blade
stuck in her rib cage. He'd go for tendons or arteries, or her eyes, or her neck. She lifted her elbows
to provide some shield and to protect the insides of
her arms. "You can't hurt me," she reminded him.
"You still need the password."

"I have a Plan B," Iron Jacket said.

He dipped forward and thrust his knife at her
and she sidestepped to the left of his arm, just
enough for him to pass her. She was at his shoulder,
almost behind him, forcing him to pivot in order
to come after her. He thrust at her again with the
knife, and this time she stepped forward, holding
on to his right arm with her left and moving toward
his centerline, close to his chest. By using her body
to block his view of his knife, the move would buy
her a second, maybe. Her right fist tucked at her
breast, thumb snug against her index finger, elbow
behind her, she thrust her fist forward, into his
throat, aiming for the notch below his Adam's apple.
He dodged and she connected a little to the left, her
knuckles driving hard into the meat of his neck. He
let out a howl of fury and she dove away from him,
to the couch, snapped up the throwing star she'd
hidden under the book there, and whirled back to
face him.

His eyes were pink with rage. His mouth

twitched and he made a noise like a low growl. She held the throwing star vertically and raised it above her head, ready to strike.

"That's why you took Mia Turner," she said. "To make her do movies."

"She had star potential, Beth. Just like you. Mel always said the secret was to find a good girl."

Kick snapped her arm forward and released the star, shifting her weight onto her front foot. Iron Jacket grunted as the five-bladed star sank in his chest. His face went scarlet. He pulled the star free from his chest muscle and tossed it to the floor. The knife now in his left hand, he came at her. The bloody notch of torn fabric on his shirt was the only hint she'd injured him. It hadn't slowed him at all.

"When I kill you," he said, "I'm going to film it and put it all over the Internet. One last Beth Movie. All your fans can imagine themselves fucking your corpse."

She tried to step around him again, but he backhanded her. This time she didn't see it coming; he was too close. She flew sideways and was barely able to relax into the fall. She hit the floor, slid, rolled, and bounced back onto her feet.

Blood ran from her nose. She spit some out of her mouth. Her cheek blazed.

"That's enough, Beth," Iron Jacket said.

"Stop calling me that." Kick looked him in the eye, stepped forward, transferred her weight, consciously relaxed the muscles in her striking arm, straightened it, and jammed it into his solar plexus.

He managed to catch her wrist just in time, and he pulled her into his arms and wrapped her in a bear hug, the knife still in his hand, now inches from her face. She kicked and clawed at him, sputtering, growling at him. "Shh, Beth," he said, tightening the pressure around her chest. She remembered his smell. His sweat. She remembered the feel of his hand on her arm in the pool. "Beth, I'm not going to let you go until you calm down." She twisted, trying to get free, but her feet were off the floor and she couldn't get leverage. "Shh, Beth," he said again. "You need to relax now, okay?" Tears slid down her cheeks and she nodded. She exhaled a shaky breath as she let her body go limp. "Good," he said. "Good."

"Enough," Bishop said.

Kick jerked her head up at the sound of his voice.

He was propped against the wall, like it was the only thing keeping him upright. His face was half covered in blood and he was grimacing in pain. But his eyes were open. He was conscious. And he had Kick's Glock held between his bound hands. "Step away from her," Bishop said.

Iron Jacket's grip didn't loosen. The knife glinted near Kick's eye. If Bishop took a nonlethal shot, Iron Jacket would cut her throat. Bishop would have to go for his head. And then Iron Jacket would be dead.

Kick could not let that happen.

"Wait," she gasped. "What about Adam?" She

didn't want to be the reason Adam was lost. She needed Bishop to understand. "You wanted to punish him, didn't you?" Kick said to Iron Jacket. The heat of his body was all around her, pushing into her. " 'You don't come out of the box until you know the rules'—that's what Mel used to say. You killed your wife before she could rescue Adam. And you put him back in his box to teach him a lesson." She didn't know how much Bishop had overheard about Josie Reed, about Mia, about any of it. It didn't matter. The effect was the same. Adam Rice was in a box. It had been only two days. "He's still alive."

But Iron Jacket was the only one who knew where that box was.

She could see Bishop doing mental calculations. Sweat beaded his face. She didn't know how much longer he'd be able to stay upright.

Each of Iron Jacket's breaths compressed her lungs, making it harder to take in air. "Trapped in the dark," he said. "No food or water, not knowing if anyone is ever coming back for him. Does that bring back memories, Beth? How many months did Mel keep you in the box?"

Beth didn't like being alone. That was the worst part. Days and days of no one at all. . . .

"I like it when you cry, Beth," Iron Jacket said. "It reminds me of the Desert Rose."

Kick shook her head, trying to block it out. "No, no, no, no."

"Stay focused . . . on Adam, Kick," Bishop said. "Nothing he says . . . matters."

"Once I got you out of the pool, you did everything we told you," Iron Jacket said. Kick felt something break inside her, like glass cracking. "A real natural. I wish to God we'd gotten it all on film." She was crying now, shoulders shaking, tears running down her cheeks. "Mel. Me. Klugman. We had a party. We broke her in. She was a real little wildcat."

"Stop," Bishop said.

Beth felt numb. She didn't care what happened to her anymore. They had to protect Adam.

"You want to see how good she is at following directions?" Iron Jacket asked Bishop. He opened his arms, and she felt her feet touch the floor. "Sit down, Beth."

She did what he said. She sat in the big chair and brought her knees to her chest and made herself as small as she could.

"Mel was a master, wasn't he?" Iron Jacket said with appreciation.

Bishop was only a few feet from the chair and she watched him over her knees as he slipped a few inches down the wall. The Glock had gone off-kilter in his hand.

"Aren't you going to shoot me?" Iron Jacket asked, coming at him.

"Not yet," Bishop said. "I need Kick to do something for me first." He made eye contact with her. "Kick," he said. "I need you to tell me where Adam is."

Beth squeezed her arms tighter around her knees.

Iron Jacket looked over his shoulder at her and chuckled as he moved his gloved hand to Bishop's throat. Iron Jacket's eyes gleamed as he took Bishop by the neck, and then he laughed with a bark of astonishment. He glanced down at the Glock that Bishop was barely managing to hold on to. "You're really going to let me do it, aren't you? You're not going to fight back at all." Iron Jacket's voice trembled with excitement, his fingers dancing along Bishop's neck. Dominating a trussed-up kid was one thing, but a grown man submitting willingly—that was a whole other level of enjoyment.

She couldn't look away. Bishop was staring right at her, pleading with her. It felt like he was looking at her through a peephole, a gray eye in a hole in a black wall. "He's in a box where you were kept, Kick," he said. The words buzzed around her ears like flies. "It's where he found the Scrabble tile," Bishop said. "You know where he is. You've got this."

The muscles in Iron Jacket's arm flexed, and he lifted his heels and leaned forward, so his weight was behind the hand he had pressing into Bishop's throat. Iron Jacket's face twisted into a snarl. Bishop made a guttural noise like air being slowly let out of a balloon.

She couldn't see the Glock anymore. It was somewhere lost between them.

"You feel that?" Iron Jacket said to Bishop in a harsh whisper. "Your pulse throbbing? Give it a minute. And it will start to slow."

• • •

Beth rocked in the chair. She had to think. Think, think, think. *Where are you, Adam?* It had to be close to the house where they found Josie Reed's body. Mia was moved three times over a period of a few hours. Bishop had said that Josie Reed's absentee landlord owned a lot of properties in the neighborhood. The house next door fulfilled all the requirements: set back from the street, fenced-in backyard—and two houses side by side provided more protection from nosy neighbors.

When the police had knocked, the three-legged dog's owners had not been home, because the dog had been abandoned. Maybe they never came home. Kick had thought the dog had been tied to that tree all day, but what if it had been longer than that?

Beth had had a dog once.

• • •

Now Monster was dead. Iron Jacket had killed him.

Bishop's eyes were glassy half slits. His forehead and temples were a latticework of engorged veins. His mouth was open, making tiny, silent gulping motions.

Iron Jacket's eyes rolled back with half-mad pleasure. "Mmm," he moaned. "There." He smiled at Bishop. "Feel that? Ba dump. Ba . . . dump. Ba . . . dump."

• • •

"Hide," Beth whispered. *"Get somewhere safe."*

Visualize a backyard.

The tire swing is warm from the sun. Kick's father is kneeling beside her in the grass. In his palm there are two cherries, twin berries connected by a short stem. A large cherry tree is rare, he says, exceptional, like she is. He points heavenward, and she leans her head back and lets her eyes travel up the rope that tethers the tire to a branch, to the green leaves and red berries up above. They have the biggest cherry tree of all. Her father eats one of the twin berries and she reaches for the other one. His fingers are long, his palm smooth, his thumb has a bump at the end.

She knows that hand. It's not her father's hand. It's Mel's.

• • •

Kick snapped her eyes open. "I know where Adam is," she said.

Bishop fired.

45

THE TELEVISION IN KICK'S hospital room was tuned to coverage of the sensational rescue of Adam Rice. The footage was five hours old, but they kept replaying it in a loop, shots of the bomb squad going into the house in their crazy bomb squad suits, followed by the Seattle police and the paramedics. In the blaze of a billion news lights, the house looked dingy and exposed.

Kick was riveted by the images, even knowing how it turned out. She held her breath as the camera stayed focused on the house's front door, waiting for some news from the first responders inside. It felt like years that they were in there, or maybe the TV correspondents just made it seem like years. Then the door opened, and the media pressed closer, and a young uniformed cop appeared on the porch. He hesitated. Then he gave a buoyant thumbs-up. You could have heard the cheer on the other side of the world.

"That's my favorite part," Kick said.

"How many times have you watched this?" Frank asked.

"A bazillion," Kick said. "Shh."

On the TV, the cop held open the front door as paramedics rushed a shape on a gurney to a waiting ambulance. A wall of patrol cops jogged alongside, using their bodies to block the news cameras. As the TV reporters lined the perimeter of the yard to file their reports, Kick caught a glimpse of a three-legged collie being led away by animal control. For Iron Jacket, the dog had been an extra layer of security, to dissuade unwanted visitors. But Kick liked to think that the dog had betrayed Iron Jacket, too, and that it barked madly that night as if to say, *Here, you jackasses, try here*.

"How did you know?"

"The cherry tree," Kick said. "I remembered it. Then everything else made sense."

A nurse came in, pushing a hospital stretcher, and wheeled it parallel to Kick's bed. Her fitted mint-green scrubs had the words *Trident Medical Group* stitched on the chest. "We're all ready for you, Miss Lannigan," the nurse said.

Frank stood awkwardly. "She won't have contact with him, right?" he asked.

"They'll be in separate operating theaters," the nurse assured him. She depressed the stretcher's brake with her foot and came around to Kick's shoulder. "He's under heavy guard. Everything's been arranged."

Kick scooted sideways onto the stretcher and lay down while the nurse checked her IV port. Frank turned away. Kick knew his resolve was crumbling.

"Swear to me you won't call Paula, Frank," she said, lifting her head. "I mean it. I'm an adult."

"I won't call Paula," Frank muttered.

Kick put her head back down. The ceiling of the room was bone white. Two sprinkler spigots looked back at her like eyes. Frank came around to the stretcher's bedside.

"Any news from Bishop?" she asked.

"They sent a chopper for him," Frank said. "He's probably shot full of steroids and painkillers and being a pain in the ass at the scene right now," he added, with a glance at the TV.

The news was in the happy cycle now: the joyful reunion, the celebrating crowds, the parade of psychiatrists optimistic about his reintegration. The next cycle would reveal all the missed chances law enforcement had to find him sooner; leak details of his abuse; feature the same parade of psychiatrists, now armed with new and darker predictions; and, finally, showcase the real experts, the kidnap moms, in expensive clothes bought with their children's settlement money, hawking books and dispensing sage advice.

Iron Jacket was dead, but the investigation into the extent of his crimes was just getting started. For now, "Dennis" was the only clue they had to his real identity. "I know you have other places to be," Kick said.

Frank laid a hand on her forearm. "I show up when you need me, kid," he said. "That's our deal."

The stretcher jerked as the nurse lifted the

brake, and Kick flinched. "Here we go," the nurse announced cheerily. She gave the stretcher a push and wheeled it out into the hall. Frank was right next to her again as soon as they cleared the door.

"Check on James for me tonight, okay?" Kick asked.

"You sure you want to go through with it?" Frank asked one last time.

"It's a kidney," Kick said with false bravado. "I have another one, right?"

46

WHEN KICK WOKE UP, she was not in the hospital room. The ceiling was not white. It was crisscrossed with timber beams. She lifted her wrist. The IV port was still there; a tube snaked to a bag hanging on an IV pole. She tried to lift her head but was struck by a nauseating wall of pain.

"Take it easy," Bishop said.

"Where am I?" Kick whispered.

"At my house," Bishop said. "The surgery went well. Both yours and Mel's."

Kick's head was fuzzy from morphine. It hurt to breathe. "Good," she said.

Bishop looked at her over his folded hands. He was wearing a collared shirt and a tie, and Kick wondered why he was so dressed up, then realized he was probably just trying to hide the bruises that purpled his neck.

"Did Frank call you?" she asked weakly.

He hesitated. "I know people at the hospital," he said.

Kick tried to smile. "You just want the password," she said. "You think I'll mutter it in my sleep."

Bishop gazed at her thoughtfully. She could see the bulk of the bandages on his shoulder under his shirt. The small lesions on his face had been expertly stitched with clear sutures. But his cheek was swollen and bruised, and a blood vessel in his right eye had ruptured, coloring the white of the eye red. "I already know the password," he said.

There was no smirk, no hint that he was kidding.

"The Scrabble letters you hid," he said. "You said they were always the same letters. Mia had the *E*. You had the *K*. What other letters did you hide? Do you remember what you were spelling?"

She still didn't understand. "Nothing, probably."

"What words does a kid that age know how to spell?" He took her hand, and her heart jumped. "Kit. Kick. Beth. So many names," he said, turning over her hand in his. He put his thumb on her palm. "But as far as the Social Security office goes, you just have one." His thumb drew a line down the inside of her wrist and hooked under the plastic hospital bracelet that encircled it. "It's your legal name," he said. "Kathleen."

Flashes of memory splintered through Kick's brain. *A, H, N.* She remembered those letters, feeling them in the dark, memorizing them. "I was spelling my name," she murmured. Not Kit—not her nickname—but her legal name, the important one. "That's the password?"

"That's the password," Bishop said.

"You tried it?"

"We found the banking account number on Iron Jacket's BlackBerry."

Kick hesitated. "How much is there?"

"Thirty million and change."

She inhaled so sharply, it felt like her stitches might burst, and she had to let the pain ebb before she could talk again. "I don't want to touch it," she said.

"It's yours to touch or not touch," Bishop said. "Just keep it offshore or you're going to run into some legal issues."

Kick's body was somehow both floaty and full of stones. Maybe it was the painkillers. Maybe this is how she was going to feel from now on.

Bishop stood and straightened his tie with the hand of his good arm.

"How's the throat?" Kick asked.

"Fine," Bishop said. But she could hear the strain in his voice when he spoke, like his vocal cords were still swollen. He stepped back, toward the open door. "But do me a favor," he said, rolling a wheelchair into the room. "Try to be just a tiny bit faster next time."

He parked the wheelchair at her bedside and offered her his elbow like he expected her to take it and jump to her feet. Kick looked at him like he was out of his mind. "I just had an organ removed," she reminded him.

His expression didn't waver. His elbow remained at the ready. He stared at her, his left eye half filled with blood.

The wheelchair had a steel frame and black vinyl upholstery. It didn't look particularly comfortable.

"The recovery protocol requires you to be up and active as soon as possible," he said.

"I can't sit up," Kick said.

"I'll help you," Bishop said. He put his hand behind her back and supported her as she gritted her teeth and elbowed herself up into a sitting position. Every contraction of her stomach muscles made Kick grunt in pain, but she somehow managed to get upright. She didn't get any time to rest. Bishop lifted one of her arms and ducked under it so that it was around his neck, and then he took her by the waist. "This might hurt," he said. He pivoted her around so that her bare legs slid off the bed and the only reason that Kick didn't scream profanities was because it hurt too much to talk. The instant the toes of her socks touched the floor, Bishop lifted her to her feet. Kick's knees buckled and Bishop barely managed to keep her off the floor. By the time he was able to grapple her into the chair, they were both panting. Kick scowled up at Bishop, who sat perched on the edge of the bed nursing his injured shoulder. "Don't ever do that again," she said.

Bishop dragged a blanket off the bed and piled it on her lap, and then started fiddling with her IV pole.

"What's this for?" she asked about the blanket.

"I want to show you something," he said. He hooked the IV pole to the back of the wheelchair.

"I need to rest," Kick said. "I'm convalescing."

Bishop dropped to his knees in front of her chair, folded down each footrest, and forcibly placed her feet on them.

"I feel like you're not listening to me," Kick said.

"Think of it as an opportunity for fresh air," Bishop said.

There was no point arguing. Kick didn't even like fresh air. But she also wasn't looking forward to getting manhandled back into the bed, so if Bishop wanted to wheel her around the grounds, then what the hell. She straightened the blanket on her lap and sat back as Bishop steered her out of the guest room and down the hall.

A glass door led outside to a vast expanse of lawn that stretched to the edge of woods on one side, and to the beach on the other. Beyond the strip of rocky shore, the chilly water of Puget Sound looked like glass. Two seagulls fought over the scraps of something dead on the beach. The air tasted like salt. Kick lifted her face to the sun and felt another wave of pain medicine hit.

She was jerked back to the moment by a faint but familiar sound—the distant hum of chopper rotors. Kick scanned the sky, but didn't see a helicopter. The seagulls started to squawk loudly at each other. She was only barely aware of them—she was focused on the helicopter. But the squawking continued. It almost sounded like they were calling Kick's name.

"I think someone is trying to get your attention," Bishop said.

He pointed a finger across the lawn where two figures sat on a garden bench at the edge of the woods. One of the figures was a woman, the other appeared to be a slight young man, wearing what looked like a robe over pajamas. Kick inhaled in surprise, and then glanced uncertainly up at Bishop. Bishop gave her a nod. Grinning, Kick placed her trembling hands on the chair's wheels and rolled herself forward a few feet.

James waved at her from across the yard.

Kick made a sound somewhere between a laugh and a sob.

The grass swirled and flattened between them. The thrum of helicopter blades was clearly audible now. Kick's eyes went to the vacant helipad, and then skyward, where a chopper approached over the trees.

"I'll be back in a few weeks," Bishop said.

"No," Kick said.

"You and James, enjoy the house for as long as you like," he said. "I've arranged for full-time medical care." The beat of the chopper's rotor echoed in Kick's ears. Bishop's necktie flapped against his shirt. "That's your private duty nurse now," Bishop said, looking across the yard.

The female figure sitting next to James stood and started walking toward them. She was wearing pink hospital scrubs. Her blond ponytail slapped sideways in the chopper's wind.

It was the paramedic.

He had hired the paramedic he'd bedded after Kick's concussion.

"You're unbelievable," she said. He really couldn't go twenty-four hours without getting laid.

"She's got an excellent bedside manner," Bishop said.

Kick gave him a sideways look.

"I'll be in touch," Bishop said. He bent down, kissed her chastely on the cheek, and then turned and headed toward the helipad.

The next thing Kick knew the paramedic had swept behind her wheelchair and was whisking her across the lawn toward James, the wind from the chopper beating at their backs.

Bishop could fly off wherever he wanted, Kick told herself. She had James, and he was the only person she really needed. Pale, hair fluttering in the wind, wearing the wrong glasses and pajamas that were several sizes too big, James was right there in front of her. Kick was nearly overcome. When the paramedic pulled her up to her brother and parked the wheelchair next to the bench, Kick and James just sat grinning at each other for a good several minutes. The slutty paramedic slipped away behind them. The chopper landed.

James offered Kick his hand and she took it.

"I missed you," Kick said. The words were lost in the whine of the helicopter's rotors, but James seemed to understand anyway. He squeezed her hand and said something back, and she, too, understood, one word: Monster.

James's eyes filled with tears. He had loved Monster almost as much as Kick had.

Kick looked sadly at their entwined hands. She still could see Monster's empty eyes as he lay lifeless in her lap. James gave her a quick squeeze. His mouth was moving, but she couldn't catch the words. He frowned, and bit the tip of his tongue, the way he did when he was figuring out how to break down a complicated concept into the simplest explanation possible. With new determination, he gestured emphatically with his chin at something behind the bench. Kick winced in pain as she shifted around to look. Douglas firs towered above them at the edge of the woods. The manicured lawn gave way to wild blackberries and old-growth trees. She scanned the dense trees, but James squeezed her hand again, and redirected her attention closer. The wind tickled the small hairs on her arms, but Kick felt bathed in warmth. The mound of raw dirt stood out on the band of green lawn. It wasn't large—just a few square feet—packed tightly so that it rose only a few inches above the grass line at its highest point. Ringed with rocks, it looked like a small garden bed waiting to be planted. Nestled at its center was a purple tennis ball.

Kick drew in a shaky breath.

Bishop had buried her dog.

The noise of the helicopter surged, and Kick looked up just as it lifted from the helipad. It hovered five feet off the ground, the frantic beat of its blades plastering her hair against her skull, and then slowly traveled overhead, gleaming white, with a black logo on the door: a *W* with a circle around it.

Kick had seen that logo before, stitched on the seats of Bishop's private plane. She craned to catch another glimpse, ignoring the pain of her incision, and as the helicopter leveled off over Puget Sound, she got one more look. This time she saw the logo for what it was. Not a *W* at all. A trident. Poseidon's trident, with its three prongs. What better to represent a company that made its fortune selling weapons than a spear? Bishop had said his boss was named David Decker Devlin. Three prongs, one for each *D* in his name.

She lowered her eyes to the hospital bracelet that encircled her wrist.

Trident Medical Group.

There had been no prisoner's rights organization behind the campaign to match Mel with a donor. Even organizations like those wouldn't touch someone like him, a dying pedophile, a child abductor, a child pornographer. Kidney donations required going through all kinds of mental and physical health hoops, but not this time. It was like they had been waiting for her call. She had been in surgery within hours. Everything paid for. Mel whisked out of prison. She knew of only person who had that kind of wealth and influence. Devlin. He'd arranged all of it. They wanted Mel alive. And now, she thought, with a sickening pang, her kidney was inside him.

"Are you okay?" James asked.

Kick sat up straight. Her incision barely bothered her at all anymore. *Change your thoughts and you change your world.* Devlin and Bishop were up to something, and she was going to find out what.

Kick lifted her arm and waved at the glinting chopper. "Smile and wave," she said to James, plastering a fake smile on her face. James gave her a nervous glance, and then raised his own hand and waved it. Kick did a covert scan of the grounds. The paramedic was wandering the path to the beach. Kick didn't know if anyone else was on the property. Not that it mattered.

She was an invited guest, and Bishop had said he'd be gone for weeks.

That gave her plenty of time to search the house.

ACKNOWLEDGMENTS

I OWE A BIG thanks to my editor, telephone counselor, and cheerleader Marysue Rucci for taking a risk on me and this series. She was and continues to be one of Kick's greatest fans, and she is the reason this book exists in the world.

I want to also thank Carolyn Reidy, Jon Karp, Cary Goldstein, Lance Fitzgerald, Andrea DeWerd, Loretta Denner, Lisa Erwin, and Louise Burke. Jackie Seow and Marlyn Dantes, you made a beautiful book jacket. Special thanks to Sarah Reidy and Grace Stearns. Sarah spent her day off texting me when I was stranded at an airport for eleven hours and is the only reason I am not in detention at JFK to this day. My editor's former assistant Emily Graff (now an S&S editor) and her current assistant Elizabeth Breeden possess both patience and organization, qualities I lack and envy them for. Thank you, Joy Harris and Adam Reed of The Joy Harris Literary Agency, for all of your awesomeness and for putting up with me. Usually the publisher avoids even telling us writers our copyeditors' names, lest we hire contract killers to track them down and kill them—but check it out, David Chesanow, I know who you are. And I'd like to thank you for a fantastic job finding the words that I meant to use, instead of the words that I used because they were kinda sorta similar. Well done, sir. No need to get the locks changed.

Elizabeth Lannigan (or as she is known in my daughter's second-grade classroom, Mrs. Lannigan) gave this character a great gift, her name. Zach Greenvoss is James's technical adviser, and I'm pretty sure he installed RAT malware on my laptop years ago. Thank you, Kelly Sue DeConnick and Matt Fraction, for continuing to inspire me creatively, for your friendship, and for "bthmmp bthmmp." Brian and Alisa Bendis supply a third of my family's weekly caloric intake. Kelley Ragland, you still influence my work in so many ways.

As always I am indebted to my weekly writing group: Chuck Palahniuk, Lidia Yuknavitch, Erin Leonard, Mary Wysong-Haeri, Diana Page Jordan, Suzy Vitello, Monica Drake, and Cheryl Strayed (Ret.). I am also lucky to have many writer friends whose work dazzles me. Special thanks to Eliza Mohan, Sophie Evans, Danielle Khoury, Nina Khoury, Piper Bloom, Daisy Ziatnik, Emily Powell, Sophie Jacqmotte-Parks, and Stella Greenvoss (København campus)—eight nine-year-old girls who teach me a lot about writing.

Finally, my husband Marc Mohan and our daughter Eliza Fantastic Mohan are simply my favorite people in the whole world. How lucky that I get to live with them.